In the Cold

Daniel H. Smith

This book is a work of fiction. Any references to historical events, people, or actual places are used fictitiously. Other names, characters, places, and events are products of the author's imagination. Any resemblance to actual events, places, or persons, living or dead, is coincidental.

Copyright © 2021 by Daniel H. Smith

All rights reserved, including the right to reproduce this book or portions thereof in any form.

PART 1

CHAPTER 1

January, 29, 1943, Maine

Trudy Honeywell turned up the collar of her khaki pea coat against the vicious wind screeching in from the coast. She pulled her woolen scarf up under her leather billed cap to better cover her ears, then blew on her slender hands and rubbed them together. That provided only a moment of fleeting relief so she shoved them deep into the coat pockets and cursed herself for leaving her gloves in the car. She was at the train station to meet the 8:10 from Boston and it had long since become a deep, enveloping dark. On top of that, the local civil defense warden had ordered a blackout drill, though she could see the station master in a window reading by candlelight.

It was almost 8:15. Late. She stomped her too-large boots on the platform to try to get her blood flowing and to deny the wind a sitting target. *At least I'm out of the snow under* the covered platform, Trudy thought as she watched it fall, steadily accumulating. Her mind wandered...

The war, she thought, had made people stop caring about the unimportant things (it seemed) like girls wearing trousers. She was glad. Because here she was: little Trudy Honeywell, standing at the train station after dark in a pair of warm, woolen, plaid trousers. The idea of a skirt made her knees and calves shiver. And then the rest of her. Heck, she wouldn't even *be* here. They'd have given the job to some fella. She smiled: she liked the job. Not looking after kids or taking in sewing or laundry or helping in her parents' hardware store, but assistant to Judge Norris. It was mainly running his errands and driving for him and his lovely wife – but she loved every minute. She was his right-hand man... so to speak.

Still, you couldn't *like* the war...and she didn't, of course. Most of the boys either shipped out or about to for training far away to fight the Nazis in Europe or the Japs in the jungle... She missed, she had to admit, getting the attention she used to get... Still...if it *hadn't* happened, the war that is, well, she was just making the best of a bad situation.

Of course, 'here' was waiting on a frigid train platform for the now even more behind schedule 8:10 from Boston. She didn't care, really, about the cold. This was exciting! Her father surely wouldn't have let her get this kind of job before the war. He would have said it was unseemly. He sure didn't think it was unseemly to make her work stocking the hardware store shelves after hours, she grunted. Trudy's mother would have nodded along and told her she should be engaged to be married by now. 19 years old, Trudy thought. Maybe that's how they did it in the roaring 20s, but... Her mother, Trudy grumbled to herself, would have her go right from one house to another without seeing a bit of the world or having any fun at all or learning anything! She recalled driving with friends to the USO show in

Portland and her parents had grounded her. She had been 18 years old at the time. Grounding an adult: "as long as you're under this roof…" They would have her settled down and married off with child in a year if they had their way.

Still, what else was there?

Her thoughts wandered from her own predicaments to the wider world. The radio, the newspapers, the newsreels…it was all so terrible. The Nazis seemed downright crummy. And what was their beef with Jews, anyway, Trudy wondered? Her dad always said they were great money men…but then again, he did say "don't Jew me!" to his friends when he thought they were cheating him…

Anyway, the fact remained that the war *was* a reality right now and doing her part meant working as assistant to the judge in the absence of any capable young man to do the task – she would be glad for that, at least. And, she thought, who knows? Maybe once the war was over the Judge would be so impressed with the job she had done that he would keep her on (even if it was *mildly* unseemly). That might lead… anywhere! She could be a professional woman, like in the movies…

Of course, what Trudy really wanted, what she'd said to friends a million times (and even her parents once or twice, met with a scowl) was to get out of town. Out of Maine. See something – anything at all. When she thought about staying, she could immediately see years, decades – a lifetime down the road. A husband, church socials, children…maybe she could teach school one day but... she could see herself old, quiet, having never really lived at all, even if it had been all just as it should have been. Her somewhat wild and short-ish blond hair now long and gray, severely contained in a tightly pulled bun on top of her head, and her pert pink cheeks turned colorless and wrinkled, the look of mischief replaced with a faraway stare, sitting by a window as another Maine winter settled in outside a window. She still dreamed of maybe, just maybe, going to college.

"It'll be an all-girls school, Ma!" she remembered discussing with her mother. Just once.

"Even if we had the money – which we don't – what good would it do you? Trudy, honey, that's dream stuff."

When she told her parents that she might want to be an actress she remembered her mother nodding and with a sigh saying "There's no money in it."

Trudy checked her watch. 8:22. Were the trains always this late?

She knew the name she had written on the sheet of thick paper that she now held under her arm but looked at it again. "Agent Asa Mori." She had added the "Agent" part herself to be respectful and hoped it was correct. Judge Norris had only given her a name; no title. The FBI didn't have things like sergeants and lieutenants and captains, did they? Anyway, the judge had entrusted her to go to the train station in his dark crimson 1940 Nash Ambassador and retrieve this (hopefully) *Agent* Mori and bring him to the judge for... something.

Huh, funny, she thought: *Trudy Honeywell was working with the FBI!*

Sort of. Anyway, she wondered what her friends might say if she told them.

What kind of name was 'Asa Mori' anyway, Trudy wondered? She knew old Asa Pike that had been a lobsterman... Mori: what was that? French? Asa did sound like an old timer's name. Trudy figured he'd be a no-nonsense old G-man like in the gangster films and newsreels; she kept imagining that he would look like Walter Huston...

At long last she heard the whistle in the distance. She looked but the train was not yet visible, though she could feel a slight vibration in the air radiating from the frigid metal of the train tracks. They were icy blue, slinking off in parallel lines before disappearing in the dimness and flurrying snow. 8:28 according to her watch. She straightened the sign under her arm and resumed her march on the platform.

The train came out of the trees abruptly like a jungle predator, loud and bearing down quickly. Without realizing, Trudy took a couple of steps back. The light on the front of the train flooded the inky dark area in front of it. She supposed they didn't radio ahead to tell them they were conducting a blackout drill. The light was blinding as it approached, it reflected off the snow on the ground, the smoke from the engine and the red brick of the station, and made it a muddy tangerine color. The locomotive brought a rush of wind toward Trudy and caused a chill up her spine.

The metallic shriek of the brakes brought the enormous locomotive to a stop with a heavy exhaling hiss. She held the sign out in front of her to alert Agent Mori that he was expected and the freezing air bit at her hands. The dry, lazy snowflakes swirled about her in a vortex. An ancient porter in a cap with a square bill stepped off and looked at Trudy.

"End of the line miss." He said. "Only one passenger on board."

"Only one?" Trudy repeated, forgetting to lower the sign.

The side of the silver car gleamed. The minuteman logo of the Boston and Maine Railroad Company looked off to the right, clutching his trusty musket in his left hand. Descending the stairs behind the porter (who moved away quickly down the platform) was a man entirely unsuited for the environment. He wore a gray hound's-tooth jacket and dark gray vest with a slate-colored tie. He had black and white wing tip shoes and looked less like a federal agent and more like a nightclub singer that the bobbysoxers would swoon over. His gray fedora and his lone suitcase hung from his left hand. His hair was slicked back like Cary Grant and seemed like an oily helmet that the snow couldn't quite cling to. Also...

"Oh my god." Trudy whispered to nobody, though maybe just a bit too loud. "He's a damn Jap."

CHAPTER 2

January 22, 1943, Maine

"Did you see we made the papers again, dear?" Lillian Norris said. "We had another one."

She was 66 years old, a touch of gray, but still mainly brunette. She was lively, plain-looking, whip-smart, and devoted utterly to her brilliant and occasionally dotty husband. She wore her hair short to try to keep the misbehaving curls in line but usually lost that battle. She'd prepared a breakfast of sausages, poached eggs on toast, grapefruit halves and coffee and she and the judge sat at opposite ends of their rather large maple breakfast table and read sections of the paper. Lillian still held the front section and had been pondering it since she'd first taken it from the front porch. War news always topped the papers with banner headlines. The story that troubled her particularly was relegated to page eight.

11

"How's that, dear?" Judge Norris asked. He hadn't yet touched his food, struggling as he was to get his false teeth properly into place. He was only five years older than Lillian, though his full head of gray-white hair and sleepy demeanor made it seem like more. Everyone still called him "Judge" though he hadn't, in point of fact, actually been one for over 10 years. Not since he'd run for the seat in the state house of representatives and won. He'd never been a great fan of politics but considered public service a duty and the job to be a nice slowing of pace compared to being a circuit court judge. He had nowhere to go this morning, really, and the weather, even at midday, wasn't likely to get over five or ten degrees. Still, he was dressed in one of his worn but professional looking black suits and polished shoes. He responded distractedly and without lowering the newspaper pages in front of him.

"We…the town, I mean… We had another…" she paused and put her hand over her heart. Perhaps she didn't like the word, "We had another fellow take his own life. It seems."

Judge Norris looked over the section he was reading and saw the sadness in his wife's eyes. "Like the others?" he asked.

She nodded.

Judge Norris said, "Let me see it, won't you?"

The front page read *Portland Press-Herald,* and below that the headline: "Churchill and Roosevelt Continue talks in Casablanca". There was something else below the fold about today being "tin can drive day" that Judge Norris couldn't quite make out. Lillian folded that away and handed him a nice, neat quarter of a paper, folded to page eight. The table was too long to simply pass the page and so she got up and brought it around to him, making sure not to disturb his breakfast.

"And eat up." She said, returning to her seat.

Judge Norris poked at the eggs with his fork but didn't actually get any to his mouth. He sipped on his black coffee but the story gave him pause before he swallowed. He said something like "Hmm."

Local police found the body of one Rupert Delisle face up in the snow on Woonsocket Rd. about 6 miles outside of the town limits. The deceased was completely without clothing and the cause of death was determined as extreme hypothermia. According to Police Captain Ballard, Delisle had no known family and was a member of the Mohawk Nation and probably still a Canadian Citizen from Quebec. This apparent suicide is a near exact copy of the suicide on December 30th of last year (just a few weeks ago) when another Indian, though this one still listed as "John Doe," carried out a similar suicide and was found on the same road, further out of town. These acts mirror those two suicides carried out last winter on December 12, 1941 and February 8, 1942, bringing the toll for such incidents to 4.

Captain Ballard said his investigation has so far shown little progress, as all of the men were loners and transient workers. All of them were employed by the Stark Lumber Corporation except for Mr. Robert Curette, the man who committed suicide last year on February 8th, who worked as a fish packer at the cannery in East Jonesport.

According to Captain Ballard: "The fact that they were all Indians makes us figure it was probably something to do with tribal traditions. One hears about Eskimos putting themselves out on a drifting piece of ice when they get old so as not to be a burden on the rest of the tribe. We figure it's something like that."

The last time Mr. Delisle was seen alive was on Saturday night, leaving the Caribou Lodge on Jefferson Street. One patron, James Lufkin, also an employee of Stark Lumber, said he had seen him leave "in quite a drunken state."

Captain Ballard said that the odd manner in which the men took their own lives led him to think at first that they may have had some kind of suicide pact, though as yet there is no proof that the men even knew each other. Ballard went on to say that as of now there is no reason to suspect foul play.

There was a silence for a bit as Judge Norris considered the information his wife had shown him. Her demeanor may not have betrayed any agitation, but the Judge could tell just from her voice, the way she carefully enunciated every syllable, that she was adamant about this.

"What do you think?" Lillian asked.

"Curious. Very curious."

Judge Norris shoved a bit of now cold egg and toast between his dentures and made a gesture of apology for his mouth being full. Lillian smoothed her dress patiently and waited. She was familiar with this stalling gambit and knew just to wait it out. Judge Norris washed it down with a long gulp of the strong, black coffee.

"Well then?" Lillian said, eyebrows raised.

The Judge turned his hands up and shrugged. "What do I think? It's awful. Tragic. Very sad."

"Well, of course that." Lillian said. "I mean the rest. The way the investigation seems to be going. *Or not going.* I'll be honest, Joshua, I don't think they even *care*!"

She was more passionate about this than he had even originally thought, the Judge realized, having dragged out his first name. "Dear, that's harsh, don't you think?"

"I don't know. I hope it will end up being so. But it just seems...I just don't know."

There was a silence, then the cracking in the wood cook stove, which was blazing so that the outsides were glowing reddish-orange. There was a short howl of wind from outside, where the windows held back the frigid January air and caught the natural geometry of ice building up. Venturing too far from the stove made one susceptible to the chilling drafts even in the snug confines of their home.

The Judge offered, "Well, there is a war on."

"I know about the war, dear. I lead paper drives, rubber drives... I teach the WACs for god's sake..."

It had irked Lillian that the age limit for the Women's Army Corp was 45, since they wouldn't be in any actual fights. So, she volunteered as an instructor. The Judge knew it pleased her to simply call her a WAC. "I know you're a WAC dear, I'm very proud of you."

"Thank you, dear, but I'm just concerned about this Ballard fellow. He's supposed to be keeping things together while our man is abroad."

Pete Smith was "our man." He'd been a private in the first war and a military man for many years before returning to his home in Maine to be a small-town police captain. When war called again, he could hardly refuse. He was off somewhere, only the government knew where, training other young men to fight the Germans, as he had been taught a generation before. Captain Ballard had been his replacement, hired hastily by the Board of Selectmen.

"What do you know about him?" Lillian asked.

"Not much, really." The Judge says. "Moved here from...I'm not sure. Somewhere south. Tennessee?"

"Not even from Maine?"

"No dear. What is it you're getting at, Lillian?"

She crossed her legs and adjusted her skirt primly, then sipped at her coffee. "I just don't know. If they do care at all down there at the police station, it seems to me that they are going about it very..." she stops herself before saying the word in her head: 'half-assed.' She knew when she cursed it makes the Judge cringe a little. "Negligently."

"That's a serious claim."

"It's meant to be."

The Judge studied her face as she sipped her coffee and pretended to read a section of the paper lying next to her plate.

"I don't know what you're suggesting."

Lillian replaced her coffee cup in the saucer as if this was the question she was waiting to be asked. "Well, don't you still have your contact at the FBI?"

"You know I do. I wouldn't refer to him as a 'contact' mind you."

"Your friend, then."

"As you well know."

"Yes, well, I think it would be prudent to ask if they could look into it."

The Judge shook his head. "This is exasperating! I can't ask them to send agents here to look into some suicidal Indians!"

"If indeed suicide is the right word."

"There is a war on!"

"We've been over that."

The Judge harrumphed. "Lillian...Dear...what I mean is that the FBI is busy. Too busy for what is a local matter. And that is indeed what it is. It shows a real lack of faith in our local officials to do this with only our suspicions..."

"Are they *our* suspicions?" Lillian asked.

"It's impertinent. And it oversteps any authority I could presume to offer as justification. Really, I mean..."

Lillian fluttered her hand in the air to indicate that such trifles were of no importance. "Dear, it is men like you, *good men*, who hold communities together in trying times like this. And good women like me, for that matter. It is our duty to make sure that things don't go to hell in a handcart while the boys are away."

The Judge pondered this for a moment.

17

"You could make up any ruse." She said. "House of Representative business or what have you."

"I don't see how it is possible."

Lillian shrugged, sipped again at her coffee and leaned a bit toward the kitchen stove, thinking she would have to get up and feed it a nice green, long-burning log soon. "I don't know. That's just to tell the local… police. Dear… something just doesn't sit right with me."

Judge Norris nodded very slightly, "Yes, I know you're right." He said, with a faraway voice. "It is odd… and it doesn't sit right with me either."

CHAPTER 3

January 29, 1943, Maine

"Huh. *Agent.*" The man said, smiling. He pointed at the sign which Trudy had crafted so carefully. "I guess that's me."

He can't be a Jap, she thinks. He's just oriental. There was no trace of an accent; and that swell suit! The matinee idol hair...well, he clearly wasn't from Maine. Dear me, she thought, he's almost...*handsome.*

"Oh," Trudy said. "Is that not right? I had wondered. Lieutenant?"

"No, it's right, alright. It's just swell seeing it written out like that, is all." He sat his suitcase down with the fedora on top and ran his hands together to warm them and then buried them in the side pockets of his jacket. "I'm a little new to the game, you see."

Agent Mori was very young looking, Trudy though. Not much older than herself, she reckoned.

"You can put the sign away. You found me." He said, hopping a bit to keep moving and visibly shivering.

Trudy had been too dumbstruck to realize she was still holding out his name at him She folded it up and stashed it away. "How silly! Of course."

They stood there a bit longer until Agent Mori said. "Look, sister, I don't mean to put the rush on you but I've never been this cold in my life and I worked in an out of a fish freezer one summer. I assume you've brought a car?"

"Oh goodness! Yes, of course. Follow me." Trudy led him to the Nash and they deposited his bag in the back seat. As soon as she cranked the car to life Agent Mori began fiddling with the heater switches and seemed to be losing the battle with trying to suppress his shivering.

"Sorry." He said, nodding to the heater, for being so presumptuous as to start touching things. "It's just really, wow...*really cold!*"

"It's a bit of a drive back into town." Trudy said, "You'll have time to warm up. You didn't bring an overcoat? Doesn't it get cold in Washington?"

Trudy found herself sneaking glances over at his oriental features as bits of moonlight managed to illuminate him now and then. He held his hands up to the heat vents and then rubbed them together.

"How's that? Washing... oh, no. Just a stopover there. Highly recommend visiting though. No, I came from the West Coast. Los Angeles. Well, that's where I'm from, anyway. Actually, came in from... well, somewhere else. My coat... I had one but... well, it got misplaced."

Trudy lit up. "Los Angeles! Wow! Lucky! That's amazing! What's it like?"

Agent Mori shrugged. "Like anywhere else." He said, distractedly. "Only more so."

"Um, well, have you met any movie stars?"

Mori nodded. "Oh sure. But that was all business. I was doing some acting, you see. Until the war. Then I had to serve. That is, do my duty with the FBI. For now. I might get the call to the army, though. We'll see. Can't wait, to be honest." He felt that Trudy wanted to know who he'd met but doesn't feel right asking after his statement about duty.

"I worked on a Clark Gable picture. Then this other one with Walter Pidgeon. Oh, and I saw Myrna Loy at a coffee shop on Melrose. But that wasn't professional. Just a coincidence."

"Wow." Trudy said.

Agent Mori relaxed against the seat and stopped shivering, for the most part. The silence was a bit awkward and Trudy drove particularly slowly as the fine powder on the road has made things slippery and the trucks wouldn't be out to plow and sand the roads until morning.

"So..." she said, "If you don't mind me asking: what kind of name is Mori?"

"What kind?"

"I mean, I …"

"You mean what origin?"

Did she?

Agent Mori pulled out a small black wallet that still smelled new and held it open for her.

"It's too dark." Trudy said. "I can't see it."

With a quick metallic chafe and an aroma of flint, Agent Mori flicked on his dad's lighter, which he carried with him even though he didn't smoke. Trudy took her eyes off the road just long enough to see the letters FBI in large dark blue block letters and a photograph of Agent Mori with a boyish smile next to his name: Asahito Mori.

"Asahito? Is that Chinese?" she tried not to sound hopeful.

"Ha! I don't look Chinese!" Agent Mori clicked off the lighter and replaced it and the ID in his inside jacket pocket. "Sorry. I know that doesn't answer your question. I just like showing it to people, you know, and I haven't had many opportunities. The badge, I mean. Took me a long time to get it."

Trudy was silent, waiting. Mori said, "It's Japanese. Japanese-American, that is. Well, I am. The name is all Japanese." He extracted a comb from his pocket and attempted to put his hair back into place, though to Trudy's eye there didn't seem to be any out of place to begin with. He gave up when the mirror on the sunshade proved too dark to see in.

"I don't care, mind you." Trudy said. "I mean, it must be rough to be Japanese nowadays. Japanese-American that is. I can't stand race prejudice, really. My family were abolitionists. You know, back in...back then."

Mori nodded, amused. He said, "Good."

"You, um..." Trudy began sheepishly, "You heard that thing I said back on the platform, right?"

"Don't worry about it."

"I'm sorry about it... It just slipped out. I was surprised, is all."

He nodded. "Really. Don't worry about it. I've said it a few times myself."

"Really?"

"Oh, Sure. I remember the last time was probably Dec. 7, 1941. I picked up the evening paper and said 'you goddam Japs.'"

"I guess we all did." Trudy said, then felt odd about it. She decided to change the subject. "I like Mr. Moto!"

"The movies?"

"Yeah, ya know: *Think Fast, Mr. Moto!* Peter Lorre. Good movie."

"That was a good one." Agent Mori agreed.

"Hey, you said you did some acting...were you in that?"

"Was I in Mr. Moto? Nah. That came out when I was a teenager."

She said, "Oh, yeah." And there was a silence.

"Say," Mori says. "I don't think I caught your name."

"Trudy." She said, smiling. "Trudy Honeywell."

"Asa Mori." he said, holding out his hand. Trudy took her right hand off the wheel just long enough to shake. His hand was firm and strong but still quote cold. "You can call me Ace if you like."

"Ace..." Trudy repeated.

He thought this over. "Actually, maybe you should call me Agent Mori. Ya know, to keep things official."

"Right." Trudy said, wanting to help however she could. "That's sensible. So...how many cases is this for you? Or missions. Whatever you call them."

"Oh shoot...dozens. I couldn't tell you, honestly. Loads." He nodded. "Training missions, that is. This is my first case in the field."

Trudy lighted up with real enthusiasm. "Wow. That is exciting!"

Mori nodded and smiled with a quite satisfied air. "So, where to, Trudy Honeywell?"

"To the hotel. We've reserved a room for you. The judge has, I mean. You can get a good night's rest and get to work in the morning."

He nodded. "So, do you have any details on this case? I got the bare bones but no meat on 'em, if you know what I mean." He didn't really need a briefing but figured he could find out what a few of the locals thought, if they knew anything about it at.

Trudy looked over at him with concern. "No. Sorry. I'm just the… I mean, I'm... no. I don't know why you're here. Just that I'm to get you to the Judge."

Mori shook his head. "Okay. Guess the details will have to wait. No big deal. I hope the hotel is well heated."

CHAPTER 4

January 22, 1943, Washington, D.C.

As special assistant to the Deputy Director of the FBI, Colin Blakeslee was important enough to warrant an office on the north side of the Washington Field office facing Pennsylvania Avenue. If one were to walk one way: there was the White House. The other way: Capitol Hill. Not that anyone would be walking for very long today, if they could avoid it. Colin could barely see far enough down the block to remember which direction either of those renowned locations was located. He stared down at a trolley car making its way through the center of the street as snow fell slowly and steadily. Everything was whitish-gray, blotted out, and slumbering.

Colin began to contemplate his own significance. He was, after all, undoubtedly an important man. In addition to his regular duties, he was a key figure in the Bureau's fight against domestic terrorism and the radical element as part of the war effort. And yet, a call from Judge Norris and he felt like a small-town law clerk again. The Judge hadn't called in years, but the reply was always "put it through" without hesitation. Judge Norris, quietly, commanded that kind of loyalty and respect. Colin had never come across a fairer man or a sharper mind – but the judge *was* in his 70's now, wasn't he? He listened as the judge laid out the story, such as it was, glancing out to the snow, disorienting as it flew about outside. With all that was going on, the judge's story seemed so…insignificant? Suicidal Indians? What was he to do about it? Still, this was the judge he was talking to. If he thought there was cause for alarm…

"Well," Colin said, "I mean, it sounds like a sad business. Sad all around. But, uh, I don't see how I can help."

The judge paused on the other end. It gave Colin time to flip the long, straight phone cord around his ashtray once, then again. He heard the line crackle, likely due to the weather. Then the judge said. "Ayuh. I know. I said the same thing to Lillian."

"How is your lovely wife?"

"Lovely. Stubborn. The same."

"We're stretched thin as a whisker now too, what with the war…"

"Ayuh. There's a war on. I said that too. Hard all around…"

"So, I mean, you see where… what I mean. About…" he trailed off.

Colin was perplexed. The Judge hadn't asked for a troop of agents or a pair…or even that a single man be sent. He hadn't even said straight out what he suspected, if anything. Still, he couldn't disappoint the Judge. But what could he do? What was there to be done?

"Well, I just wanted to let you know what was going on. That is was concerning. I know, given your position, that you'll know the right way to handle it. If indeed you think anything needs handling." The judge said.

Miss Waverly, Colin's secretary, buzzed in to tell him that the Director was on the other line. With apologies to the Judge he rung off, giving assurances that he would do what he could. But when would he have time for that? He picked up and Director Hoover barked at him. "I need the details on the Union thing today, Blakeslee. Now, if you have it."

"Uh…" he looked around his desk and said. "Yes! I do! Just in…"

"Now then! To my office…wait no. Let's all go to lunch. I'm famished. To Childs. I'll see you there in 20. Working lunch. Tell the DD and Bobby."

Child's Restaurant. One of Hoover's favorites, but Colin didn't want to venture out in the weather. His head was buzzing. He hadn't even had a chance to review the material. Some op to weed out Commies and sympathizers in the trade unions. The war powers provisions gave them a little more leeway, which they intended to use. He still had to follow up on some American Fascists they'd run an operation to infiltrate and…

I'm up to my neck as it is, Colin thinks. Still…

The Judge. He still couldn't let down the judge…

"Miss Waverly, would you come in here please!"

She did, and promptly. She was in her late 20's, a round, pretty face, dark hair trimmed above her neck and curled in the latest fashion; loosely but not one out of place. She wore a gray wool dress with a good-sized bow tied at the slender neck and carried a steno pad – always at the ready. "Yes sir?"

"Who do we have anyone around here that isn't busy?"

"Ha! No sir. Nobody I know of."

"Well, is there anyone in the offices right now that has people to spare?"

"Spare? Goodness no." she put her pencil between her teeth to show how hard she was thinking it over. "There… is a recent transfer here from the west coast. Bullock. Was training out in San Fran but he's been reassigned. Not sure to what…organized crime, I think."

"That'll do. Can you fetch him for me? And be quick about it. I've got to meet the director in 20."

Agent Phil Bullock was a small man, compact and barrel-chested with dark, wooly hair. He was also very prompt: it wasn't even five minutes before he was in Colin Blakeslee's office. Colin was already putting on his overcoat and a gray winter fedora with a black band. "Bullock?"

He nodded. "Yes sir. Phil Bullock. I'm with…"

Blakeslee waved his hand, "Later, later, I'm in such a hurry. Sorry. The director, you know… anyway, look, my secretary tells me you just transferred in from the west coast, yes?"

"Yessir." Bullock says. "San Francisco office. I was a trainer for new recruits."

"Oh, that's fine, that's fine." He looked Bullock over. For a man with dark, curly hair and thick (Blakeslee thought 'Mediterranean) eyebrows and features, he was a bit pale. "Didn't you get a famous California tan?"

"Well, San Francisco is a bit nippy this time of year, sir. And to be honest, I didn't get out of the field office much. Especially now with the war…we got busy, sure enough."

"What's your line, mainly?"

"Counterespionage. Watching the Japs and watching out for sabotage. That kind of thing."

"Oh, sounds interesting. Catch many saboteurs?"

"Well…no. Not exactly. None, in fact."

Blakeslee nodded and waved with his hand, a gesture that signaled 'walk with me.' They made their way through the office toward the elevators as agents and secretaries buzzed about around them. "I have an old friend." The Special Assistant to the Deputy Director said. "A mentor really. He contacted me today. He's concerned about his hometown. He thinks there might be something…amiss."

"Amiss?"

"Yes. He wasn't long on specifics, Bullock, if I'm to be frank, but this is a man of…" Blakeslee fumbled for the right words. "Real integrity. Last of the old breed, you know? A damned keen legal mind, too. Wasted out in the wilds of Maine, really. He really should have run for higher office instead of just in the state house like he did, I think…"

In the interest of keeping Blakeslee on track and getting him to his meeting with Hoover, Bullock offered, "And this man has some sort of…dilemma?"

"Oh, personally? No. He's a straight arrow, all right. If ever there was one. But he seems to think the situation is fishy."

Bullock asked, "What situation?"

Blakeslee laid out the little he knew. "You can check the wire for specifics. So, what do you think?"

Bullock raised his black caterpillar eyebrows and shrugged, perplexed. "Well, sir, I don't rightly know. Until I find out more. But it seems just a matter for the locals."

Blakeslee nodded slowly and adjusted his hat thoughtfully. "I know. I know."

"And I can't personally see to anything with…"

"No," Blakeslee interrupted, "I know. And this would sort of be…non-official official, if you get my meaning. When I heard you were a trainer it gave me an idea… Don't you have some young, fresh-faced fellow we could send? Call it a field training exercise."

"Non-official official?"

Blakeslee nodded. "You understand." It was a statement, not at all a question.

Bullock stammered. He wasn't sure that he *did* understand, per say, but… "I'll see what I can do."

"That's fine!" Blakeslee slapped his shoulder. "Just fine! Alright then, I'm off to be flogged…" he tipped his hat as he stepped on the elevator and as the doors closed, Bullock watched him fumble with the clasp of his briefcase. Bullock pulled out a packet of cigarettes and lighted one, drawing in a long, tired drag.

"Well, that's just swell." he said.

He had his secretary scour reports and go over the teletypes for the days in question while he tried to finish up some of the work on some smugglers they'd had under surveillance for having possible ties to Nazi groups and shipping bomb parts. That, Bullock thought, is what I *should* be working on. Instead I'm wasting an afternoon helping a higher-up impress an old boss. And that is *all* the time I intend to waste on this, Bullock thought.

Bullock was not nearly so important a person as Blakeslee and so no window to the wintery scene outside to distract him. Bullock's prim, middle-aged secretary set a few scant pages on his desk as he looked on. He removed his jacket and rolled up his sleeves. "That's it?"

"That's it." She said.

"Okay, Vera. Thanks." He made sure to remember her name. She's only been assigned to him 3 days ago.

"Thought I'd go down to the cafeteria for lunch. Want anything?" Vera asked.

He shakes his head. "No thanks." He set alight another lucky strike with the remnants of the one he just finished and stubbed the butt in the rapidly filling ashtray. "I'm gonna work this through lunch and be done with it."

Bullock smoked and read. He loosened his tie as the smoke danced and curled up toward the vents and made patterns against the brown wallpaper. He'd heard that Washington was more of a political game and that he was going to miss the relative autonomy of the west coast... but DC was where the action was – supposedly. He hoped this was the last little "errand" he'd be backed into.

There wasn't much beyond what Blakeslee had said. Two suicides last year. Two this year. No paper outside of Maine had picked up the story – why would they? From what he read, it seemed like the locals were calling it a tribal thing. Bullock thought it sounded more like a cult type of deal, but, he thought, six of one, half a dozen of the other. The cult angle may just have been his mind trying to make the case more interesting. Anyway, he could get a trainee, send them off and call it practice. Make old man Blakeslee happy...

He buzzed Vera and asked her to get the San Francisco Field office on the phone, then remembered she'd gone to lunch. He was having a hard time getting used to having a secretary – anyway, he knew the number. He dialed then asks the operator for the right extension. Long distance so it would take a minute, but with their dedicated government long distance operators it wouldn't be too long. He heard a faint hiss and the operator said, "Your party is waiting."

He asked for the extension of his old pal Harvey Feynman. Harvey was a bit of a rarity, a Jew in the FBI, but things were a little less rigid out west, both by necessity and habit. Harvey was short, balding, built like a barrel of bricks and incapable of mincing words. "How's tricks, Phil? You can't possibly be begging to come back to California yet!"

"Not yet, Harv. Not yet. Maybe soon though. They've got me running errands. You wouldn't even believe... Or they're testing the new guy, anyway..."

"Okay, okay, you need something. What it is? Lay it on me."

"Jeez, Harv. I said hello... and yeah, I need something. Or someone. I just need a victim. Oops, forgive me, I need a trainee."

33

"Lamb to the slaughter?"

"I don't think it'll be anywhere near that interesting."

"Oh, I get it." Harvey's voice is almost laughing. "So, you got wrangled into doing favors for a Director."

"Not even a Director. Not even Deputy. Special Assistant…"

"Ha!"

"So, can you send me a sacrifice?"

"No can do, Phil. I have everyone assigned…let me rephrase that – I have everyone assigned from the class that hasn't even come in yet. I have everyone scheduled and assigned for the next year! Maybe you've heard: there's a war on! Anyway, not for favors. I mean, if there were no war, maybe I could send a kid but… c'mon."

The specter of more wasted afternoons and perhaps even an obligatory trip to Maine of all places…no, Blakeslee wouldn't be able to pressure him into that. Right? He took a long drag on the Lucky and shook his head. He wished he had a window to put his feet up on the ledge of to think this problem through. Of course, if he didn't find a way, he likely never would have that window. He put his feet up on the radiator, but quickly put them down again to avoid the heat blasting from it.

"A war, you say? I hadn't heard. Well that explains things. Dammit! So, what am I gonna do?"

"You don't have anyone there? Just find some eager beaver running around to give the job a once over and write a good report so you can show the 'not even a Director' you can follow orders and put his mind at rest. Can't you find one single eager beaver in the whole FBI Washington office?"

That rang a bell. Funny, who was it that he used to call the 'eager beaver'?

Oh no. That wouldn't work. Not in DC. Damned sure not in Maine.

But then...what choice was there? And why not?

"Remember that guy?" Bullock said. "The one who was always chipper, always bright eyed and bushy-tailed? Always... you know, the eager beaver."

"Who? Which one?"

Bollock signed; exhaled silver-gray smoke. "The Jap."

"Oh hell. Yeah, of course. *Mori*... I think, was his name... You can't use him."

"Why not?"

"Why not?! He's a Jap!"

"A Japanese-American, Harv. And a helluva recruit as I recall."

"*Japanese-American*." Harvey repeats, scornfully. "But yeah, he did pretty good on the course."

"Better than good, as I recall. Damn near the top. If not the top."

"Yeah, but... I mean, even if it you could, god knows where he is. Probably got evacuated with the rest of them."

"Evacuated?" Bullock asked, nervously scratching his wooly scalp, "I was afraid of that. You think so?"

The previous year, a couple of months after the Imperial Japanese Air Force laid waste to Pearl Harbor, President Roosevelt had issued Executive Order 9066, allowing the Army to "exclude" anyone they chose from designated "military areas." These areas included southern Arizona, all of California and the western halves of Washington state and Oregon. Lt. General John L. DeWitt was the mastermind, feeling that the potential for Japanese fifth column activity for sabotage was too great. With that, some 100,000 Japanese immigrants, and many *Nisei*, native born Americans of Japanese descent, were ordered to leave their homes and lives and move inland. Camps were set up, like overnight boom towns, in the Sierra Nevada's, in Utah… all the way out to Arkansas.

"No idea." Harv said. "Makes sense though."

It was coming back to him now. Bullock remembered the last time he saw the kid – the kid's last day as a trainee. He was amazed that Mori, of Japanese descent, got as far as he did in the FBI training, and admired the kid. But of course, after Pearl Harbor… He was starting to feel this might be a good way to set things right. Even if sending an oriental, specifically, one of Japanese descent, out to Maine was… risky. He decided to trust the kid.

"Yeah. You think you can dig him up?"

"Shouldn't be too hard. If I remember right, he'll probably race down here like Bugs Bunny the minute after he picks up the phone." Harvey paused a moment, thinking it over. "Maybe it'll be better to get one of the washouts. What was the guy's name, Beck? The big blond guy from Montana."

"I remember him. He was lazy. And a drinker, I think."

"Well, he was white. So, you wouldn't be rocking the boat sending someone that looks like the enemy."

"He looked like Hitler's ideal man to me. Blond, blue-eyed…"

"Okay, okay… Don't get all idealistic with me."

"I don't want someone who couldn't hack it to go in and muck it up. Last thing I need is trouble. Mori would've been a fine agent if, you know, the war…"

"Just sounds like it might be asking for trouble."

"Don't have much choice, do I? Anyway, can you find him for me?"

"You're 3000 miles away and I'm still running your errands. Sure. I'll dig him up for you. But I'd appreciate it if, you know, whatever happens… keep my name out of it."

"You got it. Yer a pal, Harv. Call me when you know anything."

He replaced the handset in the cradle with a hard, plastic clack. Bullock was satisfied that the solution was a workable one and immediately returned to work, not giving the matter much thought until the phone rang again just 40 minutes later. Vera was back and announced, "Agent Feynman from the San Francisco office is on the line."

"Bad news, Phil."

"You couldn't find him?"

"No, I found him. It wasn't hard. He was on a list here…he's in Manzanar."

"That's one of the camps, right?"

"Yup."

"Okay, so, he's just cooling his heels then, yeah? That's not bad news. He's finished all the training courses, right? So, he's good. We're on."

Harvey isn't convinced. "What? Look, I'm not even sure what the protocol is here, Phil. I mean, what do we do, just show up and…"

"You worry too much. Write a note on FBI letterhead. Or get a friendly judge. If you even need one. I don't care. Whatever you need to do. I guarantee you nobody will put up a stink. Just send someone to get him."

CHAPTER 5

January 29, 1943, Maine

For such a small town, the Mansfield Hotel, was actually quite nice. This was fortunate because it was also the *only* hotel in town. It had once been a grand old mansion for a prosperous family in the century past: an owner of a cannery for the fish and shellfish riches so close off shore. It was a glistening white building even in moonlight with rounded corner alcoves that made it seem like a castle: New England-style.

Trudy pulled into a space close to the front of the hotel, chucked the long Nash gearshift into first and shut off the car. When Trudy had first started driving for the judge, the Nash had intimidated her somewhat, even though she'd been driving to make deliveries for her parents' store since she was 14. She had grown to really enjoy tooling around in the swanky

Ambassador though, even if it did make her feel a little big for her britches (as her mother would say.)

Mori felt the immediate loss of warmth with real lament and gave the gleaming silver dashboard a tap, hoping to get a last bit of contact heat. "Okay." he said, stepping reluctantly back out into the icy night air. "I mean it's no Beverly Wilshire but it'll do. Especially considering where I've been bunking lately."

"Oh?" Trudy said, "Been roughing it?"

Trudy watched a strange thing happen to Mori's face before he answered. He looked off with a pause and there seemed to be a shadow darken what to this point had been a downright cheery (and she had even thought *handsome*, hadn't she?) countenance. Then, just as soon as the gloom appeared, it was replaced with a smirk. "Roughing it? Yeah, but that's job, isn't it?"

"I... guess so." Trudy said.

"Let's get inside before we're popsicles, Trudy Honeywell." He took his suitcase from her. It was awkward enough having a girl driver but he had to draw the line at the petite blond in her little leather billed cap dragging his few belongings into the hotel.

Inside was an even more pleasant surprise. He might have expected sparse, Puritan New England furnishings and hard couches under short ceilings but the lobby was spacious and decorated in a quite modern way. Art deco sofas of a chocolaty color with silver arms and legs, a painting of the hotel hanging over the stone slab fireplace. Mori proceeded directly to fire and held out his hands. Trudy followed.

"You gotta get some warmer clothes." She said.

He just nodded. The lamps had red shades and soft bulbs and cast a warm, glowing light around. With the blackout curtains drawn it seemed like a most inviting cave somehow out of time and space. Warmer and now content, Mori headed to the front desk and rang the bell.

"I've never stayed here." Trudy said, as they waited for the night manager. "I came here for Julie Abernathy's wedding reception. It was in the reception room. Well, Julie *King* now."

The Night Manager emerged from the back rather sleepily and stopped well short of the desk before he began to stare at Mori with something akin, Trudy thought, to the look one would display finding a bear going through their trash. He buttoned his jacket nervously and smoothed the flyaway straps of hair over the large bald area on top of his head. His nose, which seemed to hang in a little red ball at the end of his face, turned up a bit as if he'd stepped in something. "Yes?"

"Checking in." Mori said with enthusiasm. It had been a long trip and he was eager to hit a pillow with the side of his head. "Nice place you've got here."

"Yeeeesssss." The Night Manager said. "You have a reservation?"

"Yup!" Trudy offered helpfully. "It'll be under Judge Norris."

"And who are you?" the Night Manager asked, addressing Trudy.

"Trudy Honeywell." She says.

"And you aren't *with* this man, are you?"

"With? I don't…"

"She's the driver!" Mori said, attempting to help.

"I'm Judge Norris's assistant." She corrected him. "And, I've just met this gentleman tonight, actually. I picked him up at the train station."

The Night Manager narrowed his eyes at her and seemed to lean into the two of them. Mori was tall for an oriental, Trudy thought, at least as far as she knew... She had heard they were short. He stood as tall as the Night Manager, yet the latter seemed to loom in very disconcerting way.

"That is to say," Agent Mori offered with a helpful smile, "She collected me there in her capacity as Judge Norris's assistant. I'm here on official business, see." He removed his FBI identification and handed it to the Night Manager.

He patted down his strands of hair once more and tugged at his blood red tie as he took the wallet, then looked closer, pulling it with both hands up close to that bulbous nose. He examined it at length. Witheringly, he said the words, "*Asahito Mori*?"

Mori nodded. "You got it."

"It says here '*provisional*' next to your name."

"Yes."

"As in *temporary*?"

"Those do mean the same thing, yes."

"Japanese FBI agent?

"*American* FBI agent." Agent Mori said, raising a finger and giving a small chuckle. "Of Japanese ancestry."

The Night Manager continued his glare and held the identification card far away from his face like a far-sighted man might, though he no longer was looking at it. "Yes, well, at any rate, there must be some mistake. I do see a reservation for Judge Norris but I can't imagine how such an error can have occurred. We are all filled up, you see. Not a room to be had."

"Are you sure?" Trudy said. "I called and spoke to the fellow myself a couple of days ago. I don't remember his name...but he said it was all arranged!"

"Yes, clearly an error was made. Terribly sorry but we're all filled up."

Agent Mori straightened his collar, which he had turned up against the wind, back into place and smoothed out his still immaculate hair and tie. "I'll bet a lot of people underestimate the drawing appeal of Maine this time of year. They might think that the days of constantly below zero temperatures would discourage tourists and lead to a downturn for hotels and the like but I understand. I do. I find it bracing."

The Night Manager just grunted.

"Well, wait, so you mean there's no place for him to stay?"

"No room for him here, Miss." The Night Manager said.

"Well, nothing to be done." Agent Mori said. He shrugged and picked up his suitcase. "Honest mistake. No room at the inn, I guess. Don't have a manger out back, do ya? Or even a cowshed? Doghouse?"

"I'm afraid not." The Night Manager said, sighing impatiently.

"Well, we'll just have to try the next place. Good night, old timer!" Agent Mori was out the door with Trudy trailing on his heels.

"That's funny." She said, cranking the Nash to life. "I called and made the reservation for the judge myself. Really I did."

"There are almost no cars in the parking lot, nobody was relaxing in the lobby or even in the bar and it is Maine in the middle of winter. There may not have been a single soul in that entire hotel, Trudy."

"Then…?" she looked at him, but he just smirked, raising as eyebrow. "Oh."

"Yeah. Well, no sweat. Let's go to the next one. I'd be afraid that curmudgeon would spit in my coffee anyway."

"Next one?"

Agent Mori took some of the heat blasting from the vents and rubbed it between his hands. "Next hotel."

"Next…there is no next one."

"This is the only hotel in town? In the entire town?"

Trudy nodded. "Yeah. The only one I know of."

"Well…old ladies with a room to let then? Can't we just go to one of them?"

She shrunk a bit and pulled the bill of her cap down. "I guess we could…if I knew of any. And it's late. I'm not sure we can just show up… I could take you to the Judge's house. He'd put you up, I know. And he's got a real nice house…but it's late. I'd hate to disturb them. They're older folks, you know…"

Agent Mori held up his hand. "Alright, alright…got any bright ideas? I don't think I can sleep in the car. I'll run out of gas and freeze to death and won't even notice…"

She pulled the bill of her cap even lower, covering her eyes almost. "I have one idea…can you be very quiet?"

"Like a ninja." Mori said.

"A what?"

"I can be very quiet." He said.

CHAPTER 6

February 22, 1942, San Francisco, CA

The San Francisco field office was a giant slab of a five-story building looming right off the corner of Front Street and Golden Gate Avenue with an imposing edifice of brick below and stone on the upper levels. On top of the usual crimes being investigated, the business inside was now devoted heavily to the war effort, counter-espionage, and detecting and stopping sabotage. It had been just over two short months, following the attack on Pearl Harbor, of flurried activity and rearrangement of priorities. Asahito Mori, still a trainee, pulled up in the back of a beaten Plymouth Yellow Cab and looked up at the building with real enthusiasm. He hadn't seen the place since before Christmas and was eager to get back to it. After the attack on Pearl Harbor he'd continued his training for a few days but things with the other trainees had gotten tense. After that he'd been sent home. He didn't despair though, as Bullock had told him to just take it easy, and wait for things to get back to normal. Well, normal as they could be with a war going on and you looking a bit too much like the enemy. Secretly, Mori believed this was to his advantage and envisaged scenarios where he was assigned to a deep undercover operation, rooting out spies working for the Japanese Empire. Nobody he knew, of course, but spies sent over, trying to blend in. He also knew he'd done better than just about any of the other trainees on almost every test and the nickname "Ace" wasn't just a play on words for his name. This call from Bullock was expected and welcomed and he was figuring he'd have his choice of assignments out of the box. He didn't so much walk down the bustling, wide hallways to his appointment with Bullock, as glide.

Bullock was higher on the food chain in San Francisco and actually had an office with a window, and it looked out over some rather nice homes lined up down the avenue and clear out to the heights. He called Mori in and the eager beaver sat in his guest chair across the desk, barely containing his smile.

"You alright, Mori? Just hear a good joke or something?" Bullock asked, loosening his tie and setting fire to a Lucky Strike.

"Just fine, sir. Couldn't be better." That smile, that pomaded hair…he should be the first and only Japanese matinee idol, Bullock thought.

He pointed the pack of Lucky's at Mori as an offer but the younger man waved politely. "No thanks."

"Have a good rest, Mori? I know being on leave was… unexpected. But, ya know, so was Pearl Harbor, right?"

Mori smiled dutifully. "Just glad to be back. Eager to get to work, sir."

"Okay, well, Mori, look, I gotta say, your file is outstanding. You've really outdone yourself here. Physical tests all top-notch. Shooting, tactical...Your intelligence tests are all great. Good work. You've really put in the work and... it didn't go unnoticed."

"Gimme something harder next time!" he waved and straightened his tie. It was blue with a beige diamond in the center. He'd worn his dark blue suit, and white oxford shirt, wanting to fit in with the conservative look the agents all had. "I kid. I'm glad I was able to do so well. It was a tough road, but I set my mind to it and..."

"Yeah," Bullock interrupted. "Top marks, all around. Really. Listen..." he drags on the Lucky, stalling, "I guess you've noticed you're the only, uh, Japanese in the class."

"No kidding?" Mori waved his hand. Another joke. "In the whole FBI trainee class, I think, actually."

"Yeah, and, do you follow the news?"

"I do like to stay informed." Mori said.

"Then you've no doubt heard about Executive Order 9066?"

Mori nodded. The conversation might be about to get touchy. "Yeah. Of course."

"Got any family that have been interred?" he didn't ask the question with malice, but there was an antenna in there, to see just how raw Mori might have been feeling about it.

"Family? No. None left, sir, actually. There was only my pop and he passed a few years ago."

Bullock paused and looked at a sea gull passing by outside the window. He felt like he was about to ruin the kid's life.

Mori sat up so straight he seemed to be holding up the chair. "I don't like to second guess President Roosevelt. Big fan of The Man, no question. I'm sure he had his reasons. Or the Army did. You know, I suspect it was one of his more reactionary advisors, but that's neither here nor there. Locking people up with no due process is going to be a big to-do, I can tell you...I have to say I think it was a mistake. But when he sees what a contribution Japanese Americans can make..." Mori leaned forward and pointed his finger onto Bullock's green desk blotter for emphasis. "And I think it could be the difference that wins the war for Uncle Sam...he'll let them get back to what they do best!"

"Which is?"

"Adapting!" Mori punctuated the word by pointing his finger in the air with passion. "Wherever a Japanese goes, they adapt! My father, may he rest in peace, left Japan a penniless farmer but came to America and prospered in the fruit business. He learned English, became a pillar of the community, and made it possible for me to be here now." He spread his hands wide, to display his own adaptation, his own prosperity. The description of his father's life may have seemed a bit... exaggerated to those that knew him, but to Mori it was... mostly true.

Bullock nodded. "So, you're first generation?"

Nisei, Mori thinks, but doesn't say aloud. He may not be fluent, but that is certainly one word he knows well. "Yessir."

"I gotta ask you, Mori...why the FBI? Why'd you wanna join up with us?" Bullock flipped through his file.

Mori flashed that 100-watt smile. "Why does anyone want to be a G-man, sir? Make a difference. With the people who can really do it."

Bullock smiled, amused. "Not the fame and glory and all the money, huh?'

Mori shrugged, "We'll see what happens."

Bullock was not feeling any better about the news he had to impart. He stabbed out his Lucky and watched the remaining smoke curl up to ever so slightly darken the paint on the ceiling.

"I think this is where I can do the most good." Mori went on, spine straight as a flagpole once more. "Especially now with the war on. We all have to do our part for the war effort and I'm convinced now more than ever that this is where I can do the most good."

"Not in the Army?"

"I tried to sign up at a couple of recruiting stations but they wouldn't take me cuz I'm Japanese descent." He hadn't really meant to tell Bullock that, rather hoping he imagined him eagerly waiting by the phone to come back to the FBI.

"Too bad," Bullock said, "but yeah, they won't… and they definitely won't now."

"Why do you say that, sir?"

Bullock hesitated, he tried to sit up as straight as Mori and look him in the eye but it felt like he was stabbing the kid in the guts. "Well, the Executive Order… it means you *can't* get in the Army now. You can't be classified 1A because…" he pointed at Mori's face. Awkwardly meaning to say, because of your heritage but trailed off. "You'll be classified IV-C. Do you know what that…"?

"Enemy alien." Mori said flatly.

"Yeah, and they're, the Army I mean, they're gonna clear out the coast of any Japanese. Jap-Americans, I mean. You said you haven't any family… have you got somewhere in the country to go? Somewhere inland?"

Mori shook his head. "No."

"Well, they're setting up camps I heard. To evacuate the people to."

"Camps?" the term "concentration camps" was in the news a lot, as it seemed like Hitler's favorite way to stash away opponents. The parallel was not comforting.

"Centers. Evacuation, uh, centers." Bullock tried to cover. "If that happens, and you go. I mean, I guess if you want to stay in contact with us. If you hear anything, you know, in the cam… the centers, any, you know, fifth column activity, we can talk. We can try to look out for you…"

Mori moved to the edge of the rickety chair. "Is this an undercover assignment?"

Bullock half shrugged, half nodded. "Sure. Of sorts."

Mori held up a finger to ask a question. "So, is there something *specific*, a person or gang or what have you… Someone or something you want me to investigate?"

"No, no, look, nothing like that. Just keep us in the loop."

"That's just being an informant. You want me to go to a camp and rat on the people there? When and if this comes to pass?"

Bullock scratched his black, wooly scalp, started to think maybe is wasn't the right time to ask.

"I don't like to tell tales about what we trainees say amongst ourselves during training." Mori said, trying to maintain his composure. "But there was a kind of understanding amongst us that the better you did in training, well, you kind of had your pick of assignments. Within reason, of course."

Bullock lights another Lucky and snaps his lighter closed with a loud click. "Nobody has their pick of anything. And anyway, well, you aren't the typical trainee, are you, Mori?"

"No. I'm quite a bit better, as I've seen."

Bullock sighed and leaned back. His wooden office chair squeaked and he blew another stream of smoke straight upward toward the ceiling.

"Sir," Mori tried again, "You can take my word for it: there are no more loyal Americans than Japanese immigrants. I'd stake my life on it. Anyway, what you're asking me to do is be a... a rat. Something you could get any bum to do that lived in the neighborhood. It isn't work for an agent. I don't even speak Japanese!"

"How do you not speak Japanese?"

"Not very much I mean. Most *Nisei* don't. At least the ones I know. Look, I grew up with just my father. He was always at work. I speak *Spanish* fluently, if that helps. We lived in a largely Mexican neighborhood, see, and..."

"Spanish. Sheesh. Mori, look..." Bullock held up a hand. "Save your breath. I'm sorry. Really. But your status flags you... I mean, obviously now the FBI is... out. But later on, if you want to stay in contact as I suggested..."

"I can't be a snake in the grass to a lot of innocent people." Mori shook his head and thrust out his chin. "I'm afraid the idea isn't at all satisfactory."

Bullock grimaced and nodded. "I understand."

Mori sat for a moment, realizing that he would now have to find another path but unsure what the next move should be. He half expected to be arrested, although he knew it was the army that would be rousting people if... when this whole stupid "evacuation" thing went forward. He wanted out of San Francisco in a hurry and wondered who was left back home in L.A. He stood and made to leave, looking back from the pebbled glass with Bullock's name on it back to the man himself.

"Sorry, kid." Bullock said, truthfully. "Good luck."

Mori walked away, down the black and white chessboard floor. He tried to leave hastily but somehow casually, feeling like he didn't recognize the building or even the country anymore. In one of those coincidences that have a way of altering the direction of a life, he ran into one of his main rivals in the training school for the first of two times, and by far the less consequential. It was Jack Taylor, another recruit from L.A., like himself, though from Brentwood. Mori spent most of his childhood in East LA: Boyle Heights, Chavez Ravine... Taylor had a long cowboy face and crisp, sandy blond hair. He loomed over Mori at six feet three and was carrying an unlit pipe. He looked more like Randolph Scott, Mori thought, than the real McCoy.

"Ace." Jack said. "Just in with the brass, eh? What's the story?"

Jack was a good shooter and a heck of a physical specimen, even if his size made him a bit slow on the course and his intelligence tests, while fine, weren't quite what Mori's were.

"Can't really say, Jackie-boy. Hush-hush, you know." He smirked conspiratorially.

Jack nodded, and Mori, despite himself, thought there might have been skepticism in his face. "See you at graduation then?"

"You know it. Unless the Army drags me off." He turned away, down the hallway and to the elevators, thinking it wasn't likely he would ever see the inside of the building again.

CHAPTER 7

January 29, 1943, Maine

Trudy pulled the Nash up in front of a whitewashed storefront. Mori could read the sign for just for a moment before she extinguished the headlights: *Honeywell Hardware*.

"Nice alliteration." he said.

The good people of the town had extinguished their lights for the blackout drill like responsible citizens but Mori could still see around the town square somewhat. There was a gazebo bandstand in the middle of the town common and it looked like the area around it has been flooded for an ice rink. He could see a clothing store, a grocery store, a gas station and a bridge leading off; beyond it a hill and darkened houses. All of these surrounded and faced the bandstand. It was idyllic, he thought, or probably would be in daylight. A picture post card.

Trudy held up her index finger to her lips in a shushing motion and Mori nodded. He grabbed his suitcase and followed her up the short steps and into the hardware store. Trudy opened it in such a way that the bell on the door only makes a hollow metal tap (she seemed to have some experience sneaking in) and waved at him to follow.

"My folks are probably asleep. We live upstairs above the store." She whispered this and kept moving through the aisles, which she seemed to know very well. "They probably conked out after Abbot and Costello. So, you'll be good here until morning anyway. And then I'll explain it all to Dad."

He whispered, "Okay." And shuffled along behind her, making out various items in the dark: hammers, levels, snow shovels, a row of shotguns.

Trudy ushered him into a back room with no windows. She set light to a kerosene lantern and some surrounding shelves, rough and hand-built, piled up with extra stock, came into view. There was a desk with a vice bolted to the corner and a Bakelite radio on top, pushed to the back. Next to the desk was a cast iron wood stove that looked like a giant toaster and a small pile of logs next to it. A few feet from the stove was a small, bare, army style cot with a tiny pillow. Trudy stooped and opened the wire latch on the stove door and stabbed inside with a metal poker. She examined the waning coals and threw some kindling on top, let it fire brightly, then a bigger log and closed the door again. "That ought to make it through the night." She said. "Gimme just a sec!" she said and disappeared back into the store.

Mori looked at the heavy canvas of the cot and sighed as he remembered the look of the lush couches at the Hotel. He had been traveling quite a while and the idea of what the beds at the hotel looked like was something he was trying to put out of his mind, Still, his fatigue was such that the canvas started to look better and better. Also, it had, he reminded himself, a certain and very recent familiarity...

Trudy returned with some sheets and a blanket and went about fixing up the cot as best she could. "If this looks like an army cot that's because it is. My dad bought it from some guy who was in the first war. But it's super comfy! Well, kinda...anyway, I nap on it sometimes. Dad too. He naps like every day at lunch. Anyway, it's all yours tonight. Better than out in the snow, anyway, right?"

"Definitely. But, um, your Dad may want it back in the morning."

"I'll explain everything to him. He can be a hothead, but he'll understand. Really."

"Trudy, thanks for everything." Mori said. "Putting me up and all. I'm sure that's above and beyond what your job requires."

"Aw, it's no problem. I can't believe that jerk at the hotel! What a snob! Chucking you out on your ear in the dead of winter and in the middle of night. Who does that?" she tugged on the bill of the cap again. It was a little nervous gesture, it seemed. He always tried not to pay much attention to Caucasian girls, even the cute ones. It was best just to avoid the trouble. Still, it was hard to deny that Trudy certainly was appealing.

"Well, I appreciate it, anyway." He sat his suitcase down with his hat and jacket on top. The room was fairly small and without windows and the fire had already started to warm things considerably. He kicked off his shoes and wiggled his almost numb toes next to the stove. They started to prickle and tingle and he wished he'd worn (or owned) a pair of socks thicker than the rather smart gray ones with the arrows on them that he was sporting just then.

Mori longed to lay down and drift off to sleep but was still a bit wired from the long trip. He dug a book from his suitcase and sat it next to him on the cot. "Try to wake up before your dad does, okay Trudy? I don't want him coming in and finding a handsome Japanese-American stranger in his stockroom."

"Oh, I will. He makes an awful racket when he gets up. Snores when he sleeps. Always loud…come to think of it he makes an awful racket doing just about anything. Do you have everything you need?"

"I'll be just fine, Trudy. Thanks."

"Whatcha reading?"

"This?" he picked up his dog-eared paperback and passed it over to her. She sat at the chair by the desk and looked it over.

"*The Big Sleep*" she reads aloud, and her eyes widen as she looks at the blond on the cover, covered only in a bed sheet with a gun in her hand. "Never heard of it."

"It's about a detective from L.A. Reminds me of home."

"I guess your job takes you away from home a lot, eh?"

Agent Mori nodded. "The job? Well… sure. But, you know, life in general."

She flipped through. "Any good? Looks a little racy…"

"Good? Heck yeah." He leaned in conspiratorially, "Me and Phillip Marlowe - that's the main character in the book, see, well, we're a lot alike. Well, I mean, he's a Caucasian of course, and kind of depressed, I think, and kinda fast with women…but upstairs," he tapped at his temple. "We're peas in a pod."

"Wow." Trudy said.

"Give it a read."

She looked at the cover again. "Hadn't better let Dad catch me with it…but okay! Looks exciting. L.A. sounds amazing! I've never been anywhere, really. Portland a few times. Went to a baseball game in Boston with my Dad when I was really little. But I will, someday. Maybe I'll make something of myself in the war effort. Women are doing a lot now."

"How old are you, Trudy, if you don't mind my asking?"

"I don't mind. I'm 20. Well, almost 20."

"And you're concerned about your Dad catching you with a book?"

"No. It's just… looks a little racy is all. I've read plenty. I'm a modern woman, really. I'm going to go to college to be an actress!" she blurted out this last bit a little louder than she'd meant to. She looked behind her as if her father would be coming down at any minute to admonish her to get to sleep. But she knew he slept like a rock. "I mean, I might. I'm thinking about it, anway."

"Well, you don't need to go to college for that. Though I guess some of the best ones do."

"Yeah? You think I've got what it takes?"

"Sure! You could walk on right now and get a bunch of parts. Best friend roles to start, probably. But once they glam you up...sure thing. You've got the looks. The rest is just acting the part."

"Acting the part." She repeated, slowly.

Mori nodded. "Yup."

She looked the book over again and stuffed it into her jacket pocket with a faraway smile. "Get some sleep. I'll get you first thing in the morning."

He thanked her again and she was off. In a few moments the wood stove had gotten the small room so warm that he kicked off the blanket. A few minutes after that he was fast asleep.

CHAPTER 8

July 19, 1942, Los Angeles, CA

Sofia stroked the hair on the side of Mori's head, around the ear and fluttered her elegant nails at the stubble on his neckline. It sent a contented shiver down his spine. "Billy, you should come along tonight. It'll be a gas, really."

She knew him as Billy Kim, aspiring actor and Korean-American. When he purchased the fake ID, he saw no reason not to adopt the entire persona. Breaking the law made him feel a bit queasy, even as convinced as he was that the law was unjust. Yet things like meeting Sofia Villaraigosa, who sat across from him, stroking his hair and looking affectionately into his eyes – he felt that he had made, unquestionably, the right decision. She was shooting a scene today and was dolled up in a harem girl outfit of sparkling gold fabric. She occasionally had to reposition the chiffon veils around her face and ample cleavage.

"Tell me about your scene." Mori said.

She smiled and clapped excitedly. Her English was quite good but occasionally she had to reach back for the right Spanish word. "It's so fun! Bob Hope finds himself in our Harem, see, and we girls parade by him and he says something...*travieso*[1] and I smile over my shoulder and keep walking."

Sofia was what Hollywood casting agents called *exotic*. Descended from Mexican aristocrats, she had smoky almond shaped eyes, and skin like coffee and cream. With her astonishing figure and wavy sable-colored hair, Sofia got a lot of work as Harem girls, jungle temptresses, eye-catching maids...usually non-speaking parts, even though her accent wasn't terribly pronounced.

They sat together in the Paramount Commissary on the corner of a little metal table. Around them, an astounding array of people, from spacemen in silver jumpsuits to gangsters with spats and period piece bit players in comically large hoop skirts and bustles. All of them chattered away over their chops, chicken or sandwiches. Mori had ordered a simple hamburger and milk. Sofia was picking at a fruit plate and coffee. Mori has no need for costume today: his last paying gig as an extra was a week or so back and his face was mainly covered. He had been a henchman in a sci-fi serial called "The Space Rangers" and only had to nod when given orders by the alien bad guy, who was dressed like a silver painted monk. He'd had a role as a jungle extra in something called "White Cargo" awhile before that and even had a scene where Walter Pidgeon walked in front of him. Still, work was sparse. He had a friend who was going to get him into another serial but it was shooting on the cheap up in the hills and not starting for a few weeks. For now, he was making a few bucks helping build sets. Honestly, it was all a lot of fun, and

---

[1] naughty

he barely thought about the FBI, or even the war. Yet every time there was war news it nagged at him to be excluded.

"Is that Veronica Lake?" Sofia asked, nodding over to a platinum blond eating spaghetti by the shade of a potted fern.

He squinted for a moment. "Nah. Stand in."

Sofia nodded, a little disappointed. She adjusted her veils for modesty, though it was something of a losing battle. "I'm going dancing tonight with some of the girls. I feel like I might dance all night! I'd like to dance a few with you."

"I'd like that too." Sofia had been in the back seat of the convertible, waiting to shoot a scene and in between takes Mori had hopped over the fender and into the seat beside her. He started asking all about her in Spanish: that had been a week before. Ever since then they'd been seeing each other every day and going to parties every night.

Sofia clutched his arm and turned it slowly to look at his wristwatch. She had to get back to the set. She enjoyed touching him, tracing the lines on his palm, running her hands through his hair, clutching his arm as they walked and leaning in. "You're not going to leave too and go off to the war, are you Billy?"

He shrugged. "When my number is called, I'll go. Have to. I want to."

She pouted and swats him on the arm. "You want to? You want to leave me?"

"No, honey. If I could take you along, I would. Well, not... you know what I mean. Anyway, it might be a long time from now."

"I don't know. The way everyone is getting their draft notices…"

"I'm here now. And I'll stay as long as I can."

Her dark brown eyes still looked a little sad but she smiled a bit for him. They walked back to the sound stage where the red light was still out indicating filming had not yet resumed. Mori got a bit sad himself actually, thinking about it. If he'd met her under his own name – well, it would never work knowing he'd lied from the very start. Anyway, when he looked at her he knew she was that rare breed of shooting star: she'd either Anglicize her name, work out the accent and become a real movie star or marry a millionaire and be waited on her whole life, which he couldn't deny he rather thought she deserved. Mori knew he was going to be get into the war sooner or later in some capacity and, after that, well, it probably wouldn't be the sort of life she was built for.

"As long as you can." She said. She planted a soft kiss on his lips and entered the soundstage, running her hand down his arm, clutching his hand until she was gone and there remained her scent of jasmine and cinnamon. Mori stood there with a dumbstruck smile until the red light came on and reminded him that he had to get back to work too.

That evening, he decided to walk to meet up with Sofia at the nightclub (she was going in a group with a bunch of other starlets.) It was at the "Zamboanga South Seas Club" off of Slauson Ave. Mori decided to walk the few blocks in the humid night air, breathing it in and admiring the rhythmic movement of the palms that lined the street as they swayed overhead. It was a pleasant sensation and he felt very… alive. Usually he had a niggling feeling of wasting time and feeling useless, restless, without purpose. Working on the movies, meeting Sofia – maybe it was enough to keep him occupied. At any rate, as cars passed and people walked along around him in his home city – he felt a kind of peace.

The club was crowded, dimly lit, loaded with cigarette smoke and laughter. There were booths made of bamboo and upholstered in fabric with artsy shells and fish on them. The seats at the raised bar had grass skirts dangling from the back and bamboo rafters across the ceiling and some lighting that made it seem like a giant south seas hut right off an LA thruway. Or that was the general idea, anyway. The congestion made it hotter inside and he couldn't spot Sofia anywhere. Maybe she's late, he thought. She was the "grand entrance" type. He stepped back outside to get some air and cool off. On the sidewalk he met some Mexican guys waiting for women as well and they conversed in Spanish for a few minutes. They were decked out in colorful zoot suits and hats with feathers. One has a long gold chain that matched his gold tooth. They talked about their neighborhood, and it turned out to be only two blocks from where Mori had grown up.

"Coreano, ¿eh? Bueno, tu español es excelente. ¡Ni siquiera tienes acento gringo!"[2] Said Ignacio, the one with the gold chain.

Mori heard somebody angrily grunt "motherfucker!" from nearby and turned to see who uttered such a word.

Three Caucasian servicemen were eyeballing them. They were navy men, out in uniform. The same voice, from a tough looking, dark haired one said "We go off to the service so they can stay here and brush up against our women in their goddam monkey suits."

Another one said, "Wetbacks."

---

[2] "Korean, eh? Well, your Spanish is excellent. You don't even have a gringo accent!"

65

"Gringo jerk off…" said Ignacio.

"We're going too, you know, gringo!" Said one of Ignacio's pals. "My cousin Guillermo went to basic two weeks ago! Fuck you!"

Mori could see the writing on the wall here and wanted no part of it. He much preferred an unbloodied face to meet Sofia with – to say nothing of staying off the radar with police, should they happen by. Still, even after such a brief encounter, he felt a certain loyalty to his be-zoot suited companions. He needn't have worried though. Other Mexicans saw what was transpiring and approached to put their two cents in, some of them were Navy men too, by the looks of it. From across the street, other Caucasian servicemen came to the scene as well. Mori exchanged a look with a Negro serviceman who shook his head quickly and then faded into the crowd as if he wasn't there. Mori followed his lead.

The crowd continued to build but Mori could only hear the melee now, with people cheering, shouting and admonishing in turn. He heard some bottles breaking and some angry shouts. Police started to appear on the edges of the crowd, but the combatants either hadn't noticed or didn't care. There might have been a dozen or more people on each side fighting by that point, Mori reckoned, and far more onlookers. He continued to slip away from the fight, and the police…

Until he backed directly into an unyielding body that felt like a brick wall. Slowly, he turned to see. At first, he thought he'd accidently bumped into Randolph Scott.

"Ace?" said Jack Taylor.

"Jack." Mori said, and he started to get a real feeling of his goose being quite well done indeed. There was a young policeman at Jack's side. Jack looked to be on the job: light jacket, small brimmed fedora, bulge under his left arm where he was clearly carrying a heater, FBI standard issue .38 no doubt.

"You've been missed, Ace."

"I'm touched. Hope I haven't worried anyone?"

"Well, there was speculation where you might be anyway. You just...disappeared. Rumor in the office said someone saw a document with your name on that said you were supposed to be on a bus to Manzanar. No word that you ever did get on that bus though." Jack made a motion at Mori and the policeman interpreted this as a sign to search Mori's suit. The policeman patted Mori down and took the wallet from his inside jacket pocket, then handed it to Jack. He flipped it open and rifled around inside.

"William Kim?" Jack read, thinking it really very funny. "Korean, eh?"

He shrugged.

"Bet it seems like a small world right now."

"You could say that..."

"Cuff him and wait here." Jack said to the policeman. "Load him on the paddy wagon when they get here."

Mori sighed as the metal shackles were applied really snugly to his wrists. At least they cuffed him with his hands in front. Jack draped Mori's jacket over the cuffs.

Jack withdrew the fake ID and stuffed the wallet with just a few dollars and some movie stubs back into Mori's jacket pocket. "I'll get rid of this for you." He said, holding the ID between his first two fingers. "If they catch you with it, they might call you a spy. Call it a courtesy for an old colleague." He left and faded into the crowd as if he'd just been an ill spirit and Mori was left with the young policeman. Worst of all, he *had* done Mori a favor, really, disposing of the fake driver's license and he really didn't want any fond feelings for Jack or the Bureau. A phony ID might have meant real trouble and he felt stupid for even having done it.

It took a while for the paddy wagons. The fight dragged on and the cops, it seemed, waited for everyone to get their licks in. Mori couldn't really see through the crowd very well but it didn't look as if one side or the other had gotten the upper hand. By the time he was loaded onto the police vehicle he had been standing with the cop for around fifteen minutes, listening to the crowd "ooh" and "ahh", shouting encouragement and curses. Mori fought back the creeping sensation of doom, seeing men in the same uniform fighting each other for reasons of race or language... he shook his head. In the back of the panel wagon the heavy black doors slammed shut. He didn't recognize any of his fellow detainees. He saw the cop who was watching him point in his direction. Giving instruction. Likely from Jack, about what to do with him, no doubt. He scanned the crowd for Sofia but didn't notice her anywhere. Race fights like this would go on for a year or more, even as the war raged. The next summer, 1943, it would come to a head and the papers would call them the "zoot suit riots." Mori would be long gone by then.

The paddy wagon rumbled to life and he looked around at his bloodied fellow riders. They cursed and shouted and raged at strangers outside on the pavement. Mori looked back again to the throng, dressed swankily, looking shocked but energized, laughing, cursing, drinking... He thought he could hear steel drum music from the club over the hum of the crowd – back to normal. He looked again for Sofia but couldn't see her anywhere. He thought of her all the way to the police station, but he never saw her again.

CHAPTER 9

January 30, 1943, Maine

"Alright, now get up real slow and don't try anything funny!"

Mori felt the tiny, cold circle of a gun barrel in his shoulder and fought the urge to jump up, startled. He didn't know the voice and couldn't turn to see who was speaking.

"Okay, okay. Take it easy." Mori said and slowly rose to his feet as best he could. He still didn't dare look around just yet but he thought he saw light coming from the door behind him: it must be morning, he thought. He felt as though he had just closed his eyes.

"Shut your mouth! Not a word, Hero-Heeto!" the voice hissed and jammed the heater hard into the tense muscle between his shoulder blades. He imagined whoever it was looking him over as he slept, examining his features... he had a shiver.

"Plug him." said a voice behind the other one, a younger voice, Mori thought.

"Nah...might be a spy. Then we gotta find out what he knows and what he's doing here."

Mori attempted a look over his shoulder and caught a quick peripheral look at his new acquaintances. Both were in police uniforms, but he didn't get much of a chance to examine their faces.

"Turn around and keep the hands up!"

Mori had raised his hands carefully. "Officers..." he tried again. "If I may..."

The policeman directly behind him got very close to his ear; close enough for Mori to tell he'd had both beer and onions fairly recently. "Boy...shut up. If you know what's good for you."

Exasperated, Agent Mori simply said, "Check my inside coat pocket."

He felt a thump against the back of his head. Handle of the gun, likely. Just a love tap; a warning, but enough to make him see little stars, a rush of blood, and jangle his nerves. The cop stepped slowly to the jacket, which was resting on the office chair, and kept the gun trained on Mori while he rummaged through the pocket. The cop was a big man, 40 years old or so probably, sandy brown hair that fell into his face, though it was shaved closely around the sides. His face was doughy though he seems to be in good shape otherwise, and he had a wide, flared nose and just the sliver of lips for a mouth. His eyes were small, close set, and dark. The gun was even bigger than Mori had first thought: an enormous Smith and Wesson .45. The cop fished out the ID and looked it over at length, as if he couldn't quite reconcile who was in front of him and what the identification card said. He continued looking perplexed for a while, then he seemed amused and a smirk split his face in a way Mori found disagreeable to look at.

"Agent Ass-a-Heeto-More-Eye." The cop said. According to his name tag his name was Captain Edward Ballard. "Provisional."

Agent Mori nodded. "Asa is fine. Or Agent Mori if you prefer to keep it professional. May I put my hands down?"

"If you wanna get shot, maybe. Otherwise, I'd keep them right where they are."

"Provisional?" the voice from the doorway said. "What's that mean?" It did indeed say "provisional" on Mori's ID. Bullock couldn't very well have legally issued him the credentials of a full agent, but since he had been a trainee anyway, the provisional designation was wide enough to accommodate him.

"It means bullshit." Captain Ballard said, and moved the hair off his forehead with his non-gun hand. The gun hand was still pointing the .45 at Mori, though his elbow had dropped to his waist, almost casually.

"I assure you I am who I say I am...who that identification says I am, that is."

Captain Ballard approached. The barrel of that huge gun poked into Mori's gut, brushing his undershirt. "Oh, of course. You're a Jap in the FBI and you're on the coast of Maine on a mission...right?"

"Mission? That's not the word, really. But, now that you ment..."

Captain Ballard's eyes narrowed. "Did you sneak in from Canada? You headed to the naval bases in Kittery? You looking for secrets to send home to Tojo and the boys?! Huh?!"

"Captain, again, really...I can assure you...I'm an American. I'm not a spy! Call Washington. They'll vouch for me."

"Even if you ain't a spy, you sure ain't an American."

Mori decided to ignore that. "Call Special Agent Phillip Bullock. He's my direct superior. This is just a misunderstanding. Trudy! Talk to Trudy. She'll tell you..."

"Little girl is upstairs. My deputy is talking to her and her parents now. Hopefully, she isn't an accomplice."

"She...no. I mean, there isn't anything to...talk to Judge Norris."

Captain Ballard eyed him suspiciously. "Why would I do that, exactly?"

Mori felt he'd better tread lightly. "He's an important man and...I believed he's already been briefed as to the situation. My arrival, that is, and the reason."

"Which is..." the Captain then held up a hand. "Know what? Save it. We'll get your bullshit story down at the station." He clapped handcuffs on Mori, tight and quick and the metal was frigid against the skin on his wrists.

"Shoes?" he nodded toward his two-tone wingtips.

"You'll live." Ballard said, shaking his head. "Claypool." Ballard called to the other man, a very fit man with curly, sandy hair and about six foot three, easily, "Go make sure the square is clear."

Of course, the square *was* clear, as it was just sunup and the town had yet to awaken from a heavy winter slumber. Ballard clutched Agent Mori's arm like a bird of prey with a tasty morsel in its talon and led him roughly down the center aisle of the store and onto the street. For a moment, Mori thought he heard Trudy upstairs loudly pleading something he couldn't quite make out.

When the thin material of his stockings hit the icy blacktop and the wet snow soaked them through, it robbed Mori's body of what little heat it had in an instant. He began to shiver violently but tried to control it, not wanting to show weakness in front of the police. Mori was almost thankful that Ballard was rushing him forward so hurriedly on the sidewalk as it gave his feet less time to remain on the cold ground. He couldn't see a squad car and decided not to enquire about it but just to endure the walk. Ballard led him out of the town square, around the brick drug store and across some railroad tracks. It wasn't far until he saw a building with a clock tower that said "Town Hall" which had an office off to the side that carried the town seal and the word "Police." They ascended a small incline and the dry powder that had gathered and hadn't yet been plowed no longer sends daggers into the soles of his feet: he could no longer feel them at all.

This is all a misunderstanding, he wanted to say, and easily put right, but he held his tongue for now as he was led inside the police station, which was really just one large room, a smaller office to the side, three desks in rows, two to one side, one on the other, and a single jail cell in the back. Looked like in the westerns, Mori thought. These two are a bit scary, he couldn't help but admit to himself, but he remained confident that when everything was straightened out, they could work together and put this behind them.

Mori was deposited in the cell. There was a long-ish bench and a dented paint can on the floor that seemed rather unmistakably the only way to relieve oneself. Looking out on the police station Mori could see the ancient wooden desks and a door off to the side that was probably Captain Ballard's office, though "Captain Smith" was painted on the marbled glass. The one the captain had called "Claypool" was staring in on him like a hunter who just seen his trap get sprung. There was another, unoccupied desk with a nameplate on it: *Officer Falkenham*. Ballard scrutinized the FBI credentials in his hands at length, turning it over even and looking at the new leather of the wallet around it.

Captain Ballard leaned against the desk behind him with a practiced ease and folded his long arms in a manner that left him looking pensive, with the FBI identification still dangling from the end of his left hand. It is warm in the station, and sweat formed on his brow. Mori too felt the heat begin to prickle his skin, his head began to beat and his throat to burn. He didn't seem able to sweat and he shivered still, despite himself. He was feeling quite ill, suddenly.

"Awright." Ballard said, "Now that you're all safe and sound why don't you tell me your bullshit story."

Mori did his best to smile good naturedly. "Really, Captain, as much as I respect and even appreciate your vigilance, everything I've told you is true."

"You're an FBI agent? That's the story?" he looked at the ID again and then tossed it on the desk. He wiped the hair out of his eyes and shook his head. "How old are you?"

"That isn't really relevant, Captain."

"Relevant? Are you shitting me? What are you? Twenty?"

"Twenty-three, Captain."

"Un-huh…new to the game then, eh?"

Mori's sick feeling only worsened. His head was buzzing and now that he could sweat again, he couldn't seem to stop. Beads of it trickled down him, increasing his shivering. He nodded.

"So, what are you doing here?"

Mori knew, even as he grew increasingly light-headed and as his head thumped and he tried to direct all of his energy into suppressing his shivering, that he must play his part to protect the local situation. Calling out the judge as the prime mover to the local cops wasn't something he should do, even if they already suspected. "The Bureau took note of the suicides here over the past two winters. I'm here to review the situation and make a report."

Neither the Captain nor Claypool moved at all or seemed to have much of a reaction. Claypool then broke the silence by putting his feet up on the desk and smirking. "They sent you up here for *that*?"

"Bullshit." Ballard said again. "With the goddam war on they send a little twenty-three-year-old Jap, never arrested anyone in his life up here to my town…"

"This is very much a part of the war effort." Mori said, starting to wing it with his story a bit. "I'm with the civil r-r-rights desk." He couldn't manage to keep the shivering out of his speech. He tried to hug himself warm and wished he could throw off the cuffs and run back for his jacket. He was so cold that even if they pulled their guns to stop him, he thought he might still try it, if he had been strong enough. "Axis propaganda uses the stuff here on the home front in their campaigns to discredit the USA overseas. With our allies, even. They say that the way the negro is treated here is no different than the way they treat the Jews over there and so what do we have to say about it? And with all the suicides here being Indians...well, they figure they could say how can we find fault with the Germans suspending the civil liberties of the Jews when they did the same thing to the Indians, even if it was 50 or 100 years ago. Propaganda is a tool of war, gentlemen. And one of..."

"Awright, shut up. So, you're here from the *civil rights desk* at the FBI. That's your story?"

"Of course. How would I know about it otherwise?"

"You could read a damn paper and make it up. Like a spy."

"Call Agent Phil B-b-bullock. In Washington. He'll verify everything." His shivering had become harder to control, he felt as if he were having spasms. His throat was dry and he couldn't keep his eyes focused.

Ballard approached the bars of the cell slowly, then rapped his knuckles against the metal. "And Judge Norris? Why did you mention him? Why does he know all this before me...hell, why does he know this at all?"

"He's the local representative in the state legislature. I'm sure it was just a matter of protocol."

"Protocol would have been going through *me!*" He said it through his teeth, with some irritation.

Captain Ballard loomed beyond the bars like a silhouette blocking out the sun. His presence suddenly made Mori feel quite vulnerable. His soaked and exposed stockinged feet were now entirely numb. "N-n-no offense was intended, Captain."

"Well, I hope, Mr...." He clearly and purposefully avoided saying "Agent" as he picked up the ID and examined it again, "*More-eye*, that you can understand how I might be skeptical of your bullshit story..."

"I do wish you wouldn't keep saying..."

"And some Jap fella, oh excuse me, Japanese-*American* fella appears out of nowhere, doesn't check in with this department, doesn't send advance word of his arrival – in fact, nobody does. The FBI doesn't send advance word..." Ballard leaned back on the desk, his shadow receded and he tossed the ID back on top of the blotter.

"I think I see your point, Captain."

"I'm so glad."

Officer Claypool laughed at this. The short guffaw came from behind a newspaper he was looking at, though he didn't seem to be reading it, and his feet were up on the desk. He was a hulk of a man. Mori could see his shoulders around the sides of the paper.

Mori's teeth chattered. He was a good judge of his body usually and though he almost never got sick he felt it coming on him now very strongly. "May I ask why I'm being held?"

Captain Ballard shrugged and played with the leather strap on the holster of his Colt pistol. "Wanna call it trespassing?"

"Trudy invited me to use the room when I was turned away…"

"*Trudy*, is it? How familiar!" he shook his head. "Well, I was gonna say 'suspicion of espionage' but I didn't want to hurt your feelings."

"Captain…" he felt weak and tried to get up from the bench to emphasize his case but found it more difficult than he imagined it would be. "Please. Just call Washington. I report to Agent Phillip Bullock. He'll explain everything."

Ballard nodded. "In due time." He said. He spun away and took his heavy winter coat from the rack by the door. "Claypool! Watch him!" He put the coat on quickly, wrapped a muffler around his neck and put his Captains cap on top.

"You going somewhere?"

The Captain just repeated "Watch him!" and was quickly out the door.

Claypool watched him go and then when the door was closed, immediately turned his attention to Mori. He walked up to the bars, examining Mori again like a monkey in the zoo, as before. "I've never seen a Jap up close before." He said.

"Is it ev-v-verything you'd hoped?" Mori asked. He knew it is warm in the station – he just couldn't seem to *feel* it. He tried to recede into himself, to make himself small and conserve heat and energy.

"Seen 'em in the movies, I guess. Charlie Chan and that… Or is that Chinese? That's Chinese, ain't it? Well, whatever you call it. You really a spy?"

"I'm an FBI agent, Officer Claypool."

Officer Claypool though that was very funny indeed. When he made that guffaw of his it made his tiny lips pucker like he was whistling and his square jaw jut outward and make a little snapping noise. "Un-huh." He said.

"Officer Claypool, may I have a glass of water?"

He didn't budge, just stared, and didn't get any water.

"Officer, a glass of water, if you…"

Officer Claypool backed away from the bars and said. "Wait 'til the Captain gets back!" He went back to the desk, put up his feet and resumed reading the newspaper, or at least holding it as if he were.

Mori didn't have the strength to protest. He decided to curl up on the bench. It was terrifically uncomfortable but laying down took away some of the buzzing is his head. He wanted to rub some feeling back into his feet but couldn't. He looked at the scratches and wood grain of the bench's surface, taking in the swirls and jagged terrain as if his eyes had become a telescope to a distant, hostile planet. The bench was so unforgiving that ordinarily it would have been nearly impossible to sleep on. He shivered and sweat, his black hair was drenched and he caught a whiff of the scent of his pomade before he drifted into unconsciousness.

CHAPTER 10

January 25, 1943, Manzanar Internment Camp, California

"So, what does that mean? You're sprung?"

Miyakawa looks at Mori dumfounded. He couldn't believe the kid's dumb luck. Miyakawa was about ten years older than Mori and he had a wife, two daughters and mother-in-law all in Manzanar with him. He was rather fat, and probably the best friend Mori had made in the camp. Miyakawa was in charge of the commissary for their sector, based on his experience on the outside having run a hash house in Long Beach. On that experience alone, he'd been thrust into the position of preparing meals for hundreds of people a day. That was the sort of ad hoc division of labor that happened often in Manzanar. Mori acted as his de facto assistant. His main job was preparing enormous pots of rice and opening number ten cans of fruit, vegetables or gold-lacquered c-ration cans of stew, beans, or whatever the army trucked in. He'd gotten the rhythm of opening the large number 10 cans down pat: slide the big can under the metal bar, slap down the mechanism and listen as the metal tooth slams into the can and the hiss of air escapes. Mori's arms would whirl and he'd unleash the contents of army surplus foodstuffs to crowds of mostly miserable, stunned Japanese-American faces, most trying to make the best of things, leery of the future.

Manzanar, along with the other camps, had the peculiar distinction of being the newest towns in America, and they looked the part. They were spread out through the west (but not too close to the Pacific Coast) and in the South, all filled with these Japanese-Americans, expelled from their west coast homes by the Army. They had to end up somewhere – and so there they were. As hordes of families moved in, the building continued and builders struggled to keep up. In the rush, many of the living quarters, especially, grew more and more shoddy. They were comprised of wooden frame barracks in neat little rows, clad with tar paper, clapboard or tin and usually uninsulated. The wind whipped through and left high sierra dust over every surface. Usually several families were crammed into the living quarters, mothers, fathers, children and grandparents, sleeping two or sometimes more to a bunk in the light of bare bulbs hanging by wires from the pitched ceilings. The grid system layout was likely meant for efficiency and clarity but really just made it seem more institutional, with all the streets named after letters, all the buildings square and difficult to make homey.

If he had allowed himself to get down about his lot, Mori figured it would be easy to find the whole thing depressing. He was honestly surprised more people weren't. Mostly, the internees were indignant, shocked but still proud. There were some panicky types, and a few that succumbed to hopelessness, but mostly they were making the best of things, riding it out and hoping for the best. He liked listening to the older folks; they reminded him of his father. He'd never really thought of himself as "proud" of being Japanese-American, but these people and their wherewithal... maybe pride was the word.

After being detained by Jack, it was only a few days later that a bus with caged windows pulled into the gates at Manzanar and unceremoniously dumped him and the rest of the people on the overloaded bus there. However incomplete the barracks may have looked, the guard towers looked sound and sturdy, staffed by young Caucasian Soldiers with high powered rifles.

Mori tried at first to bunk with everyone else but found that he by himself, a young man and unattached, was inevitably separating a family or getting in the way of their privacy, such as it was. It didn't feel right, since he was alone and had no family: might as well let relatives stay together rather than take up an awkward bunk in their midst, he figured. He found that he could easily fit a cot into the area behind the wall with ovens in the kitchen building. He sought out Miyakawa and volunteered his services for the privilege of a warm and quiet place to sleep. For a few months, as others slept in the dusty barracks trying to find enough wood to feed their stoves and stave off the autumn and then winter winds, Mori slept like a baby behind the cook ovens.

Mori had never really lived with a majority of people who were of the same descent as he was...and the adjustment was an awkward one at times. He managed to win over a few people – like Mrs. Matsuoka, an ancient bibliophile who had managed to drag an enormous trunk of books with her – but for the most part he kept to himself or played cards with Miyakawa. His free time was fleeting, anyway: there was always work to be done in the kitchen, and he rather enjoyed the busy pace. His usual day was getting up at 5 and prepping enormous pots of oatmeal and opening cans of fruit preserves as Miyakawa and others did the cooking. Then he would help clean and set up for lunch. When he received orders from Miyakawa he always responded "Yes Chef!" because he'd read it in a book that it was the proper response for a sous chef, the lieutenant of the kitchen. He'd take an hour or so in the afternoon and called it "siesta." It was usually then that he would read whatever Mrs. Matsuoka had for him or pal around with Miyakawa. Dinner was soon to follow and after that he usually fell into his cot, too tired to even read. Occasionally he would venture out in pursuit of that rare delicacy that was foreign to him: Japanese-American girls. When he learned to play at their speed, he got along with them okay.

Food was never at a shortage, at least not while Mori had been there, though he'd heard that at first, deliveries were sometimes short or late. People also planted gardens in between the roads and living quarter blocks. They even had an orchard growing. "Let's just ride this out until we don't suspect you anymore," the government seemed to be saying. But there was no escaping the cramped quarters, the teeming concentration of humanity, the outhouse smells wafting through the camp, the din of voices. There was no escaping the slapdash hospitals and the diseases that accompany people and thrive when they're jammed together. There was no escaping also, naturally, the guard towers placed around the perimeter strategically, and inside those: the men with rifles.

"Just like you said." Miyakawa said as he shook his head.

"Hmm? What did I say?"

"You said you'd be out of here in no time. That you knew you'd be needed for the war effort or something like that. I wasn't listening because I thought it was some crazy gag."

Mori was busy packing. He had dragged his two suitcases out from under his cot and was stowing away his few belongings. He put his warm clothes in one and his other things, suits, books, toiletries and the like in the other, smaller case. "Well, a little wishful thinking, I suppose. But I knew..." what did he know? "Let's say I let it be known I had a purpose. Value. And I... thought positive and..."

"Positive thinking got you out of here?" Miyakawa said, leaning on the door jamb.

"No." Mori said, hastily folding some socks. "Just understanding your strengths, honing them, and not letting anything like wars or Caucasians stop you from carrying them out."

"Destiny." Miyakawa said.

"Dest...no. No. It's like you're not listening..."

Miyakawa shrugged and smiled. He would miss messing with his friend Mori. "But what if you're wrong?"

"I'm not."

"No, I mean, one...ya know, what if *one*..." Miyakawa made a circle in the air with his finger to mean, Mori supposed, everyone, "anyone, a person, thinks they are meant to be something and they are wrong."

Mori nodded. "Yeah, it probably happens. But I think if you do a thing long enough, maybe you were designed for it. I find the brain rebels against even simple things that bore it."

"So, I guess I was meant to run a greasy spoon, eh?"

"I've seen you in action. You're an inventive chef. Don't sell yourself short."

"Chef! Ha!" Mori's occasional haughtiness always tickled Miyakawa. "Anyway, I'm pretty sure the restaurant has been repossessed by the landlord by now. My neighbor said he'd write to me and let me know but he hasn't yet." This wasn't just pessimism on Miyakawa's part. Many of the Japanese-Americans who had been evacuated from the coast either had to sell their belongings that they couldn't take, usually for pennies on the dollar, or abandon them outright.

Miyakawa waved a dismissive hand. "Anyway, hurry up and get out of here before they leave without you."

Mori packed his overcoat in his bigger suitcase. It was warm by the ovens and an unusually warm winter day overall and he didn't think he'd need it. He then set the cases at his sides and extended a hand to his friend. "Goodbye Miyakawa." He said. "If I can ever do anything for you…"

"If you're ever in Long Beach…" He thinks it over as he shakes Mori's hand "Well, I guess I Might be too, someday. Maybe." He shrugged again. His face was shiny with a bit of sweat and he smiled. He adjusted his white peaked chef's cap and nodded. "Good Luck, Ace."

"You too. Oh, I left a couple of books on the bed that I borrowed from Mrs. Matsuoka. Will you return them to her for me?"

"You got it." Miyakawa extends a meaty right hand and they share a goodbye handshake.

Mori departed the commissary with a final nod to his friend and goes back out in the crisp dry air, breathing deeply. He could see the majestic blue and white Sierra Mountains rising up and making the otherwise imposing barbed-wire fencing seem puny. He held one suitcase in either hand and stepped quickly. He was wearing his two-tone wing tips instead of the beaten second-hand army boots that he'd worn holes in the bottoms for the last few months. The idea of freedom, even if only long enough to do this job, whatever it was, for the FBI, was enough to make him break out in a wide smile. People looked on and pointed.

He smiled despite himself when he thought of the sign outside the front gate. "Manzanar War Relocation Center" it read. He hadn't been up to the front since he'd arrived, nor bothered to sneak a look at that gateway to freedom. The longing was strong enough, he thought, without feeding it. Now he would see the sign and, he *hoped*, for the last time.

He wanted to keep a level head but it was difficult not to be a little giddy. As he approached the south perimeter fence there was an area where some of the interned had planted a garden and constructed a wooden bridge over a small stream. It looked almost like a Buddhist shrine, he thought, though he'd only known such things by books, or a description by older folks. He paused in front of the bridge, thinking about what he had once told Agent Bullock about Japanese-American wherewithal as he looked at the bridge. Was this not a sterling example, he thought? He withdrew the letter from his inside pocket to give it another look.

The FBI letterhead and Agent Bullock's signature. He still needed a minute to take it in. Still, it was as he'd predicted, wasn't it? To himself, certainly, and to anyone that would listen. He was accepted provisionally and immediately upon receipt of the letter as an official agent in training with the Federal Bureau of Investigations. It was his ticket out of Manzanar and to his future and his purpose. Persevere, adapt, excel, he thought, nodding. He replaced the letter and was in such a haze of delight that his usually quite keen reflexes and senses failed to notice that he'd been sneaked up on. Someone pushed him from behind as he was picking his suitcases up once more. He managed to hang onto the smaller of the two cases and also to not lose his feet as he was propelled forward and onto the handmade bridge. He turned with some surprise and found two men staring him down.

"Going somewhere?" said the taller of the two. He was quite tall (for a Japanese, especially) almost six feet, lean muscle and spotty chin whiskers. He had a gaunt face and a hard look and squinted a lot. His name was Matsui and Mori had met him before. It had been when Mori had been making out, actually rather innocently, Mori recalled, under a pear tree by the hospital quarters with Matsui's on-again-off-again girlfriend, Eve Kashino. The other was a shorter guy Mori had seen around. His name was Sasaki, Mori remembered, and though diminutive he was barrel-chested with big meaty fists. He wore a rag around his head as if he thought it made him look like a samurai. They both wore the green army surplus coats.

"Congratulate me, boys." Mori said. "Got my ticket punched! I'm gone! Hey, Matsui, no hard feelings about Evie, right? I didn't even know she was your…"

"Hard Feelings? Nah., I don't care about that pig." Matsui shrugged. The tiny slits of his eyes glimmered. Mori didn't find the reassurance convincing. "So, what'd you do? Get a work pass to go pick lettuce in the sticks?" Volunteering for jobs on the outside that were deemed essential to the war effort (but not of great security concern) was one way internees could get out of the relocation camps. Generally, it was agricultural work.

"Lettuce? No. I've got a job. You see…"

"Job?" Matsui pretended to think it over and to be impressed. "Wow. Ain't that something? Sounds important. But if you ain't going out picking the Caucasian's fruit for them, then what are you doing? What kinda job can a Jap get anyway? And yet *you've* got a job …" Matsui pointed to the mountains, the air, the outside world, "…*out there*."

Mori nodded. "Yeah."

"Okay, so, what kinda job?"

"Fellas, I'm running a little late, I gotta get…"

"What kinda job?" Matsui repeated, with some menace.

"I don't think I'm at liberty to say." Mori said, if they were set on putting the knuckles to him, perhaps he could provoke them into doing something stupid.

Sasaki finally spoke. "*Kuso Inu!*"[3] He hissed.

"That's *rude*, Katsuo, don't you know that Mori here doesn't speak Japanese! He's All-American!"

The fact was that most of the Nisei either spoke no Japanese at all or weren't anywhere near fluent. Mori could barely follow along to most conversations in Japanese, and it helped if the participants spoke slowly. Growing up near the barrio, playing baseball with the Mexican kids at Elysian Park in Chavez Ravine and going to schools that usually had mostly Mexican and Latin American fellow students gave him his Spanish but… In Manzanar, the grievance felt, particularly by a lot of younger men towards the government, took the form of a Japanese pride, speaking the language and railing against anyone collaborating with the Army or authorities.

"That's okay." Mori said. "I know what that one means." Indeed, this particular insult couldn't be taken literally. Though Sasaki had called him a dog what he'd really meant was 'informer.' The implication was that they believed Mori was

---

[3] "*Fucking Dog!*"

being releases as a payment for having informed on his fellow interred. If they had shared these feelings with others, which they almost certainly had, there might be others to join in on the beating, providing anyone believed them. That these were the only two meant perhaps that Matsui's reputation as a blowhard had led to skepticism of his claims. It was a sad thing, really, Mori reflected. He'd never met a more loyal group of Americans than Japanese-Americans and yet the government seemed to be trying to do whatever it could to alienate them.

Adding insult to injury was the recent issuing of the "Statement of United States Citizen of Japanese Ancestry" a few months back, or Defense Department Form 304A. Mori knew it was a well-meaning attempt by the government to allow leave and travel to those interned but it struck a lot of them as an affront. Aside from being interned, which most could even almost understand in the panic of war, this document, which most called the 'loyalty questionnaire' seemed like Uncle Sam slapping them right across the face. Question 28 on the loyalty questionnaire asked if they would swear unqualified allegiance to the USA and defend against foreign or domestic foes, forswearing any allegiance to the Japanese Emperor. Most of the Nisei were insulted to be asked to renounce an allegiance they hadn't made. Most of the *Issei*, or first-generation immigrants, were not allowed to be full citizens under US law – making the renunciation of Japanese citizenship tricky.

Another result was the perhaps predictable reaction of the likes of Matsui and Sasaki.

"*Watashi wa kare no kubi o kowasubekida!*"[4]

Mori thought Sasaki was suggesting he should suffer a broken neck, or something like that. The malice was clear, in any event.

---

[4] "I should break his neck!"

That Sasaki kept with speaking Japanese was starting to amuse Mori. He thought he had heard Sasaki was Nisei from Inglewood. Anyway, the war department needed interpreters. This was all such a waste! "Gents, as I said, I've got people waiting on me, see? So, I've got to hurry."

Matsui nodded. "You're in a hurry. That's right. You said. Well, let me lighten your load so you'll get along faster." Quickly, and before Mori could protest, Matsui lifted the larger of Mori's suitcases, the one loaded with his warm clothes, and gave it a half spin before whipping it back around and high into the air. The case came down with a tremendous splash in the creek. Mori paused and looked on, disappointedly, debating whether he had the time or inclination to fish them out. He watched the case sink and counted it a loss. It was a cheap case he bought in a second hand store: so be it. Nothing was going to keep him there longer than was necessary.

"Thanks fellas. You're right. That ought to save me some time." He turned to leave and walked to the end of the bridge, feeling the creaking of the thin, strung-together logs.

"Hey!"

Mori heard the shout and knew they are rushing him. He turned and held up his hand. "Alright wait a minute!"

For some reason, they did. They stopped dead in their tracks and looked at him with a fierce anger mixed with confusion. It may have been because Mori didn't flee but calmly sat down his remaining suitcase and took off his jacket, folding it and placing it on top. He moved to his left a bit to more open ground and nodded. "Okay." He sighed. "If you insist." He held up his hands in a defensive stance and waved the two of them on.

This seemed to infuriate the both of them and they rushed off the bridge in Mori's direction. When they were upon him, he dropped and focused a kick with his heel into Sasaki's shin. He figured that in order to stand up to both of their attacks he would have to deliver incapacitating blows to one and deal with the other one on one. Sasaki was clearly the slower of the two and so more likely to receive such a blow without being able to parry. The shin kick gave Mori a few moments to regroup and focus on Matsui. It was quite a solid kick and he heard Sasaki scream loudly in pain as the hard and sharp stacked leather sole impacted with great force. Unfortunately, Mori doesn't move away in time and Sasaki falls on top of him. He managed to throw the squat man off and move away as Matsui pursued, but his attacker landed a stinging blow on the back of his head. He spun away and got back on his feet. Sasaki tried to stand but couldn't, and he held his damaged shin.

    Matsui was strong and quick but he left himself open with big, loping swings of his arms and Mori was able to quickly get inside and jab to his body enough that Matsui was forced to back away. Sasaki leaned on a pathway stone that has been placed by the evacuees. He'd be back in soon, Mori thought, throwing him a sideways glance. He rolled up his sleeves and waited for Matsui to charge, which took only a few seconds, raging as he was. Matsui was flailing and making mistakes. Still, he smartly kept low and tried to take Mori off his feet. Mori saw it coming though and put out his two hands like catching a basketball and deflected Matsui to one side.

    Sasaki got up and limped toward him. He got there quicker than Mori expected and grabbed his arm and tried to put it behind his back. Mori turned enough though, to almost be facing the stout man who was clawing at his forearm and landed his fist directly into Sasaki's Adam's apple. He pulled the punch to not do too much damage but it put Sasaki down again. Matsui seized the opportunity to wrap Mori up in a bear hug from behind. Sasaki couldn't assist, and he held his throat and struggled for breath. Matsui didn't want to let Mori have his arms back and so he wrapped his legs around and toppled his prey to the ground. Mori was winded by the weight of the other man falling hard on him and coughed roughly. It was a firm impact on his ribs, but Mori didn't focus on it. Matsui pinned him with his body weight and began to punch at Mori's side. The angle and lack of torque made these blows only a little painful at worst but still Mori couldn't shake the other man off. Sasaki came hobbling over, approximating a run and meant to kick Mori in the face but he wound up and missed entirely in his effort to not also kick Matsui, who was right atop Mori, breathing in his ear.

"*Seiko Suru!*"[5] Sasaki screamed. Mori was impressed that he was sticking with the Japanese.

Mori estimated the location of Matsui's nose behind his head and, with as much force as he could muster, whipped his head backwards into it. Immediately, Matsui broke away from Mori, cursing and screaming. Mori saw dark red blood fall into the dirt and spurt outward from Matsui's fingers, which were clutching his nose. The blood got in his eyes and obscured his vision. He tripped on a path stone and fell backwards onto the dry grass.

In the distance a few people gathered to watch the goings-on, though there had been no attempt to intervene. An elderly, disapproving voice calls out to them to stop such nonsense.

The amount of blood burbling from Matsui's face startled all of them but it was Sasaki who first broke out of the haze to grab Mori around the head. He pulled his him down with great strength and was trying to slam Mori's face into his

---

[5] "Fuck you!"

knee. Mori managed to raise his elbows and block the short kicks. Sasaki cursed him and clawed at him.

Mori dropped all his weight to the ground but Sasaki hung on and they rolled in the dirt. Matsui wasn't able to wipe the blood out of his eyes enough to reenter the fray, and at any rate he was too shocked to feel like wanting to and he staggered around, trying to regain his equilibrium. At last Mori and Sasaki broke free of each other and regained their feet. Sasaki charged, telegraphing his movements badly. Mori hopped to the right and as Sasaki missed an open body tackle, Mori lifted his foot and brought it down hard, sideways on the stout man's knee joint.

Sasaki's knee bent inward quite unnaturally and he fell to the dirt with a scream. Mori thought he may have heard a snapping sound but doubted it was broken. Still, it seemed like he wouldn't be getting up any time soon. Sasaki pulled the samurai rag from his head and bit it in an effort to manage his pain. Both of Mori's attackers were down and unwilling or unable, it seemed, to reengage. Mori was left covered in the dry, dusty red clay and feeling a bit awkward. He looked over them both as they tried to curse him but were out of breath or tending to their injuries.

Mori brushed off his shirt and trousers but the Manzanar dust seemed to be part adhesive and still managed to cling to him. He had a few droplets of blood – Matsui's – on his shirt below his left shoulder. He took a handkerchief from his pocket and began dabbing at it. Sasaki crawled over to his friend, who was still holding his face and sitting on a pavestone.

"Look, fellas," Mori said. "Sorry about this, but I mean, you *did* start it…" he pulled on his jacket, glad that it covered the flecks of blood on his shirt.

"Dirty...sucker-punching son of a bitch..." Sasaki coughed the first things he had said in English. He did sound like he was from LA, Mori thought.

Mori went to replace the handkerchief in his pocket but instead walked over and handed it to Matsui. The man sat a moment looking at it put then snatched it quickly and held it to his nose. The blood spray had been impressive and a bit disconcerting. For Matsui, certainly.

"Broke my damn nose." Matsui said, holding the handkerchief gently to the gore on his face.

Mori nodded. "Probably..." he didn't seem to know how to disengage but had no time to linger. "Well, alright. Good luck, boys." He retrieved his remaining case and walked the rest of the way to the administration building without looking back. Honestly, the two of them had gotten in a couple of good licks but Mori didn't allow it to show, even though the back of his head and neck were throbbing.

The girl behind the desk in the administration building was very efficient looking and Mori thought he'd seen her before at a dance in one of the mess halls. She dressed sharply in a tan sweater and brown skirt. Her face was very expressive, especially for a Japanese girl, Mori thought. As she looked him up and down, she smirked. "Have a little trouble getting here?" she asked.

"I was in such a hurry I tripped and fell on the way." Mori said.

"Kind of a klutz, are you?"

He shrugged. "Do I have time to wash up?"

She nodded toward a door with rows of wooden slats. "I guess. The State Troopers are waiting outside for you."

Mori peered through the blinds with a smile. The back end of a black and white Chevy, red light mounted top and center, and two staties waiting inside, engine running. He could think of a more comfortable ride, but he would take this one, no problem.

Mori put the rush on and reemerged from the bathroom in under two minutes with hands and face cleaned with the rough camp soap, his clothes patted as clean as he could get them and his hair combed back into place with fresh pomade applied. He felt considerably better. The girl pushed a small paper cup of water and a bottle of aspirin across the desk toward him.

He took three, downed them with the warm water and said "Thanks."

"Looked like a nasty tumble." She said. "Sign here." She puts a carbon document in front of him. He signed it and she handed him the copy, which he pocketed without a look.

"You're really good at this." Mori said. "Were you a secretary on the outside?"

She smirked and looked him in the eye sharply. "I just graduated from law school."

Mori nodded. "Wow." He said. "You from LA? I might need you in the future."

"San Jose." She said. "And I'm sure you'll get along fine."

He nodded, said thanks and met his ride outside. The State Trooper got out and said, "You Mori?"

"That's me, Trooper... Davis." He said, reading the man's gleaming name tag. Before even being asked, he climbed in the back seat, tossing his small case of worldly belongings beside him. "Thanks so much." He said, settling in on the tatty leather seats behind the back-seat cage.

The troopers consulted a file folder, no doubt with a picture inside, and then looked Mori up and down. The staties nodded to each other and then drove off as cold dust swirled around the car. Mori looked back only once to get a picture in his memory of the camp disappearing behind him. The wire-strung wooden fence opened and they drove through. When they closed, Mori felt as if a weight has been removed from around his neck.

"Are we driving to LA?" Mori asked.

"No sir," said the trooper in the passenger seat, a young man probably not even as old as Mori. "We'll take you back to town and you'll be taking the bus to LA from there."

Mori nodded, smiling, thinking of the picture in his mind of Manzanar receding in the distance. Suddenly everything felt right. The snow on the mountains in the distance was almost preternaturally white and the air through the window, rolled down just an inch, was bracingly fresh and cold. They rode back to town in near silence.

CHAPTER 11

January 30, 1943, Maine

Mori woke up in a very nice room with two old Caucasian men standing over him, which immediately made him fear the worst. He came to his wits right away though, having little confidence in the existence of an afterlife and being doubtful in any case that, if it did exist, it would have looked like this. The two men were both elderly, one with snowy white hair and a funereal suit and the other in his shirtsleeves and with a bit of misty sweat on his brow. This was a doctor, Mori figured, from his manner and the way his grey eyes were sizing him up.

"Gentlemen?" Mori said through a cough. He felt alright but his throat was terribly dry. The doctor poured him a glass of water from a clear pitcher on the bedside table. He sipped and nodded, feeling rather vulnerable in his undershirt and shorts, even with a large and heavy down-filled comforter folded at his waist.

"Agent Mori isn't it?" said the man in the suit. "You took quite ill…"

"Yes, yes, I know. I'm terribly sorry."

"Well, there isn't anything to apologize for…"

Mori got up and slid on his pants and socks to feel a bit less exposed. He was irritated with himself for succumbing to illness. Did I pass out? He wondered. Mortifying. He couldn't have anyone in this town thinking he was weak, and right off the bat too. He'd have to work hard to overcome any such perception. He knew this but he still felt a bit tired and frail.

The Doctor said, "Don't feel like you have to get up if you're still feeling ill. Take things slowly."

Mori smiled that electric smile. "Not a bit ill. Eager to get to work, really." He looked around the room. "Is this the hotel then?"

"Yes. Terribly sorry they turned you away last night. The manager was, well, how does one say it? Being a… bit of a cretin. I suppose his surprise at your…person, was overwhelming to him."

"I imagine," Mori said. "He is the one who called the police, I suppose. Likely with some scared story of a Japanese spy or other. Ha!"

The doctor and the judge looked at other. "I have to be going." The doctor said. He looked at Mori with a blank expression. "Try to get some rest. Stay warm. Drink a lot of fluids." He smirked. "And try to stay out of the jailhouse." It took the doctor a ridiculously long time to reequip himself for the out of doors. He put on his gray sport jacket, then his heavy down overcoat, his hat with ear flaps and a khaki-colored muffler.

"I will." Mori said. "All of those things."

The room was warm and comfortable. The judge sat in one of the straight-backed chairs at a gleamingly polished lacquered table. The lights were dim and the air seemed calm and gauzy. Mori made the bed hastily before sitting in the chair next to him, with effort, his spine straight as the chairback.

Judge Norris introduced himself formally and shook Mori's hand. Still firm for an old man, but soft, papery skin. He then rested his hands on his knees and leaned back. "I've spoken with the management here at the hotel. You can stay as long as you need to. As long as your investigation requires. You'll get no further problem from the staff."

"Great. Thanks. Say, I don't suppose you've spoken to Special Agent Bullock about any of this, have you?"

The Judge held up his hand and nodded assurance. "I have. I was referred to him by, well, a friend, also at the bureau and I told him you had arrived and seemed very capable. I didn't feel the need to mention the rest until I spoke to you. I did mention being surprised by your... person. But he explained and I said that I understood completely, given the manpower shortage with the war and all... And he did say you were indeed very capable."

Mori wanted to defend himself as more than a consolation prize but was mollified by the description and let it go. He also decided to let the Judge speak as much as he could. He needed all the information he could get.

"As for Captain Ballard...I've spoken to him as well... He's a...strange sort. Proud, I suppose. I think his pride smarts a bit with having someone – and that someone being *you* specifically, coming in on... his investigation. And it is his, I suppose. But, then..." the Judge trailed off.

"If he'd been expecting anyone at all, it wouldn't have been someone with my face. Still, I think maybe he went a bit overboard, just from a peek at my, uh, oriental mug."

"Perhaps. You can understand, though. He's probably never seen a Japanese face outside of a newsreel. I haven't, for that matter... And with the war and all..."

Mori decided to change the subject. "You're the reason I'm here, aren't you?"

"I suppose I am." Judge Norris said. He rubbed his eyes, which were reddish and watery, the way an old man's eyes get. He folded his hands around his midsection and looked at his thumbs contemplatively. "Well, Lillian, really." He said.

"Your wife?"

Judge Norris looked up, as if not having realized he'd said it aloud. "What? Oh, er, yes. She...*we*... That is, think perhaps that a bit of outside expertise..." he gestured toward Mori uncertainly, "Would be in order. You see, with the war, our regular police force, such as it was, always a small contingent mind you, are away doing their bit. We are left with...inexperienced men."

Mori sat forward on the edge of the chair. "I would have guessed that Captain Ballard had quite a bit of experience, by the way he carried himself."

Judge Norris nodded. "Yes. Perhaps I'm putting a euphemism where it doesn't belong." He sighed heavily. "I suppose I am reluctant to say what I fear might be the case. That it isn't the Captain's experience that might be in question. But rather his...methods. Or, more likely, his... sensibilities."

Mori thought he may be still too euphemistic but didn't say so. "So, you believe the Captain may not be up to this investigation? More to the point: that he just doesn't care enough to investigate it properly. I assume you think that is because the men were all Indians?"

"By golly." The Judge said. "And they say that we New Englanders are blunt!"

Mori studied the Judge for a moment, noting that although age had clearly weathered him, his mind was still perfectly intact behind the imperfect body. He had a trace of that regional accent, drawing out some vowels, dropping the r's at the end of some words and adding it to others where they wouldn't ordinarily be. He held his head up and spoke with kindness but firmness. His was a clean, purpose-driven life, Mori thought.

"Lillian would say that, I think." The Judge said. "And I think I would say at least that, yes."

"I don't suppose I can count on much cooperation, then." Mori said.

"Forgive me, my boy," The judge leaned toward him with fatherly concern and folded his hands in front of him on the table. "You seem bright, capable, eager... all of the things I would have hoped for in an agent of the FBI but I'm not sure that by my – presumption, I suppose I'd call it, that I haven't unleashed something worse."

"My being Japanese-American, you mean, I think."

"I do." The Judge reached out and tapped Mori on the knee to show no hard feelings or ill will. "Don't take my meaning wrong, son, really. I don't question your loyalty or your capability. But I am worried about the reaction of the town. Most people only see an oriental face in the newsreels and hear them called the enemy. Some families have boys over in the Pacific, or soon will have. They may not be kind to you."

"I would prefer kindness, of course." Mori said, puffing out his chest a bit. "But it isn't essential to get the job done. I'm confident that I can win them over. And if not, well, I can handle myself."

The Judge was tip-toeing around something he wanted very much didn't want to say but felt he needed to. Mori cut him off at the pass: "I know what you're meaning is though, really I do. Folks read the papers of see the newsreels and the rows of Japanese soldiers marching off on the word of their emperor alone to take over the world. Mindless like drones in a beehive and the emperor is the queen bee. Any Japanese must be under the same mind control. Must be...beholden in the same way. The whole fifth column thing. I know a man of the world like yourself wouldn't think such thoughts, but many do."

The judge almost chuckled at "man of the world."

"Actually," the Judge says, "I was too old even during the last war. And they gave me some exemption that I didn't want. Too old – to hear it now makes me laugh. I suppose I should count myself fortunate to have not had to take up arms in defense of my country. And content myself with hoping I have been of service in other ways. I say this as a very old man... I hope without regret. They don't say war is hell for nothing. But it is hard to not want to say you'd been there and done your part when you were needed. My father told me about serving under Colonel Chamberlain at Gettysburg. The stories were thrilling but he always paused before he could finish a story. He was always overcome. I know that my boyish adoration was a distortion of the real suffering he saw and felt. The real death he witnessed."

Mori nodded. "My father was a soldier also, for a brief time as a very young man. He was drafted to go and fight the Russians in 1904…"

"Port Arthur?" The Judge asked.

Mori nodded. "There was never any choice for him and I think that rubbed him the wrong way. I know a lot of boys got drafted but the war with the Russians, my father said, was just over some rocky islands in the Pacific, and the greater glory of the Japanese Empire. I think his experience in the war is why he left, in the end, and came to America."

The Judge said, "You know, you speak like a much older man sometimes. Is there a Japanese word for 'wise beyond your years'?"

"Probably." Mori said.

The Judge chuckled. "Where are you from?"

"Los Angeles: near Chavez Ravine." Mori smiled. The wind whipped at the window and prompted him to say. "It's nice. Probably about 65 or 70 degrees or so this time of year. Good to remember a sweater."

The Judge wagged a finger at him. "Speaking of which: what on earth were you thinking? Coming here without a stitch of warm clothing? It's no surprise you nearly caught your death!"

"I wasn't as badly prepared as you think…" Mori said, noting that the hint of suspicion at his patriotic loyalties had been replaced, it seemed, with almost parental concern. "I had some complications on the way and the bag with my winter clothes was...lost in transit. That said, I was still unprepared for this." He gestured towards the blustery day outside.

"I've lived here my entire life and still find the winters here... let's say, *bracing*."

There was a knock at the door, just two taps, lightly.

Mori and the Judge looked at each other as if wondering who the other was expecting. The Judge then raises a finger, remembering. "That'll be Miss Honeywell, I should think. She was very concerned. And very keen to defend you. Come in!"

It was indeed Trudy, and her leather cap poked around the door and then a wisp of blond hair. "Hiya, Judge. Hiya Agent Mori. Everything okay? Feeling better?"

"Right as rain." Mori said, though he felt a little exposed without shoes or at least a proper shirt, to say nothing of a jacket...

"Swell." She said, looking relieved.

"Miss Honeywell has volunteered to act as your driver for the extent of your stay. Now that I've had a chance to speak with you, I think it is a fine arrangement. Unless you've made other arrangements?"

"No. I haven't"

"She knows the area well and is very capable. If you need anything at all you can, of course, ask me yourself, or go through Trudy here. She's been invaluable to me this past year."

"I don't want to take your driver, sir." He gestured to Trudy, then said, turning to address her, "Or to take you away from your regular duties."

Trudy looked a little concerned that she was being rejected but the Judge stood and began pulling on his overcoat and hat. "Nonsense. You'll need her. And the car. I don't think you'll find a car for hire in this town."

Mori didn't protest any more. He liked the idea, honestly. It would feel good to have an ally. Even a 19-year-old Caucasian girl. They don't have to be trouble, he figured, if you stay away from the funny business. "Well, then, I accept. Thanks, Tr… Miss Honeywell."

"Swell." She said, smiling.

"I'm off." The Judge said. "I'm catching a ride home with the Doctor. I believe he should still be waiting for me in the lobby. Hopefully, he's already ordered a pot of coffee." He reached out for Mori's hand to shake it. Mori returned the gesture. "Good luck."

"Thanks."

"Boy, did they ever give me a going over about you!" Trudy said, after the judge had left. "The deputy asked me questions for an hour! Then the Captain too. What a pain."

"Not a warm welcome for me either, I gotta say."

Trudy chortled. "Well, get some rest. The doc said it's the best thing for you. I'll come get you in the morning. We've got somewhere important to get you to."

"Where?"

"Essentials." She said, swinging around the door to his room on her way out. "Trust me. See you tomorrow."

CHAPTER 12

January 26-30, 1943

In fact, the state troopers took Mori no further than a bus stop, miles down the road. As he watched the back of their car recede into the high Sierra dust, he saw a sign that said only "Lone Pine." He wondered if it were the name of a town, a landmark of some kind or just, perhaps, a literal, solitary tree. There weren't many around, so it might have been significant. The majestic blue-hued mountains rose around him and long stretches of arid flatlands with short sagebrush surrounded him and swayed in the breeze.

The troopers had given him a buff-colored envelope. Mori didn't ask but assumed the FBI office in San Francisco had arranged it and sent it down. Inside: a bus ticket (a single stop, then on to LA), some cash, and a plane ticket. This last one excited Mori considerably. The idea of flying on a plane! He never had flown before, of course. He was almost giddy at the idea of watching the sun glint on the silver wings as they passed over the country.

The bus ride was a slog though. After what seemed hours with almost no traffic either way, a nearly empty bus picked him up, the driver punched his ticket without a word or even looking up and waved him back. Mori started to almost get an otherworldly feel about things. He sat, looked off into the lonely flat ground and watched the dust play outside as the bus raced along.

The closer he got to LA, the more excited he got. The lone stop on the 4-hour trip was in a place called Homestead that seemed to only be the bus station and an attached general store, which was old, dull, and smelled of feet and rotting fruit. He did manage to finally grab a bite to eat though: just a simple cheese sandwich and lemonade but it perked him up considerably. It started to dawn on him that he wouldn't get a chance to stop and visit anyone or see the old haunts. His bus ticket had him arriving in LA with only an hour to get from the bus station to LA Municipal Airport. Who would even be left to visit, anyway, he wondered? Even most of his non-Japanese-American acquaintances (which was most of them) were probably drafted. There might have been a few girls to visit… he smirked: but no time.

In his excitement he almost didn't notice how stocked with military aircraft the airport was. He had never actually been to the airport, having never flown before, but the military presence was palpable. Indeed, later that year, the city would turn over control of the airport to the US government for the duration of the war. For now, though, Mori could only think about the plane: how it would feel to hear the engines roaring, speeding into the horizon, breaking the bond with the earth and looking down from above.

He was not disappointed.

He raced from the bus station to a cab and dashed to Mines Field (the airport) just in time to make his flight. The smell of the city was tantalizing, like a pie cooling on a window sill, but, he knew, ever out of reach, as it would be for the foreseeable future. It was the smell of heat and people and chili from the Mexican places near Echo Park and the dirt on the ballfields in Koreatown. Plus, the sun was going down and everything was turning a shimmery dark auburn and purple and brought to mind a thousand such nights in his memories. He thought of one night a couple of years ago, in a borrowed convertible Chevy, the top up for privacy but the windows open for the breeze and to hear the speaker clipped onto the inside of the door at the drive-in movie. It was summer though, and the movie had been a good one: *Blood and Sand* with Rita Hayworth. Mori only knew it was good because he went back to watch it a few days later; that evening had mainly been spent in the arms of Yolanda Garza, who, when he looked back, resembled Rita Hayworth more than a little bit...

Mori snapped out of it. The recollections were giving him a bit of melancholy that he could ill-afford. Anyway, he had the distraction of being shown to his seat by a blond in a blue skirt and jacket with a big TWA pin above her not inconsiderable bosom. She smiled and didn't even ask "where are you from?" like he'd been expecting. TWA stewardesses were women of the world, he thought.

Mori had a window seat and looked out over the wing, where the sunlight was casting back a steely orange glow from the silver skin and rivets dotting the exterior. Passengers were seated in groups of four facing each other and the others didn't seem nearly as excited as he was. He tried to appear more sophisticated and aloof but when the engines started and the plane turned and began to taxi, he couldn't help but exhale and say "Wow!"

"First time flying?" said the man next to him. He was mostly bald with a build made at buffet lines and a suit that still bore some of the evidence, but his face was round and friendly.

Mori hesitated, not wanting to admit it, "Yeah. First time. Quite a thing, isn't it? You fly a lot?"

The man bobbed his head. "Oh yeah. All the time. I'm in sales. Pork, to be precise."

Mori stopped listening. He felt his stomach shrink and contort as the plane tore from the ground and the engines raised it into the sky. The ascent kept the sunlight dancing on the wing for him a bit longer. "Wow." He said again.

"Yeah, it's really something… say, friend," the man asked, "where you from?"

It took only about 16 hours to cross the entire country, a marvel that Mori could hardly believe. That included three stops to refuel. They served lamb chops, baked potatoes, and cheesecake and coffee for dessert. I am, he thought, drinking coffee in the sky, hurtling at a speed man had only now just reached, in the metal tube that was the DC-3's fuselage. Even when it was really too dark to see outside his window, he left the little curtains open and watched.

"This trip used to take a day and half or more." Mori's salesman companion said in the morning. Had to change planes, stop to gas up every little bit. Had to sleep over. Usually in Kansas City. I don't care for Kansas City, myself…"

Still buzzing with elation from his first airplane ride, his destination gave him some reason to be giddy. Washington DC: the seat of government and where a typed note in his packet had told him to meet Agent Bullock at the Lincoln Memorial at 1pm. Obviously, he'd never been to the nation's capital, or, for that matter, east of the desert outside of LA until now. He touched down and bade farewell to his fellow traveler, and went and booked a cheap hotel, stashed his suitcase, then hailed another cab to Lincoln Memorial. He was quite a bit early and was glad for it. He asked to be let off at the corner of 19th and Constitution Avenue and cut across the snowy field to the reflecting pool. The trees were dark and wet and reached up to the gray sky all along the length of the pool, which looked to be frozen over, though just barely, as it was about 30 degrees. He breathed the cold air deeply into his lungs as he shuffled along. His clothes weren't keeping out the cold but he was still excited enough not to really care or notice. There were a few random people about, some passing through, a few stopping and admiring, then moving on. It wasn't an ideal day for tourists.

As he got closer, he could see the marble likeness of the Great Emancipator in his chair. In person, it seemed a bit melancholy, with Lincoln's head pointing down, as if heavy with worry. He stopped a few yards short of the long stairs rising to the foot of the columns that surrounded the memorial. The wind whistled a bit and he pulled the collar of his jacket tight at the throat, still staring at Lincoln with awe.

"Jeez, Mori. Did you come from California with no overcoat?" It was Bullock. Mori hadn't even seen or heard him approach. Bullock's bull-necked frame seemed even thicker in a black wool coat with his spongey hair sticking out from a dark fedora pulled low on his head. "You'll freeze to death out here. Hell, you won't make it five minutes up in Maine."

Mori tears his eyes away from the Lincoln statue, "Long story. I'll pick one up on the way. Haven't had a chance." He looks back. "Amazing, isn't it, sir?"

"Lincoln? Yeah. Pretty nice."

"You come here a lot?"

"Well, the office, the DOJ building, that is, is only a couple of miles that way," Bullock pointed northeast, "on Pennsylvania Avenue… but now that I think about is, this is actually is only my second time."

"I think I'd come here every day." Mori said. "Have lunch here, maybe."

"Speaking of, let's go get some coffee, huh? Get warmed up. I'll fill you in."

The walk to a diner called Lennie's, just a whole in the wall, really, with a smell of strong coffee and two giant windows looking out onto a busy side street.

"You're really at the center of things, sir, I envy you." Mori said this as he shoveled corned beef hash with fried eggs into his mouth and then dunked some donuts, eagerly devouring the sodden, hot, cakey mess.

"You can really put it away, you know that?" Bullock smoked and sipped his coffee, which was almost tan with cream. "Look, Mori, about this… situation."

Mori nodded and wiped away any bits that may have been hanging about his lip. He wished he'd had time to shave. "Yes sir, please, continue."

"First, know this: don't go up there and… make waves, and all that. This isn't an investigation. This is…" he struggles, then stabs out his cigarette and shakes his head. "You know what this is? Politics. My boss has a dotty old mentor that thinks he can pull in a favor to traipse all the way up to his little shit burg and… never mind. The way they work here in the east, Mori, I tell ya…" but he doesn't. He sipped his coffee and fired up another smoke.

"What was I saying?"

"You were telling me about the case."

Bullock pointed his two fingers at Mori, the Lucky clamped between them. "Not a case." He said, smoke dancing with the rebuke. "Don't think of it that way. Think of it as…" he shrugged, searching for the right word, "Like research. Just go up, look things over, talk to the local cops, write a report and come back. Try to make the old fellow – the judge, make him feel like you're working on it. But don't make any commitments. Whatever you find, make a recommendation, tread lightly, and come back."

"Tread lightly…" Mori repeated.

"Very lightly. You'll have to identify as FBI but do so… casually. Don't make a big show about it. Tell them it's all, you know, a formality or something. Also, Mori, it's likely most of these hicks have never even seen a Japanese person…"

Mori opened his mouth, but Bullock cut him off.

"*Japanese-American*… so, you know. Be on your best behavior."

"I always am."

"Yeah, I believe it." Bullock said. He reached into his jacket pocket and pulled out a small black leather wallet and handed it to Mori.

113

Mori opened it; his face became radiant. "Holy Moley..."

"Yeah, I thought you'd like that."

"Provisional?"

"Obviously. I can't make you an agent by snapping my fingers, but since you passed training... this is allowed. Sort of..."

"And a gun?"

"Obviously no gun, Mori, Jesus. Have you been listening?"

"Of course, of course." He thought the Lincoln Monument was the highlight of the day but this was something else. Agent Asahito Mori, Provisional. He read it again and again but it didn't get old.

"Tell them you're with the FBI's civil rights desk and you're doing a report just to tamp down any propaganda efforts by the enemy. Mistreating minorities and all that. Might help explain you being Japanese. Japanese-American. You know..."

Mori decided not to dive in to most of that. "*Is there* a Civil Rights desk?"

"Yeah... Well, not really. Not officially. There are some guys that handle that stuff, from what I understand. Cracker lynch mobs, *German-American Bund*, anti-Semites, that sort of thing."

"Ah."

From somewhere in his coat, Bullock retrieved another buff colored envelope. Vera had enclosed the news clippings, a train ticket in Mori's name, DC to Maine, leaving the next day, and eight ten dollar bills that Bullock had liberated from petty cash. Bullock then proceeded to tell him what he knew about the case, which wasn't much. Mori read the clippings, then read them again. It wasn't much.

They finished their meal, Bullock paid and they went back onto the street in the chilly afternoon air. It was already starting to get dark, or so it seemed with the deep gray overcast sky and a slight chill cutting into the wind. Mori felt a wave of tiredness overcoming him. The trip across the country had been thrilling but now he was feeling the results of such a long journey. Bullock wished him luck.

"I haven't gotten a car yet out here." He explained. "So, I'm getting a cab. Can I take you somewhere?"

Mori explained that his hotel was nearby and that it wouldn't be necessary. Bullock wished him luck again and said to stay in touch. "And use some of that petty cash to get a warm coat, eh?"

Mori watched Bullock go as he said this then trudged the couple of blocks to his hotel. He was exhausted and collapsed onto the bed, (he did fold his jacket and trousers over a chair though. No sense in wrecking them) before collapsing face first onto the bed. It was standard issue but after Manzanar and his cot it was like a feather bed at the Ritz. He slept long and deeply, well past the time he should have the next day and had to rush to make his train, leaving him no time at all to shop for a winter coat.

CHAPTER 13

January 31, 1943, Maine

True to her word, Trudy arrived first thing in the morning, before Mori has even finished his ham, eggs, donuts, and coffee. The snooty night manager was also just getting off his shift at the time and didn't even look at Mori in the dining area as he left through the lobby.

Trudy drove Mori to a store called "Frank's Toggery." It was a low brick building with a faded green awning jammed between a gun store and a corner pharmacy. She slammed the Nash's gearshift all the way up and said, "First, you need to dress properly. You're gonna end up even worse next time without dressing for winter in Maine. Especially this far Down East. You know, it isn't supposed to get above ten degrees for weeks."

Mori had been hovering near the heat vent, still shivering a bit, though grateful that the Nash heated up quickly and with vigor. "I guess it takes a while to get used to the temperature, eh?"

"Stimulating, ain't it?"

"That's one word for it."

"Don't worry, Agent Mori." Trudy said. "We'll get you squared away."

She ushered him into Frank's, which was packed to the rafters with apparel of all kinds. He could see pants, shirts, coats, hats, crammed onto racks, stuffed onto dark brown ancient wooden shelves, sometimes just sitting stacked on narrow tables. There weren't any aisles, per say, and the proper way of shopping seemed to just be to contort and meander through the assemblage as if spelunking.

"Impressive, huh?" Trudy said.

"Well, it isn't Bullocks Wiltshire or anything," Mori said, "but it'll do."

"What's the Bollocks..."

"Wiltshire. A Department Store. Well, *the* department store. Huge thing on Wiltshire Boulevard. Giant, fancy chandeliers everywhere, marble floors, huge copper plated tower with a light on top you can see for blocks..."

"Wow. Sounds dynamite!"

"Oh yeah, its killer all right."

"You sound homesick, if you don't mind me saying."

"I think I might be."

"Already?"

"Haven't actually been home in a while, to tell you the truth." He picks up scarf, thinks it'll go well with his hat. Only a buck 75.

"On assignment for the FBI?" she asked, expecting an exciting story of G-men and gangsters, like a James Cagney movie.

"Not exactly. I'll have to tell you about it sometime."

She frowned a little. "Okay. Well, pick yourself a good heavy overcoat. I'll fetch the rest." He looks through a rack of coats, all of them very heavy, and very much like they were meant for geezers. He wondered if old Frank (wherever he was, and *if* he was) had updated anything since the 20s… He also wonders what she meant by "the rest."

Trudy returned with a stack of clothing items in her arms that she laid down on one of the tables in front of Mori. He said, "Holy Moley, what is all this?"

Lugging all of the items and setting them down as quickly as she did caused the leather cap fly off her head and her blond curls to fly about willy-nilly. Mori retrieved the cap for her and she said "Thanks." She tucked the hair back under once more. "You ready?"

"I guess so…"

"First, gloves. Lined with rabbit fur. They'll keep your fingers from breaking off like icicles…"

He took them. Basic black, good fit, comfy. He nodded.

"Socks." Trudy said. "Heavy, wool. But not itchy." She handed them to Mori.

"Really thick." He said. "Don't think they'll work with my shoes."

"Yeah," Trudy said. "Ditch the fancy shoes. "These…" she pulls out a pair of black leather boots with a high shine and two horizontal buckles across the shin area. "weatherproof. They'll keep out the wet and the cold. Keep your piggies from freezing, I swear. You a nine?"

"Eleven." He said.

She nods. "Okay, be right back." She takes back the boots and heads off again to find the right size. He looks at the pile of clothes. On top is what looks like a full body suit made of gray flannel, with buttons from neck to midsection.

"Long johns." Trudy said when she returned. "You'll thank me for those."

"Long johns?"

"Long underwear."

Mori reddened a little.

Trudy turned them over to reveal a flap in the ass region and two buttons keeping it in place. "Keep you toasty warm and also they're convenient for when you gotta, you know…"

"Got it. Yeah, I think I've seen these in Bugs Bunny cartoons." Mori said, as he folded the garment and replaced it on the pile.

"Here." Trudy said, and handed him a hat. It was red, with more rabbit fur lining and two flaps that fell over the ears and could be secured below the chin with a small buckle. "Frank only had it in red."

"I don't think so."

"Try it on."

He turned it over in his hands. "I appreciate the help, Trudy, really, but this thing is, ah... I'd feel a bit naked without my hat, you know?" he doffed his fedora.

Trudy giggled and bit the end of her thumb. Mori reminded himself to not, under any circumstances, find her adorable. "I just wanted to see if I could get you to try it on. Ha!"

She snatches back the mad bomber cap and throws him a knitted black ring. "Put this on under your hat. It'll keep your ears warm. Warm enough, anyway."

Mori did, putting on the ring, which looked like a stretchy knitted circle, five inches or so wide, like a winter cap someone had cut the top from. Then he replaced his fedora.

Frank, an ancient and hulking man in a dull green sweater and half-moon glasses emerged to be visible for the first time since they'd arrived in order to take his money. He started writing out a receipt and he looked Mori up and down once and, in a heavy down east accent said, "You ain't from around heah, I take it, Mistah?"

"No sir. California."

"Oh ayuh?" Frank said, carefully tearing off the small carbon copy. He handed it to Mori, who put it in the pocket of the overcoat, which he was definitely wearing outside.

"California, you say? Mmmm, you'll be glad you got them long johns then." The rest of the apparel was wrapped by Frank slowly and carefully in brown paper from an enormous roll which sat on the counter on an ornate cast iron holder. He then bound the parcel with twine and gave a nod. Trudy bade Frank goodbye and he only waved without a word before disappearing once more into a back room.

They emerged again into the daylight. The sky was no longer overcast but a dazzling mid-morning blue. Without the cloud cover, the temperature had dipped even more and Mori was suddenly very glad for his overcoat, headgear, and gloves and looked forward for a chance to get back to the hotel to don the rest of the winter clothes when he next needed to go out.

The scene before him, he thought, was like something from the cover of *Colliers* or *The Saturday Evening Post*. Despite the frigid temperatures, people were out on the town common, ice skating on the area around the bandstand which had been flooded to make a rink. A large truck roared past on the other side of the common, the enormous snowplow on the front pushing a great mound of fluttery snow out of the road and onto the curb. There was chatter and laughing and people's breath shot from their mouths in wispy white clouds, which amused Mori no end. Kids in full body snow suits, with their scarves whipping around them as they skated, laughed, fell on the ice and got up, tittered and laughed some more.

A kid in a floppy blue knit cap with a pom-pom at the end ran up to Mori. He had a pair of worn, brown ice skates knotted together by the laces slung over his shoulder. "Hey! You really a G-man?"

"Is that how you talk to grown-ups?" Trudy said to the kid.

"Yeah." The kid said.

"Yes, I am." Mori said, proudly.

"You're Mr. and Mrs. Donovan's kid, aren't you? Cliff, right?"

"Yeah, that's me." The kid, Cliff, said. "Where are you from?" he asked, scrutinizing Mori's face intensely.

"Don't judge his parents too harshly." Trudy said, "just because the kid is rude. They're good people."

"I ain't rude!" said the kid.

"California." Mori said, then patted the kid's pom-pom and moved along to the skating rink. The answer didn't seem to satisfy the kid.

Trudy had to keep up as Mori glad-handed with the locals, pretending to fall but nimbly staying on his feet on the ice. Laughing at jokes older than the people telling them. Pretending to play snowball baseball with a group of kids. Mori never did spell out for anyone why he was there. He knew in a small town like this, it would get around in no time and might shut things down before they could get started, to say nothing of worsening his relationship with the police, which he would need. He really just wanted to get the feel for the place and see of the dead men were on anyone's radar at all. Nobody mentioned it.

PART 2

CHAPTER 14

January 31, 1943

Mori figured that there was no time like the present to set things right with the police. Chief Ballard was, he told himself, very likely a decent guy and a good cop. After he smoothed things over, he was sure they could get on with things. He was good at smoothing things over. Still, it was eating at him, Ballard seemed like a hard man and there was something in his eyes, to say nothing of his demeanor, that told Mori he had his work cut out for him.

The long johns were a life saver, and the boots as well. He'd gone back to the hotel just to get all of the warm clothes on, only to leave again on his peacemaking mission with the locals. Trudy had asked if he wanted her to tag along but he thought it better to approach them man to man. She dropped him at the town hall and he walked toward the sign that said

"Police" over the door. He remembered it from the day before yesterday and having been led in bodily, feet freezing and soaked, arms shackled tightly – but it was still a haze. Mori wondered, if he could remember a little better, perhaps he wouldn't be going back.

He knocked as he entered and the bell over the door chimed, drowning it out. All three of the town's policemen were there this time. Ballard sat at his desk, looking pink and beefy like a well-marbled steak. Claypool was buzzing around but stopped and looked amused as Mori entered. The other man, Officer Falkenham, Mori presumed, was rather non-descript: sandy colored hair, trimmed mustache, squarish glasses that looked to be the same color as his hair. He was the only one that didn't seem to be sweating in the heat being thrown by the wood stove in the corner. Mori noticed and removed his coat and unwound his scarf. "Gentlemen!" he said, warmly. "How is everybody today?"

They all just looked at him and said nothing.

"I myself am feeling much better." Mori said, folding his new winter coat primly over a wooden swivel chair that creaked at the slightest touch, then the scarf on top. "Not used to the climate, I guess. But better now anyway."

"Well, goddam. Imagine my relief." Ballard said, smirking. "May we help you with something, Mr. More-eye?"

Mori decided against corrections on the title or the pronunciation for the moment. "Well, the case, of course. I did want to pick your brains. See the case files…"

"What's that now? The case files? You want to see our case files?"

"Well, of course…"

Ballard began to chuckle harder. Claypool exhaled a laugh through his nose, muttered, "Jesus Christ…"

In the silence that followed, Mori stuck out his hand to Officer Falkenham. "We haven't met, yet, Officer. I'm…"

Falkenham shook it quickly. "Yeah, I know. I know." Then waved his hands at Mori to never mind with the rest.

Quiet again. Mori tried another approach: "Case files. Yes. Or we could begin by discussing it here, now, face to face. And you could…"

Ballard interrupted, "Do you think we have nothing better to do than just rehash old cases so that some *fed*, a "provisional" one at that, can write a report? That's all you're doing, isn't it? I took your advice and called down to Washington. Phil Bullock, you said? Looked him up: sure enough. He says you're here to write a report. "Anti-propaganda campaign" he said. For the war effort. So the Nazis can't say we don't treat our *ethnic and religious minorities* like they do. Or the Japs. I mean…" Ballard had been leaning back in his chair but now sat forward and folded his thick forearms in front of him on his desk. "How can we possibly criticize the Japs for running through Manchuria, killing everyone, raping every woman, hell, probably everyone, man or woman, boy and girl… I mean, how can we criticize that when somewhere in America, there might be a dead Indian? That's about the size of it, right?"

"Well, this investigation is a means of proving that your department…"

"Investigation? You don't have no investigation, Mr. More-eye…"

"Agent, if you please, Captain. Mori. More – ee."

"Provisional." Ballard said.

127

Mori nodded.

"As I was saying, the investigation closed. From what I was told, you have a report to write. That is it. Hell, you could've done that from Washington, or wherever the hell you came from. Anyway, that reminds me: how can you even be here? I thought they were taking all the Japs to relocation centers to keep them safe, or something like that. Keep them safe..." Ballard scoffed. "While Americans go get shot."

Mori had heard this line before: that the Army had all the Japanese-Americans in the camps for their own good. Mori doubted Ballard even believed it but was undoubtedly using it to get his goat. He decided not to take the bait. "The investigation is closed? Wasn't the last... suicide, just a couple of weeks ago?"

"*Closed* because they killed themselves. Ain't much else to investigate." Ballard shook his finger at Mori. "And you see, that right there. The way you said "suicide." The way you paused. Did you hear a pause, Claypool?"

"I did." Claypool said, eyes burning a hole through Mori's forehead.

"Lou?"

Falkenham nodded, sighed. "Distinctly."

"Are you *implying* Agent Mori, *provisional*, that there is some reason to doubt the findings of this department?"

"No, Captain. I haven't even seen the case files. How could I?"

"And you won't." Ballard leaned back again, folded his fingers over his round, solid gut. Before Mori could protest, the Captain said, "As a courtesy to the F. B. I." he drew the letters out contemptuously, "I will have some case summaries prepared for you. Can you do that Lou?"

"No problem, Captain." Falkenham said.

"No indeed. No problem. If it was, we wouldn't be doing it. I shall consider this courtesy the last necessary interaction with you for your little... report for the *Civil rights desk* or whatever it's called..."

Mori bristled but tried to maintain his smile. He leaned on a chair and began to squeeze the hard wood back. "That may not be entirely satisfactory, Captain. I may need to visit the locations where the bodies were found, talk to family, friends..."

"They didn't have any family and friends, boy, but if you want to run around looking at the snowbanks they were found in, be my guest."

"And," said Mori, "I might need a look at the bodies."

Ballard laughed and shook his head. "Not a chance."

All sorts of ideas came into Mori's head: subpoenas, cooperation between brother officers, the best interest of justice... but he knew this was a brick wall he couldn't break through; that he would just have to go around. He relaxed his grip on the chair, smiled widely. "Naturally, any help you can give is appreciated. And any help when your men..." he spread his hand out at both junior officers, "can fit into their schedules is likewise appreciated."

Ballard said nothing, just smirked unhappily. Mori remained, smiling a bit, nodding.

"I, uh, can have those summaries for you later today." Falkenham said after a bit, just to break the silence.

"Good of you, Officer Falkenham." Mori said. "thanks."

"Yeah, okay. Sure thing."

Mori furrowed his brow a moment, "Say, about your name. 'Falkenham.' It's the anglicization of the German name 'Falkenhayn.' You aren't related to the famous German general Erich Von Falkenhayn, are you? Distant maybe?"

Ballard looked perplexed. Mori explained, "Von Falkenhayn was a German Chief of Staff of the Army in the last war. He died, oh, twenty years ago."

"Um, I... funny you should say, actually... my folks said we might be related to some German Army big shot. Probably not though. They like to talk big... and going around saying you're related to a German army bigwig isn't such a hot idea these days, you know?"

Mori almost felt bad for Sgt. Falkenham. He was clearly the least hostile and most intelligent of the group, though Mori also sensed a sort of self-serving intelligence from the Captain. Claypool: he pegged as just a yes man. A giant, flat topped, beef slab of a yes man.

"Don't worry about it, Lou." Ballard said, lighting a camel, exhaling straight at Mori, "We won't run you off just because you've got kraut in you. Or put you in a camp." Ballard takes a long drag and there is a snap in the woodstove from a burning log. "That brings me back to my questions though, Agent Mori... *Provisional*... how are you even here again? I mean, you are supposed to be, uh, what was the word? *Evacuated?* To some... evacuation facility. So, you and the rest couldn't get up to any fifth column activity. Yet here you stand before me. How is that possible?"

130

"The Executive Order," Mori began, crossing his arms and taking a professional tone, "was to evacuate the west coast. California, Oregon, Washington, some of Arizona... not to lock up all people of Japanese descent. Move them inland to avoid, as you said, fifth column activity. Of which there has been none. And will be none. No more loyal Americans than..."

"You think the policy is harsh, then? But sound policy, wouldn't you say? I'm surprised FDR had the balls to do it, frankly. He's usually such a bleeding heart, Commie..."

"No, I don't believe it's sound policy, Captain. Or even constitutional. Anyway, there are no more loyal Americans than Japanese Americans. There haven't been any cases of fifth col..."

"No, I don't expect you would." Ballard interrupted once more. His accent was a strange muddle. Clearly, he'd spent time in the South, and maybe even mid-west but it was all very hard to place and spoken too loudly. "And don't get me wrong: the Germans now, the Nazis," his pronunciation sounded like "natzees", "they're just doing too much. It's too far. They hate the Communists. Okay, good. They realize that's the real menace in the world. You gotta give them that at least, right? And the Jewish thing. Communism is a Jewish invention, sure. But all the fuss... Germans just need everything in a neat little box. That's what I think. So, they need to drive all the Jews out. Americans, we know that a separate people living among you, you know... it can be useful. If you handle 'em right. I was a young officer in Kentucky for a while. Did you know that, Mori?"

"No."

"People talk about the negro problem all the time. Well, not around here cuz there ain't any in Maine to speak of. Maybe Portland, I dunno, but anyway... I'll tell you what: we never had a negro problem. They knew their place. We didn't give them any trouble if they stayed in line. Hell, we treated the white folks the same way. More or less. Fair is fair, right? That ought to please the civil rights desk, eh?"

"I'm curious, Captain, you seem convinced that keeping Japanese-Americans in the camps will eliminate sabotage but you told Officer Falkenham that Germans shouldn't be in camps. We're at war with Germany too, Captain. Don't you worry about German fifth column activity?"

"No, I don't, Agent…" he didn't finish Mori's name, "No, I don't. You want to know why? There is a bond, you see, that real Americans share. When you've been here awhile, you speak the language, you're white, you're a Christian… America becomes your promised land. Look, it isn't your fault. Orientals have the bond too, but with their own kind. That's why they'd sabotage. Loyalty to the emperor or some shit…"

"Blood and soil?" Mori asked.

Ballard shrugged, "I guess you could put it like that."

Mori suddenly wished he smoked. Ballard seemed to punctuate his sentences with smoky exhales, pointing the tip one way or another, frequently at Mori, like stabbing at him in the air. Mori felt he needed to counter. "I think that's probably the most un-American thing I've ever heard."

"You got a smart mouth there, dontcha?" said Claypool, leaning on his boss's chair, addressing Mori with a tiny, menacing sneer and getting a bit red-faced.

Ballard found this amusing. "As I already said: I wouldn't expect you to understand."

"I think I get the picture. Nice and clear." Mori said.

Ballard gets up from his chair and a whirl of the smoke from his camel turns in the air around him. The heat from the wood stove and the cigarette smoke have made breathing in the room a chore. Mori's long johns are dampening with sweat. The captain only sits on the edge of his desk, still lazily gesticulating with the cigarette. "I know Judge Norris got a bee in his bonnet and called one of his big shot buddies and they cared so much about appeasing the old fart that they sent their *best and brightest…*" Ballard waved his hand in the air at Mori, as if introducing him onstage with a flourish to a waiting crowd.

"So, write your little report. And if you need to go hold the old Judge's hand or wipe his ass or whatever makes him stop bellyaching like a damn woman, do that. Then get moving. If you're still here in a couple of days, I'll be very disappointed. Understand?"

"Understand? Yeah. Subtle but I think I got it."

"Subtle!" Ballard found this very funny, and he snickered, exhaling smoke through his nose like a cartoon bull. "That's the great thing about a war! Sure, war is hell and all that but it does cut out the bullshit, doesn't it? You find out who should be in charge and why. You don't waffle about decisions; you realize they have to be made and you act! Your gut tells you that all the Japs on the west coast need to be contained and you do it."

"You aren't the first to say such things, Captain. Hell, half the world is living under people who feel the same way. Only we call them the enemy."

Captain Ballard looked at first as if Mori's comment had angered him, but the redness in his face and neck then gyrated with laughter. "Go write your report, Mori. Then fuck off."

133

Mori retrieved his overcoat and scarf and draped them over his arm like a maître'd. He said, "Gentlemen." As he nodded goodbye and returned happily to the frigid outside air. Somehow, it was still morning. Only a few minutes had passed. He pulled the brim of his hat lower at the front and exhaled a cloud of pent-up breath.

"Well then…" Mori said, to nobody. "That could have gone better."

Mori spent the afternoon at the library, reading up on the locals: the who's who, the area industry, news clippings about the suicides, of which, given what a small town it was, there were surprisingly few, maps of the county… whatever came to his mind that might be helpful. Trudy got bored with that after a short while and excused herself. Mori went through all the motions of the beginning of an investigation, except for course, for consulting police files. There no longer was a newspaper in town, it had gone out of business a few years back, apparently. Nearby towns had covered the story – barely. He called them and the Portland Press Herald, the biggest paper in Maine, as well. Nobody sent a reporter to town. The reporter who wrote up the story didn't seem interested in pursuing it any further and, while acknowledging the oddness of it all, accepted and found the local PD's story pretty air-tight.

When Trudy returned five hours later, as he'd suggested, he still made her wait awhile longer while he finished notetaking. After the first few hours he'd gotten used to feeling the stares of the librarian and the few patrons who passed in and out. When he met their gaze, he flashed a blinding toothy grin and gave a little acknowledging bobbing nod – just once, to be friendly but relay that he was busy and not about to engage in conversation.

Trudy drove him back to the hotel and after a minute or so they were silent, as she could see he was deep in thought. Occasionally she would look in the rear-view mirror and see him staring at some notes he'd made in the library. She thought it odd that he sat in the back, having refused every other time to do so, even though she offered every time. His hair was glistening and perfectly pomaded in place but the lively smile at the corner of his mouth now seemed stuck in the downward position and five-o-clock shadow was adding to the gloomy countenance.

He actually wanted to invite her in for dinner but felt it wasn't appropriate. He knew these New Englanders seemed a little conservative and the last thing he needed was to cause offense. As he prepared to go inside, he said, "Well, hey…"

"Yes?"

"I… never mind."

"No, go ahead."

"I… sorry. Can't remember." He smiled widely. "Still a little loopy from being under the weather, I guess. What time tomorrow? Say, 9 am?"

"Sure," Trudy said, tugging the bill of her leather cap lower. "Nine."

In the soft light of the hotel restaurant, he ordered a minute steak and Potatoes O'Brien. The place was nearly empty, even for dinner, and Mori felt a weird sense of soft suffocation as the world got dark so quickly and the nights seemed so long. The snow outside added to this sensation. A thick blanket over everything.

During a dessert of rather good apple pie with a demitasse of strong black coffee, Mori saw Officer Falkenham walk in and up to his table.

He looked around, "Wow, dead in here." He said.

"As a visitor," Mori said, "and don't take this the wrong way, Officer, but I don't think this would be the ideal time to visit your fair town – or the state for that matter. It's a tad nippy, you see. Coffee?"

The Officer shook his head. He was carrying a buff-colored folder. "Here are the, uh, the summaries. Typed them myself."

"Officer Falkenham, please, take a seat. If you don't mind."

He did, pulling out a chair and sitting on the edge. He laid the folder next to Mori's now empty pie plate. He remained in his heavy blue weatherproof overcoat and a hat not unlike the one Trudy had tried to get him to buy, with the earflaps, only this one was dark navy colored and quite broken in.

Mori opened the folder, already discouraged at how thin it was.

"Mind if I smoke?" Falkenham asked.

"Suit yourself."

It turned out to be just four pages of sparse type. About one page for each dead man. It appeared to be basic biographical information and not much more than Mori had already seen in newspaper clippings. There were no witness interviews, nothing more than a cursory mention of any forensic information and not a single photograph.

Mori nodded and closed the folder. "Did you write these?"

"Yeah, well, I mean, the Captain dictated it, pretty much. But yeah. I typed it."

"And no photos or anything?"

"Yeah, Captain Ballard was pretty clear about that. No photos. He said he doesn't want them to get out and to sensationalize the whole thing."

"I'm with the FBI. How does he think they're going to 'get out'?"

"He's not real keen on the FBI poking in on this. Or the FBI in general, honestly."

Mori nodded. "I see."

"If you want my advice, I'd say, just write your report and go. Ballard's alright but he's... difficult. You know? He's been a cop a long time and in a lot of places..."

"Yeah, about that... does he just have a wandering spirit or is he getting run out of these towns. His sunny disposition makes me wonder. Never mind. Forget I asked. But say, Officer, have you been investigating these deaths?"

"Yeah. I help out. It's the Captain's show though. He's the expert after all. And also, I wasn't here for the first two. I mean, I was here, in town, but I wasn't a police officer yet. I just started in June. They needed cops what with the war and so I thought..."

"What kept you out? Or are you waiting on your number to be called?"

"No way. I tried. They found out I had epilepsy."

"What about the Captain? And Claypool?"

The young officer shifted uncomfortably. "I don't know. I mean, really, I don't. Anyway, I'm not sure I'd like telling other men's business. Especially to a stranger." The irritation caused Falkenham's accent to accentuate. Drawing out words at the end of sentences and dropping R's from the end of words. Mori was, Officer Falkenham said, a "straaaynnjah."

"The Captain hasn't said. Probably he's just overage. With Claypool, it's probably his brain. He's wacko." The Sargent held up his hand. "That's not fair. He's… high strung. And a little… anyway. He's alright. Maybe it's his blood pressure. I know he takes medicine for it. I dunno."

"Can you tell me anything about these deaths, Sargent? Anything that isn't in here?" he tapped the folder.

"Not really, Agent Mori. No. And not just because the Captain would tear my hide off either. They were just older guys. They didn't have anyone. No family, no friends to speak of, except work acquaintances. They were all drunks too. The winters are long here even when you have things to live for. You know?"

Mori nodded. Falkenham rapped his knuckles on the table, muffled by his thick gloves. "Okay. Well, I gotta be going. Best of luck with the report."

CHAPTER 15

February 1, 1943

Trudy knocked on Mori's hotel room door. He was clean-shaven, suit pressed and ready to go when he swung the door inward.

"Mornin' boss!" Trudy said, tugging the bill of her cap and smirking at her own joke. "Where to?"

"Come on in, Trudy." Mori said. "Want some coffee?"

Trudy had never really taken up coffee drinking but she didn't want to seem juvenile in front of Mori. "Sure thing!"

He waved her toward the table and went to fetch some papers. Trudy turned a cup right side up onto a saucer and poured some coffee into it. Steam rose and she took a sip. She scowled a bit and added two sugar cubes, stirred and sipped. She made a face, then added two more, a little cream, then thought it was just fine.

Mori returned and said, "Before we go off looking for clues…"

"Ooh, exciting."

"Yes. But before then, I need to get my head right. I think if I lay this all out, I can start to make sense of it. Do you think you could listen to me for a bit, Trudy? Let me bounce all of this off of you?"

Trudy smiled, "Yeah, you bet. I mean, sure. Whatever I can do to help."

"Great." Mori said. "I'm gonna start at the beginning and work my way to the most recent death. Okay?"

Trudy nodded enthusiastically.

"Okay… December 12, 1941… so that's, jeez, that was just a couple of days after Pearl Harbor. That's when he was found, on the 12th. So… subject's name was Winfred Moody. Worked at Stark Lumber here in town. 66 years old, said to have been born in Quebec though he spent most of his life in the US. No record of a family. Some arrests for drunkenness, vagrancy, last seen at a local bar, the *Easy Street Publick House* on the night of the 8th… Nothing about the condition of the body except 'died of exposure' which, *of course* exposure… he was found face down without a stitch of clothes on in the middle of the road… and a news clipping that says he was buried in June…"

"Yeah, "Trudy said. "Have to wait until the ground is unfrozen, otherwise it would be like trying to dig into a rock."

Mori nodded, "Of course…" he got up and opened the curtains and the mid-morning light spilled into the room. "Looks like a cold one out there today."

"Very good detective work, Agent Mori. It is! I think it's about zero degrees. May get up to five!"

"Good God, that doesn't seem possible… okay," Mori poured himself some coffee and sat again across the table from Trudy. "Where was I? That's really it for our first one. Wow. That's… no information at all. Hoo-boy… anyway. Next: two months later. February 3, 1942…" Mori tried to remember what he had been doing on that date. Waiting for the FBI to call back, most likely… "Dead man's name is Robert Curette. Again, according to my 'summaries' he had no family. Again, record of petty arrests. Again, found naked on 'Pike Road' … are you familiar with that road?'

Trudy said, "Sort of. I mean, it's not really in use much anymore. It used to go up to a lumber camp but the camp relocated, I think. Most people just call it the country road. I'm pretty sure they still plow it though…"

"They do. Snow plow driver found them both… Again, too, no close friends and nobody saw anything. Curette worked at a cannery though…"

"East Jonesport Cannery." Trudy said, authoritatively.

"Yeah."

"They're the biggest employers in the area, really. If you work anywhere, you work in the lumber mill, the cannery or off the coast on a lobster boat around here." Trudy said, with a faraway sound in her voice as if the limitations she had spoken of were unappealing to her.

141

"Three of them did work in the lumber mill." Mori said. "Stark lumber. Mr. Curette was the only one that worked at the cannery. It makes me think if there was some… foul play it probably didn't have to do with where they worked."

"Do you really think that? Foul play? Really?"

Mori shrugged. "Dotting I's. Crossing t's. That's all. But whatever the case, I'll try to put Judge Norris' mind at ease."

"I'm glad to hear that." Trudy said, sipping her syrupy coffee.

"Alright, where was I? Okay, then they start again this winter. December 30, 1942. Jeez, just a couple of days after Christmas. This one a John Doe. Worked at the Lumber Camp. No friends, no family. Barely seemed to speak to anybody. How is that possible? How did he work at this place and they didn't know his name?!"

Trudy wasn't sure how to answer, so she didn't.

"Naked. Booze in his system. Same Road. Cops found this one. The Captain himself.

"Then," Mori continued, "The last one. Rupert Delisle. Also worked at Stark Lumber. Also, Mohawk and Canadian. No family, no friends. Booze in his system, naked on Pike Road. Again."

Not sure what else to say, Trudy said, "Weird."

Mori nodded. "Some things, just, right off the top of my head, Trudy, okay? So: one person loses their clothes and gets lost in the snow. Okay. Drunken accident or, if we go ahead and believe the Captain, a suicide. It would make a copycat suicide a more likely story… but *three*?! And naked but they found no clothes along the route… did they disrobe at home and walk naked down Pike Road, this remote, long avenue to nowhere but an abandoned lumber camp and nobody saw that? In the middle of winter? I mean, even in summer you'd be likely to notice a naked Indian strolling down the road."

"Weird." Trudy said again. "But it is pretty rural out that way, Agent Mori. And at night – I dunno, maybe. I don't think anyone would come along for hours. Maybe all night."

"Okay. Perhaps. But imagine the first time the wind cuts through you at 20 or 30 below zero. I can barely stand it with all the clothes you've very nicely shown me are a necessity. Some of these men lived *miles* from Pike Road. All four just go through with it, walking down this old logging road… no second thoughts?"

"…or second thoughts too late?"

"Yes. Maybe. And maybe all their clothes were covered in snow, or blew away… god knows after reading all of this I don't think the police spent much time trying to find the garments…"

Trudy stared into her coffee as she adjusted the cup in the saucer. "You think the police are crooked? Or not doing their jobs?"

"I can't tell. I just don't think I have enough information. I can't force them to cooperate and at this point I don't even think I can sweet talk them into cooperating. It seems to me though that the best-case scenario at this point is that Captain Ballard hasn't put forth much of an effort to figure out what really happened to these men. And I think… I think it is because they were Indians."

"That's... awful." Trudy said. The room was warm from the radiator by the window blasting away but she pulled her coat closed anyway.

Mori paced to the window again, and shivered a bit looking at the cold clear sky, cloudless and strikingly blue. The snow-covered trees on the other side of the road across the parking lot stood motionless and Mori had a strange feeling of time being stopped. He didn't move again until he saw a car drive past on the road, slowly on the slick ice.

"I need more information. I need to talk to the doctor who examined the bodies. He wasn't local, worked for the state..." Mori shuffled through his well-organized notes. "A Doctor Forrestal?"

Trudy shook her head: didn't know him.

"Has an office in... Bar Harbor?"

"That's down the coast a bit. Probably take a while to get there. Two hours maybe, with the black ice. We'll have to take it easy."

"Black ice?"

"When it gets very cold like this the moisture can freeze clear over the pavement and make it slicker than grease and you can't even see it. Black ice."

"Oh. Yes. Well, take all the time you need then. Shall we?"

They left for Bar Harbor, which, Mori learned, was something of a hideaway, in the summer, for the very wealthy and influential. "All the swells." Trudy said. "The Rockefellers have a huge place there, I heard. I think they own half the town, honestly."

The town was the jewel of the Acadia National Forest, a primeval northern forest of rocky coastline dotted with lighthouses and behind them bare birch, elm, and maple trees in the midst of ramrod straight evergreens. Bar Harbor was loaded with hotels, restaurants, and attractions – mostly closed for the season. They got to the address of the doctor before noon. They'd chatted pretty much the entire ride, but not about the case. Mainly about movies and who Mori might have seen on the Paramount lot.

"You worked on *This Gun for Hire?* Really? No fooling?"

"Yup. Building sets."

"I saw that one."

"Funny. I didn't get the chance... had something come up that ate up my time."

"Was Veronica Lake nice? Was she gorgeous in person?"

"A definite yes to the second. But I never spoke to her. Seemed swell though. From a distance."

"And Alan Ladd? Is he dreamy? In person?"

"Never saw him. Sorry."

"Nuts."

Dr. Forrestal's office was small but immaculate and refined. It was on a sloping street where the smell of the ocean managed, just barely, to break through the heavy winter chill. The sign out front had the doctor's name and titles on a sign with a shiny black lacquer and all of the letters carved neatly and painted gold. The sign looked sturdy enough to stand up to the Maine winter and a Kansas hurricane.

"Shall I leave you to it? Man to man?" Trudy asked.

"Yeah, probably best."

"I'll go find a place to rustle us up some sandwiches or something then, eh?"

Trudy threw the Nash in gear sped off, leaving Mori on the sidewalk, ghostly white with frost beneath his feet. The sun was a relief and made it feel a little warmer – maybe even 10 or 15 degrees! Mori walked up the stone steps and went inside. He walked into a cozy and well-appointed waiting area of blond wood and a smell of balsam. A tall man in a white tunic and horn-rimmed glasses stood discussing the contents of a file folder with a blond nurse seated at the greeting desk. He had a neatly trimmed thin mustache that moved like an instrument as he spoke and his head, gray on the sides with dark hair on top slicked strait back, bobbed assuredly. The nurse was prim but pretty, blond curls tight but not too tight. She saw Mori first, made a gesture with her hand then pointed at him. The doctor (Mori presumed) turned to look at him. The silence was brief but awkward.

"Excuse me," Mori began. "I don't mean…"

"I think I already know who you are, if you are about to offer an introduction. News of your arrival has reached me, that is to say. I'm Dr. Forrestal. Clement Forrestal. This is Nurse Beck. Yes. We've been told that you might arrive."

"Indeed? Captain Ballard was it?"

"Yes. I must say, I thought he was pulling my leg for a moment. Except a sense of humor would be utterly out of character for the man. And anyway, here you are. In the flesh, as they say."

"Just doing my job. Being thorough."

"Of course, of course. Say, why don't you come into my office. Right this way."

Mori left his hat and overcoat with Nurse Beck and followed. Dr. Forrestal led Mori into a much larger room that was more of the same, bookshelves with glass front doors, blond wood resplendent with shine. A large window looked out onto the street and it appeared so picturesque that Mori half expected to see that Currier and Ives had signed it.

Dr. Forrestal motioned to a chair and Mori sat. The doctor, clearly fastidious, straitened the few items on the desk, first the black rotary telephone, then a small wooden box, then an ancient looking ink and pen stand. "You should know," the doctor began, "That Captain Ballard attempted to dissuade me from talking to you. He said that your inquiry is… unofficial? Is that right?"

"Well, my boss, Agent Phil Bullock with the Washington office, has instructed me to, uh, examine…"

"Yes. Quite unofficial then. I see. Why should I disclose anything to you, Mr.…? I'm sorry, the Captain told me your name but I've quite forgotten…"

"Mori. Asa Mori. Agent Mori, if you like, Doctor. I don't think it is at all appropriate for the local law enforcement to disparage and attempt to hinder the inquiries of a brother agency, to be quite honest and I think you would certainly be wrong to follow his advice."

Dr. Forrestal tented his fingers and leaned forward, "But he doesn't trust you, you see. I daresay he can't believe you *aren't* who you say you are, or he can't prove it anyway. Still, he doesn't trust you. So why should I? I've given an interview to the paper, so you can glean from that what you will. I've submitted my report to the police and they can share with you what they see fit. So, what are you asking of me? Why should I go beyond that?"

Mori was getting annoyed that everyone seemed to imply they were too busy to help or he would somehow have to jump through hoops to gain some kind of courtesy that the FBI badge (provisional or not) wasn't eliciting.

"Because four men are dead and the people who are supposed to give a damn and look into it seem to have tied it up in a neat package and thrown it in the river because they either don't want to deal with it or don't care enough to. Even if it does turn out to be just as the police reports say, it won't be for exhausting all the possibilities that it turns out to be true. There are so many stones unturned I could walk all the way from here back to LA on them. Because *I care* and one way or another, I'm going to find out anyway so you may as well just help me out now and save me the aggravation."

The Doctor raised his eyebrows, then smirked a little. "Then too, another good reason is that Captain Ballard is a bastard and I don't think I'd follow his advice on anything."

Mori looked into his lap to disguise the smile that creeped onto his face and then pretended to wipe away a bit of fuzz from his trousers. "He does make an impression."

"Indeed. Mind you, I'll tell you what I know or can recall but I can't really do more than that. I don't have any files or effects. That all stays in the town with the police. And I obviously can't give you permission to view the bodies, that, again, would be up to the police, and I don't see that happening for you… but ask away."

"Not sure where to begin, really. The police have said that all of the men died of exposure?"

Doctor Forrestal nodded and opened his right-hand desk drawer. He pulled out a briar pipe, tobacco pouch, and ashtray. "Yes, that's right." He said as he packed the pipe and then set it alight with a wooden match. "Hypothermia." He said through clenched teeth.

"And all of them naked as the day they were born?"

"That's right."

"That seems very... peculiar, wouldn't you say?" Mori said, thinking it a wild understatement.

"Well, that depends, really. There is a phenomenon among hypothermia victims, fatal cases, that is, of "paradoxical undressing." After a manic state, and nearing death, the victim will likely feel like they are burning up and shed all their clothes. And the presence of alcohol in the system only exacerbates this. Booze is a vasodilator, you see, which means it causes the blood to flow to the skin, the hands, all the places that wouldn't be getting blood flow in those conditions, so they feel hot when they're really freezing to death."

"And they all had alcohol in their systems."

"They did, to varying degrees."

"So, they may not have been naked before going out there at all. They may have experienced this... paradoxical..."

"Undressing yes. Odd that *they all* would have, I suppose. But not impossible. Ballard has his own theory, of course..."

"Yes, the tribal ritual suicides."

"Possible too, I suppose." The doctor said, puffing away.

"No clothes found though. Not so far anyway."

"No?" Doctor Forrestal said, "Well, that is a hole in my theory, I suppose. If they were experiencing the paradoxical undressing it would have been at the last stages, near death, and the garments would not have been far, I shouldn't think."

"That sounds about right." Mori began taking notes in a clipped, nearly indecipherable shorthand, "Can we start at the beginning?"

"Wherever you like."

"The first one, Winfred Moody. The one found by the snowplow driver…"

"More than found, dear boy."

"How's that?"

"Well, the driver hit the body, you see. Apparently, there had been enough of a snowstorm that night to cover the body and…" Doctor Forrestal clamped his pipe between his teeth and slapped his left hand with his right. "Scooped the corpse right up. Limbs were so stiff the arm nearly broken off clean… I don't mean to be grotesque about things, mind you…"

"No, not at all. Though, I imagine that made it difficult to determine if, say there had been a struggle. Or an altercation."

"Well, all of them, as far as I can recall, have had quite a few scars and wounds and whatnot. That said, working as a Lumberman is no easy work. Any lumberman would have a body covered in scars. Tells the tale of the trade."

"One of the men worked in the cannery also."

"Also, some back-breaking work."

"Indeed. I guess what I'm getting at is, do you think there was evidence of a struggle? Bruises, cuts, teeth newly knocked out, nails scraped on skin... is that possible?"

The Doctor began digging into the bowl of his pipe with the end of a match and he looked pensive. "Possible? Sure. I have a rather more difficult time recalling the fellows from last year. The passage of time and also, well, it wasn't a repeat of other events, you know? One of the fellows this year did have a broken hand. I could tell it wasn't long before death because of the level... well, the lack of healing and blood coagulation and what would have happened if healing were allowed to take place. If he were alive, that it. But that's not much, is it? Definitive? No. In addition to having tough jobs these fellows – well, they have hard lives. The money isn't very good, they're prone to drink and to violent and low brow amusements. Fighting, gambling, that sort of thing."

"Indians, you mean?"

"Now, now, Agent Mori," the Doctor said, reigniting his pipe. "That wasn't a comment on the race of people, just that a good many Indians in these parts, what few there are, tend to have to work in these jobs and have this sort of life... sad, in many ways, really. You know, you really do sound like a man from the Civil Rights Desk, I must say."

"Thanks."

"Wasn't strictly a compliment, dear boy. But not an insult either. Actually, there's another reason, aside from hard living, that might cause fresh lacerations and abrasions and all that... with hypothermia, once the body temperature is lowered sufficiently, the mind just… goes. The organs start to fail. Muscle coordination would all but disappear. It is likely that the severe hypothermia sufferer would fall and never be able to get back up again. When the body temperature has fallen so low as to shut down all metabolic processes… there is another phenomenon… terminal burrowing."

"And what is that?" Mori asked.

"Like a hibernating animal, the sufferer seeks the protection of an enclosed space – a burrow. They might use their last bits of strength, out of their wits, mind you, this is strictly instinctual, involuntary action triggered by the extreme hypothermia, trying to burrow into the earth – or wherever they were. But into the frozen ground and ice in this case and so tearing of the skin, signs of a struggle, well, it may not mean what it appears."

"You think that could be how one of them ended up with a broken hand?"

The Doctor looked pensive. "No. Not in that case, I don't. It was a pretty even break. Like it had been crushed."

"Goodness." Mori scribbled notes. The description the doctor painted really hit him in the gut and he couldn't shake thinking how the four men must have felt. And suffered.

Perhaps the silence was too long, as the doctor digressed: "You know, I actually went to school with a Japanese fellow."

"At Boston University?"

"How did you know that?" Dr. Forrestal asked.

Mori pointed to the degree on the wall to his left, resplendent in its shimmering walnut frame.

"Ah. Of course. Yes, in fact, at BU. Kazuo Yamashita was his name. Father was a diplomat or something. Kaz actually spoke like one of the Boston Brahmins even though he was born in… Tokyo, I think. You don't have a trace of an accent either, I notice."

"Well, I was born in East Los Angeles, so…"

"Of course." The Doctor grinned. "Anyway, haven't heard from Kaz in years."

"Might be awkward after Pearl Harbor."

"Awkward indeed. Things have been awkward for you since Pearl Harbor, I'd bet."

As if blessed with a preternatural sense of timing, Nurse Beck chose that moment to enter carrying a small tray with a cylindrical silver carafe of coffee with matching service ware. She seemed to shimmer around him with a friendly and permanent smile. "Coffee, Agent Mori?"

Nurse Beck seemed good at remembering names. "Please, Nurse Beck. Thanks."

She poured and the rich smell filled the air. "Sugar? One lump or two?"

"One, please." He usually didn't have any but for some reason he hated to correct her. Perhaps her crisp nurses' dress was snug in the right places or the simple politeness on her plain but pretty and well-scrubbed face.

She handed Mori his coffee and then prepared one for the Doctor, as she likely had hundreds of times before. She left the tray and departed, saying "Let me know if you need anything else."

"And I had heard good help was hard to find."

"Indeed." The Doctor said, seeming at peace with the world with his tawny coffee and blazing briar pipe. Mori almost hated to bring him back to the unpleasantness.

"Doctor, I'm interested in the John Doe. No identification? He had a job and nobody knew his name? What about fingerprints?"

"I can't speak to the first part. Although, that appears to be the case. No identification, I heard that from the police, yes. They were speculating that he was mute but couldn't confirm it. But as for fingerprints, I do recall they said they turned up nothing. No matches. And as for the job: I don't think they ask too many questions of the lumbermen up there. They'd lose a lot of men that way. A lot of those men go up into the woods to disappear from their pasts. Felling trees with other men who don't want to necessarily talk about their pasts either."

Mori sipped his coffee: anything warm made him feel better lately, and even the sticky sweetness didn't bother him. "Did he have any marks that might distinguish him? If we can't get a fingerprint match then maybe there's some other feature."

"I believe he was one of the ones with a tattoo, actually, now that you mention it. In fact, I'm sure of it."

"Do you remember what it was?

Dr. Forrestal chewed the pipe stem and looked at the medical books behind Mori. "Ah... no. Religious symbol, I think. On the arm. Catholic, I presume. I wasn't familiar with it. I wrote a description in the file so I wouldn't have to remember you see and the files, of course..."

"With the police, yes."

"One of the unfortunate fellows last year had a tattoo as well. Different though. Not a cross. Bigger too… sorry, don't recall what it was either. Perhaps you can persuade the police… ha! No: never mind. I was about to say you could persuade Ballard to give you a look after all but I think you'd have better luck trying to convince him that you were Herbert Hoover."

"Tattoos…" Mori said, scribbling on his notepad with one hand, balancing the coffee cup in its saucer in the other. "Is there anything about them you can tell me that you think might help? Anything at all? Anything that stood out to you?"

The Doctor shook his head. "They were all very similar. All in their 40s and 50s most likely. Indians, of course. Laborers. Alcohol present in their systems. Although not so much that I would consider that the cause. Papers like to play on the idea that all Indians are drunkards, but they didn't all have the effects of long-term drinking, I can tell you that much."

"I actually think it means they all happened to have been…" Mori was about to say 'abducted" but didn't want to set the doctor on to conjecture. "that is, started from the same place. A bar, perhaps."

The doctor nodded, unsure. "Anyway, the feet, my goodness…"

"What about the feet?"

"Well, they were just… *shredded* from the conditions. The frostbite set in fast, naturally, and then the skin froze and the icy roads would have just been taking off bits of skin… the feet would feel like solid blocks of ice, scraping along like dead flesh, which they were in way, I suppose you might say… hopefully they would have been so far gone or feeling the effects of the alcohol that they wouldn't have experienced the intense pain that might have come with every step… Dear me, tragic. Terrible, really."

Mori chatted with the Doctor awhile longer, trying to extract what he could but there was only so much he could learn. The Doctor hadn't felt autopsies to be necessary and, of course, the police hadn't pushed for them. The cause of death wasn't really in question anyway. When he departed Dr. Forrestal's office, which, cozy as it was, he did with some regret, he found Trudy waiting for him outside with the Nash running, nice and warm. He got into the front seat beside her looking deep in thought.

"Any luck?" Trudy asked, her pale face and slight, upturned nose pink from having run errands in the cold outside air.

"Not much. A little, maybe. Something, anyway. Maybe some reassurance that everything is as it should be. Or close enough."

"Well, that's good then."

Mori nodded. "It would be. If I could believe it."

Trudy puzzled at this, then shrugged. "Here." She said and handed him a brown paper bag. "Swiss cheese on rye. Some pickles. Tomato juice. Perk you right up."

"Swell, I'm starving!" Mori said, digging in. He reached into his wallet and pulled out three dollars for her. She waved it off.

"Nah, keep it. No big deal."

"No, no, take it. I've got an expense account."

Trudy smiled and snatched the bills. "Well, in that case..."

They were off again, headed back to town. Picturesque Bar Harbor receded behind them as Trudy drove and they could see the whole town in front of the harbor; tiny dark buildings in the snow, most with smoke rising to the afternoon sky. "I've never seen any place quite like this." Mori said.

"Puny compared to LA, I'm sure." Trudy said, with a young person's disdain for the familiar.

"Just different." Mori said. "And beautiful. *Unspoiled*, I guess the poets would say. Look at those islands."

Mori pointed at the line of several small islands in the Harbor, snow-covered and still.

"It's called 'Frenchman Bay'." Trudy said. "The town is called Bar Harbor but the whole..." Trudy waved her hand, adjusted her cap, then put both hands back on the wheel. "thing is called Frenchman Bay."

"No kidding? Why is that?"

"Not really sure. Revolutionary War thing, I think."

Mori pointed at the islands. "There's a Japanese creation myth. Two Gods, right? Izanagi and Izanami. And they've been given the job of making the earth solid. Livable. You know? Like, the waters receding in Genesis... So, anyway, they do and they use this swanky spear all covered in jewels, it's called an *Ame-no-nuboku*. I think. And the first drops of saltwater to fall created the islands of Japan. After that, they were supposed to go all around the world and create the rest of the world."

"Huh. Wow. Supposed to?"

"Oh, yeah, they messed up. I guess the female goddess spoke first and that was improper and that put the kibosh on the whole thing so they had to start over."

"No kidding. Huh. Just like Eve and the apple."

"Yeah, kinda, I guess."

"What I mean is, we get blamed for everything, no matter what country it is. Females, I mean. Sheesh." Trudy said, shaking her head. "Did your folks tell you that story?"

"Nah. Read it in a book."

The drove on, Bar Harbor gone and the thick trees of the Acadia Forest around them like sentinels with the road snaking though.

"Back home to the hotel?" Trudy asked.

"Yeah, Trudy, thanks. Maybe we could run by Pike Road on the way?"

"Not on the way exactly but no problem."

Mori said "Thanks." once more. "The two men from last year… they're buried. That's a lost cause. But the two from this year – I've got to get a look at the bodies. The Doctor was a good man but I don't know if he was looking closely enough. I need to get a look somehow. But I don't even know where they are."

Trudy grinned, like she'd just thought of something. "I think I might be able to help you there. But we'll cross that bridge when we come to it."

By the time they turned off the coastal road and onto the rougher ground that was Pike Road, the sun was already hanging low and threatening to plunge below the horizon. Much of the length of the area had long, flat stretches of clearing where the road snaked though. They drove this awhile until Mori asked Trudy to pull the Nash over. She did, slowly putting the gearshift all the way up into park.

"This is about six miles from the turn off. I guess this is more or less where the last body was found. No way to tell for sure."

"It's a shame the police aren't giving you more of a hand in this, Agent Mori. I don't understand it." Trudy said.

Mori got out of the warm confines of the car and onto the frozen logging road. The temperature was starting to dip. As if reading his thoughts, Trudy said, "It's a cold one. Might get down to 35 below tonight."

"Good god." Mori said. Trudy giggled.

He looked up one way, then turned and looked the other. Frozen expanse on either side. Trees standing black and forbidding in the distance. Occasional tufts of dead grass or hay poking up through the hard-packed snow. It was as desolate as any dessert he had ever seen. Once, when he had been working for a fruit company about 5 years before, he'd found himself driving a truckload of lettuce back from Barstow to Los Angeles. Before he'd even gotten halfway to Victorville, not even fifteen miles, the truck broke down. Even walking through the dessert back to Barstow to fetch a mechanic, miles in the merciless sun at midday, had not felt as hopeless and forsaken as this.

"Heck of a place to do it." Mori said, barely audible. He thought of bare skin touching the frigid, icy ground, unable to feel anything else, each second getting more and more cold until you were dead flesh and out of your wits. He shuddered.

They saw movement down the road; a car. Mori hadn't expected anyone, having been told the desolate nature of the area. They both stared at it silently, trying to make it out.

"I think it's the cops." Trudy said.

Trudy was right; he could see the dormant searchlight mounted over the left headlight and the star design on the door as the mid-30's Ford slowly approached. They watched it the whole way until Officer Falkenham, who was driving, pulled up alongside and parked while Claypool got out. He removed his winter cap with a flutter of furred earflaps and his head, with just a thin carpet of pale hair like steel wool, steamed as the cold caught his body heat.

"Everything alright?" Claypool asked.

"Just fine, officer. Thanks for asking." Mori said.

"See any strange characters out this way?" he smirked.

"One or two." Mori said, "nothing I can't handle."

"That's good, that's good. I thought you might have a delicate constitution. Like when you passed out on the floor that time…"

"Claypool!" Falkenham called from inside the car, still running, "We've gotta go!"

"…you weren't lookin' so good."

"I thank you for your concern, officer. I'm right as rain. Actually, it is lucky you've come this way. I think the tire was shimmying a little. Loose lugs, I think, probably. But there's no tire iron in the car..." he poked his thumb back at the Nash. "Could I borrow yours for a quick check?"

Claypool wasn't sure what to do for a moment, but then just said, "Yeah sure." And headed for the trunk. Falkenham, looking anywhere but *at* anyone in particular, popped the trunk then immediately returned to the driver's seat. Claypool retrieved the tire iron and Mori, one hand on the lip of the trunk, took it from him.

"Thanks." He said.

Mori went around the car, popped the hub cap off and began tightening the lug nuts. Trudy looked on, perplexed, but said nothing.

Claypool turned to Trudy, "Your folks know you're out this late and the company you're keeping? No offense, there, Ace, was it? Mr. Mo... Moto?"

"Mori..." He said, finishing up.

"But a little girl like this and all the gruesome details... you know... We went to school together, Trudy and me. She was a couple years behind..."

"Mind your business." Trudy said, making a sour lemon face at him.

Mori returned the hubcap into place with a metallic pop and handed Claypool the tire iron back.

Claypool chucked the tool back into the trunk and slammed it with unnecessary force. He then hopped onto the running board and then into the passenger seat. He slapped the roof of the car. "Okay, just making sure you weren't broken down way out here. All is well, then. You take care. Good luck with your report, Mr. Moto."

"Shut up and come on." Falkenham said to Claypool a bit louder than he wanted to, then out the window. "Okay, see you later."

They watched the Ford sputter away and turn off, disappearing beyond the bend in the distance.

"*Idiot*." Mori said.

"What was that lug nut business all about?" Trudy asked.

"Maybe nothing." Mori said. "We should go."

CHAPTER 16

February 2, 1943

The next morning, Trudy arrived again at the same time. Mori shouted, "It's open!"

He was at the mirror making minor adjustments to his hair, which had a particularly nice luster that morning, he thought. His jacket and waistcoat look like they'd been freshly pressed and his shoes had a pleasing high shine that he spent some time to achieve. "I wouldn't, if I were you." Trudy said, pointing to the shoes. "You'll ruin them out in that mess in no time."

Mori nodded. "I know, I know." He sat on the end of the bed and slipped them off. "Just wanted to have a civilized appearance for a few moments. Although these boots are growing on me." He slid into the winter boots she had picked for him, giving the trouser legs a tight fold into the furry top, and fastened the buckles.

"So, what's up today? Have we cracked it yet? Is it time for arrests? Is it some lone, savage lunatic lurking outside the city limits for unsuspecting prey?"

"I'll be heading up to Stark Lumber. You can take the day off."

"What?! I don't want to take the day off! And you don't know your way around. And, I mean, let's face it, if you just start showing up places without me there, they might think… well, god knows what they might think, seeing an oriental face."

"I appreciate your concern. And your enthusiasm. You've been a great help. And it's just for today. The lumberyard isn't any place for nice girls like you."

"*Girls*. Like I'm some Bobbysoxer with pigtails." Trudy said with a sneer, "What do you know about lumberyards anyway, Hollywood?"

"Just what everyone has been telling me. And it sounds like a few of the places I've worked in my time that aren't the most… friendly." He pinched the bill of her leather cap with his thumb and forefinger and smiled that smile. "Just for today. Trust me, okay? I'll need you back tomorrow."

She smiled back, "Does that work with most girls?"

"Some. I don't have a lot of experience with Caucasian girls so if you have any tips…"

"Not bad. A little hokey. Don't lay it on so thick."

He nodded. "Good. Good to know. But still, for today, I'd feel better… if you were out of harm's way. You know?"

164

She looked at her shoe tops to avoid letting him see in case she was smiling too wide. She had to remind herself not to go all jelly-knees over the Ja... the Oriental. "You still don't know your way around."

He pulled the corner of a folded paper out of his inside jacket pocket, then stuffed it back in and patted his chest. "Bought a map. I'll be fine. I'll miss our conversation though. Maybe the cab driver will be chatty."

She shook her head. "Cute that you think there's a taxi in this town. Let alone one that would take you way out there. Here." She tossed him the keys to the Nash.

"The Judge won't mind?"

"No. He wants you to have whatever you need to do what you have to do."

"Can I drop you at home?"

"Home?! Ugh. Heck no. Drop me at the movie house."

Trudy actually did the driving to the movie house and then she got out, leaving the driver side door open for him. The Marquee had lighted vertical letters that declared it to be *The Premier*. Quite a large and good-looking theater for such a small town, he thought. But going to the movies must be the top draw in a tiny burg like this, he figured.

Trudy read the titles, "*Hitler's Children*? Ugh. Propaganda film. Those are gruesome. *Shadow of a Doubt.* I read that was a good one."

"So, I'll pick you up here?"

"Nah, the hardware store far. I'll just hoof it when I'm done. Besides, I have a feeling you're going to be awhile..."

165

Without waiting for a response, she shut the door and, with a carefree and lilting sort of gait, made for the box office.

Mori smirked and drove off quickly. He had quite a drive before him. An hour at least, by his estimate. It didn't take long to leave Trudy's small town behind and quickly even a few scattered residences gave way to long stretches of nothing but unspoiled winter landscapes. Only occasionally did Mori encounter another car headed the other way. He tried listening to the radio but only one station was in range and after straining to hear the war news over the static, he shut it off.

The turnoff to Stark Lumber had clearly seen its share of big trucks. It was wide and had big loping turns but still looked like it could be reclaimed at any moment by the forest primeval. Mori turned and after about a further three-quarters of a mile, came to a series of four narrow buildings that looked like converted train cars covered over in wood siding and painted red with white trim. They sat all in a row, end to end on the right side of the road. Signs identified the place clearly as "Stark Lumber" but Mori had a hard time thinking such a place could be one of the largest employers in the area.

He parked the Nash and approached the building that said "office" on a sign hanging over the door. Inside there was a desk with a young man, probably no older than Mori, sitting and looking at files. There were file cabinets, stacks of boxes, some opened, some not. There was a bit of lumbering gear, boots, gloves, axe handles – the place could really, Mori thought, have used a woman's touch.

"Are you that fella?" the kid said before Mori could speak.

"Probably." Mori said, removing his hat and flicking away a bit of snow that had settled on it. "I guess I need no introduction. Flattering, I guess."

"Well," the kid said, standing and resting his arms akimbo on his hips with a swish of his ski overalls. "Word travels fast in these parts."

"Even if nothing else does."

"Oh ayuh!" the kid said, tickled, "You got that right!"

"I suppose this is good in a way. Since everybody knows I'm around and might show up they aren't inclined to shoot me on sight as a spy or some such thing."

"Or you just ain't run into 'em yet…" the Kid smiled.

"Fair enough. And you are?" Mori extended his hand.

"Art." He said, and they shook hands. "Art Miller. I'm the Camp Clerk." He had about the deepest backwoods accent Mori had heard so far and from his mouth the name sounded like "Ahhht Milluh."

"Swell to meet you, Art. Is the… manager here? Or whomever is in charge of hiring?"

"Camp Boss ain't here. But he wouldn't talk to you anyway."

"No?"

The Kid shook his head.

"Captain Ballard?"

"Ayuh. He was around."

"And he told the Camp Boss not to talk to me?"

The Kid shrugged. "I dunno. Captain was around, that's all I know. And Boyette – that's the Camp Boss – said he didn't want to see anyone matching your description."

"I see. Did he tell you not to talk to me?"

"No. He can't tell me who to talk to and who not to. He's worthless anyway. He hadn't better try to tell me…"

"So, you do know about the deaths then…"

"The Indians?" The Kid took a paper pouch out of the pocket of his ski pants. It had the words "Red Man" and the cartoon Indian on it. Perhaps the conversation had jarred the thought of it into his memory. He took a good-sized pinch of the brown strands between his thumb and forefinger and forced them into a bulge in his bottom lip next to the gums. "Sure."

"Did you know any of them?"

The kid shook his head. "Nah. The Indians tend to be the older fellas. Even the ones that ain't tend to keep to themselves. If they go into town they tend to go to the quiet bars with the other old men and just sit around, you know?"

"What about the John Doe? One of the fellas… no name? How did he work? How did you pay him?"

"Ain't hard. They come here and pick up the pay packet. Camp boss has some favorites but most of the rest get the same. Either the axmen or the river runners, they make the same. Cookees make a little less. Funny though, I know about the guy you're talking about. I never knew his name. Boyette said he did when he first hired the fella but he forgot it. Fake probably, anyway…"

"That is… extraordinary."

"Nah, he forgets all the time. He likes to drink." The Kid picked up a paper cup from the desk and spat some of the tobaccos juice into it. He did it quietly, trying to be polite. "But then, who don't?"

Mori wanted to get into the myriad of labor laws that might be going unobserved but figured that would be a waste of time. "So, they're paid in cash?"

"A 'course. What else?"

Perhaps wanting to explain further, to be helpful even, The Kid said, "I mean, they don't say a lot. Most of 'em. The Indians, I mean. They come in, they get their pay and that's it. They don't complain much, I'll give 'em that. Everyone else that comes in here wants to complain – *especially the Frenchies*. Don't even get me started. *Parlez vous* this, that, and the other thing, I swear..."

"No kidding?"

"Ayuh. The *Quebecois*. They're the best river men though."

"River men?"

"The guys who hop out onto the logs to guide them down river. Spike 'em with the *cant dog* to keep em from freezing together and keep 'em moving... 'Course we don't do as much river traffic as we used to, most of the timber gets trucked out now. We only send the pulpwood down these days; to the paper mill on the river. Say, you know, if you wanna ask about the Indians you'd probably be better off just going down and talking to them. But, ya know, like I said, they ain't apt to say much."

"Would that be alright?"

"Why not? Just go on up the road there. Indians tend to take the last camp, furthest out. 'Bout 12 miles. So, you got a little drive ahead of ya. We keep the roads up pretty well for the trucks though, so that car you got there shouldn't have trouble if you keep it steady."

"There's more than one camp?"

"Oh ayuh. Three. Well, four counting this one. And the mill, which is about a mile back on the road behind this office. These cars sleep about 15 or 20. Frenchies stay in the first, about two miles down. Keep on driving. The next one is about four miles out. Then the last one, like I said, way out… not just Indians out there but mostly, I guess. A camp is two of these…" The Kid raised his palms to the ceiling and outstretched his arms. "A sleeper and then a cook and gear car. Most will be out working this time of day though. We work sunup to sundown around here. But maybe you can catch one coming in for gear or something."

"Thanks for all your help, Art. I appreciate it."

"Don't thank me yet. They probably won't talk to you. They don't talk to nobody. But they might take your head off if you ask too many questions… or the wrong one."

"Good to know." Mori said, then replaced his hat, tipping it first in gratitude.

"Hopefully they don't think you're Tojo's first wave and start shootin' anyway."

"Yeah." Mori said.

"Say… is Japan… like they say in the papers?"

"How do you mean?"

"A bunch of, you know, mindless drones to the Emperor? All that?"

Mori shrugged. "I don't know for sure. I've never been. But I imagine that it's like anywhere: you got your true believers and your people that just go along to avoid the pain of not going along. And those that don't give a damn… but it is a dictatorship there, I know that much. So, I imagine a lot of that "patriotic zeal" is forced at gunpoint. But if you're after firsthand insight, I haven't got any for you. I'm from California."

The Kid seems even more impressed by this. "Wow."

Mori left the office and went back to the Judge's car, which was starting to look in need of a wash, covered as it was in streaks of coarse sand and snow, with harder packed versions of the same jammed into the wheel wells. How many more miles into these deep woods, he wondered with trepidation.

He took to the wide and occasionally rough road once more and after a while the landscape changed from dense forest to a wide clearing where enormous logs, all 20 or more feet long were stacked about 15 or so feet high and stretched for maybe 50 yards on the side of the road, after that came the first camp of two of the large train car bunkhouses, set back some from the road. Mori slowed down to look but saw no movement. He drove on.

Sometimes he could see through the trees to the river beyond and he could only imagine what the kid was talking about, driving logs downriver, poking at them to keep them getting snagged on the river bank or in the rocks… he had been told it was dangerous work but a single misstep would mean a plunge into the icy water. Not this time of year, perhaps, with the river frozen over, but the thought still made him shiver.

He drove past the second camp. This time he saw two men walking side by side, axes over their shoulders, covered all over in snow sticking to their wool outer things. One smoked a pipe and the smoke whipped upward like it was shooting out of a train smokestack. He drove slowly past, tipping his hat as a greeting. The two men stopped to stare until he was gone around the bend.

He supposed he could have stopped to talk to them, to anyone, really, that he came across. Yet he felt he had to speak to the Indians first. There was no reason to feel he would "poison the well" by talking to others, necessarily, or that they would know if he had or even if it mattered, but he was impatient to speak to them, whoever they were, as he felt it was closest to truth as he was likely to get. If, as the Kid remarked, he was able to get anything at all. He drove on.

Though the Kid had said there were many men at work in these woods, except for the two walking men he saw nobody and heard very little. Occasionally he saw evidence of the work they were doing. Machinery, a couple of trucks parked in a clearing, more enormous log stacks, piles of railroad track half covered in snow. It seemed to grow darker and the feeling of being swallowed up by the forest wasn't inconsiderable. The road grew rougher, usually narrower, and more like it was raising up and closing off. Swallowing him whole.

At last, he came to the last of the promised camps. Mori looked over the railroad car sized bunkhouses, covered in snow and raised over a rounded clearing. He shut off the car and got out, looking for signs of life. The cold started to gnaw at him straightaway so he donned the ear warmer, replaced his hat and pulled his fur-lined gloves from his pocket and put them on. Much better, he thought.

The bunkhouses had windows but they were too high up to see into and it didn't seem like there was anyone at home anyway. Fifteen or twenty men, the Kid had said. Must be jammed in like sardines... he started to walk around and look things over but decided against peeking inside.

Time passed.

He knew it couldn't be much past midday but the dark gray sky made it feel like perpetual dusk. Outside of the car, Mori could at last hear, far in the distance, the faint thud of axes, ripping of saws, and the voices of men shouting, though so faint he couldn't make out a single word. He couldn't make out the direction and knew it wasn't close enough for him to simply try to follow it and ask his questions. He stamped around and when he needed to warm up, he got back in the car, started the engine, and stayed until he couldn't stand the heat any longer under the layers of heavy clothing. He thought about baseball, movies, a Dashiell Hammett book he'd read, and then he remembered Sofia, and not for the first time and felt a little spark of regret and loss.

He looked back down the road he'd driven to get there, as he must have done dozens of times while he had been waiting, but this time there was... something. Someone. A black figure in the haze and... horses. Mori took a few paces forward. It was a man leading two horses that were pulling a sled full of logs. For a few moments, man and horses were motionless. Mori figured he was being scrutinized. They began again to move toward him. Mori heard a slight jingling of the bells on the horse bridles as they neared. Man and sled at last entered the clearing and when Mori could at last see a face behind a black scarf, he gave a half salute, half wave and tried to smile warmly.

"Howdy." He said.

The man didn't return the greeting but unwound the scarf and removed the knitted cap from his head. He was an Indian, with salt and pepper hair pulled straight back from his face, which was a deep mahogany color, with a hooked nose and prominent pock-marks. He had a narrow mouth and bloodless lips, which he didn't seem particularly keen on opening.

"Whatcha got there?" Mori asked, pointing, not sure where else to start.

The man looked back at the load of logs, piled about five or six feet high on a sled nearly 15 feet long. "Four-foot pulpwood." He said. "You from Bangor?"

"Bangor?"

"Company office."

Mori pointed at his chest. "Me? No."

"And you ain't here for work. Not with them clothes and that car…"

"Nope."

"And you ain't lost, since there's nowhere you belong anyway, is there? … So, you want to talk about the other thing."

"Other thing?"

"Dead Indians."

Mori nodded. "Uh… yeah. I would."

"Who are you?"

"Mori." He said, thrusting out his hand. "Asa Mori."

The man, after some hesitation, shook Mori's hand very briefly.

"I'm with the FBI."

The man only looked at him and said nothing, but his skepticism was evident. Mori felt the need to withdraw his leather wallet and flash the identification.

"Provisional?" the man asked.

Mori, not feeling like explaining, just said, "Yes."

The man shrugged, turned away and began to unhitch the horses.

Mori said, "I uh, I was wondering if we could talk about… the other thing. The… dead Indians."

"Why?"

"I just want to… just see… I'm following up some leads is all. Just making some inquires, just a formality, really."

"Okay." The man had a grating sort of monotone. He tossed the hitch into the snow and led the horses away.

"Can I trouble you to answer a few questions?"

"Don't think I can help you."

"Why not?"

"You don't know who you are or what you're doing here." The man started to walk past him and Mori stopped him, putting a hand on his arm. It might as well have been raw steel beneath, and Mori could see the hard lines on his face and the man's physique like a concrete pylon. He didn't want to start anything at any rate but certainly not with a man, even though he looked twice Mori's age, to be carved from granite by 14-hour days of hard labor. The man looked at the hand and Mori removed it.

"I just told you who I was."

"You did." The man said. He tied the horses to a hitching post by the left bunkhouse and fed them sugar cubes from his jacket pocket.

Mori, a bit flabbergasted, said with more anger than he'd intended, "Do you think cooperating with the FBI is…"

"You ain't FBI." he said.

Mori was getting tired of this line; however technically true it might have been. "No? What makes you say that?"

"You ain't white, for one thing." He patted one horse's neck. Then the other one.

Mori wasn't quite ready for that; said nothing.

"So, the badge looks real enough, I guess, even if they stamped 'provisional' on it. How'd you get it?"

"Applied and took the tests. Same as anybody else."

The man shook his head. He didn't betray a smile though he seemed, deep down, amused. "No. Not like anybody else. You had to have an *angle*. They weren't going to let you just waltz through."

Mori was speechless. He wasn't sure what the man wanted to hear.

"So, who are you?" the man asked again.

After a pause, "Agent Asa Mori…"

Without changing expression, the man started to walk away.

In desperation, Mori blurted, "My name doesn't sound overly Japanese!"

The man stopped.

"It's not like it, *Morimoto* or … whatever. It could pass for a Caucasian name if you weren't paying attention. So, I figured when I applied, they didn't notice and approved me and when I showed up in person, I sweet-talked my way into getting a try out and, I'll admit, I got lucky and had someone who… let me stay anyway."

"Japanese, huh?" He paused. "Was it?" the Man asked in a mutter, "*Morimoto?*"

"No. I mean, I don't think so. My dad never mentioned shortening it."

"Okay. Go on."

"I applied as 'Asa Mori' but my full first name is 'Asahito.' I shortened it on the application. I also applied at the San Francisco office. More Asians in San Fran so they'd be less likely to be sticky about it. And like I said, I guess I got lucky and had a fair-minded Caucasian approve and allow me through, or I don't know, maybe they just didn't want to tell me to 'Get out Jap!' at the time to my face – this was all before Pearl, mind you. After that, well *persona non grata,* of course… But while I was training I did well – very well, and got remembered when this came up…"

"So, they didn't want any part of this."

"I suppose."

"Send the Jap to clean up the mess with the dead Indians."

"No mess." Mori said. "Nobody seems to think there is a mess. Except an old judge and me. And *you*, it seems. Am I right? It was the first thing you thought when you knew I wasn't from the company office. Why is it that nobody in town seems to know or care but it is the first think you think of?"

"You expected a bunch of whites in town to care about dead Indians? I'm surprised it even made the papers."

Mori said, "I didn't know. But I don't think the whole thing has gotten a fair examination so far. That's all I know. That's all I'm trying to do. Give these guys a fair shake."

The man studied him awhile longer. "Okay." He said. He started to walk away.

"So," Mori said, "Hey! Could I…"

The man just gestured for Mori to follow. He walked to a trail Mori hadn't seen before that wound around in back of the bunkhouses and into the woods. It was a short walk and they came straightaway to a clearing that had been hacked out of the forest and had three benches made of sturdy white birch and in the middle, like an altar, a huge, flat rock, probably five feet on every side.

"Be right back." The man said and went back along the path.

"Wait, what? Where?"

"Putting the horses away. And getting something to show you." The man said, over his shoulder.

Mori was left to look around. He sat on the cold bench, which was just a log sawed in half lengthwise, as were the other two benches. They'd been worn smooth by the rear ends of many lumberjacks over the years and were shiny and gray. The rock was made more to look like an altar by the black charring in the center and the remnants of a fire, ash and old dead coals.

Shortly, the man returned, he was carrying things now, under one arm there appeared to be a cooking pot of some kind and over his shoulder... An axe. No: two axes. With his head down, he walked steadily but unhurried, and Mori began to feel perhaps he should go...

"Hey, there, u..."

The man made a gesture with the hand he was balancing the axes with as if to tell Mori to calm himself. He sat the ancient black Dutch Oven under his arm on the seat and leaned one of the axes on the bench upright. He held out the other one for Mori to look at. "What do you see?"

"I feel if I say 'an axe' I'll be missing something, yes?" Mori said.

"Does this axe look new to you, kid?"

"Uh, yeah, sort of. Clean anyway..."

"Yeah. Clean. Oiled. Not a nick, or a speck of rust. Handle is tight. And..." he picked up a stick and began shaving away bits the size of matches like they were pats of butter.

"Razor sharp." Mori said. Slight unease growing again.

The man nodded and tossed aside the stick then walked over to a stump outside the bench area and sunk the axe deep into it. He handles it like it weighed nothing and was an extension of his hand. "Delisle's axe." The man said.

"Rupert Delisle? One of the..."

"Dead men. Yeah."

"He was a friend?"

The man shrugged. "Who has friends out here? But Delisle was alright. He laughed a lot. Too much. He kept his axe like a man should, and he had a girl…"

"*A girl?* I was informed he had *nobody*. You knew this and you didn't tell the cops?! I was accusing them, at least in my head, of negligence but now it seems like maybe they aren't getting cooperation and *that's* why they aren't getting anywhere."

"They didn't want to hear what I had to say."

"How can you know something like that?"

"Same way I knew you weren't telling me the truth."

"What? Some mumbo-jumbo?"

The man shook his head. He took up the axe and began to split some small logs that were stacked behind his bench into kindling. "*Mumbo-Jumbo.*" He repeated.

"What's your name, anyway? I don't think you said."

"I didn't say."

He stacked the kindling and took a silver lighter from his coat pocket and set the small kindling tower alight. After a minute or so, as the flames flicked toward the sky, the man said, "Horace. Horace Frost."

"I didn't see your name in any of the files as a witness," Mori thought of the few typed pages, "not even to say you didn't know anything. Which would have been untrue anyway… so, the axe and all that, the girl… are you saying…"

"He didn't kill himself. Of course, he didn't."

"Because he took care of his axe?"

Frost went over to the stump and removed Delisle's axe from the stump deftly, looking rather like a middle-aged Indian King Arthur in shabby winter wear. "Bad luck, leaving it in the stump." He said, setting it next to his own.

The fire was cracking and growing and Frost fed it some more short bits of wood. He took a somewhat fatter log and cracked it open with one short blow on the altar (which is the only way Mori could think of it now.) As the section fell away, tiny reddish-black pearls fell out, looking to Mori like pebbles or seeds. Frost stared a moment, then scooped some up in his palm and put them in his mouth. Mori watched, raising one eyebrow quizzically.

"Frozen wood ants." Frost said. "Taste like cranberries."

He scooped up another palmful and waved them in Mori's direction.

"Uh, well, I…"

Frost exhaled once through his wide nostrils, which was all the laughter he seemed to allow himself.

"Actually," Mori said, "Not so big a handful. I'm new to bug eating."

Frost poured off about half and put the rest in Mori's palm. Mori had already decided to just throw them back like a shot of whisky, not thinking about it or waffling. A few of them got caught on his tongue on the way down and he almost gagged but restrained himself admirably. Frost was right about the taste too, he thought. Frost allowed himself another laugh grunt.

Satisfied that the fire was where it ought to be, Frost slipped the Dutch oven into it, leaving the metal handle out.

"Axe or no axe." Mori said, "It would be nice to have more to go on. Something a little more concrete, ya know?"

Frost said nothing.

"Like this girl: did they fight?"

"Dunno."

"He never mentioned fighting with her?"

"Not to me. Didn't seem down or anything."

"What was her name anyway? The girl."

"Dunno."

Mori rubbed his temples with his gloved hands. He noticed one of the frozen wood ants had stuck and he flicked it away. "Oh, for Pete's sake…"

"Cindy? Cheryl… something like that..."

"Is there anyone else in the camp who might know?"

Frost shrugged. "Dunno. Probably not."

Mori got up and began to pace. Partially to get his thoughts in order and partially to restore feeling to his quickly freezing legs. "See? That's the kind of stuff I need to know. And if we *are* talking foul play, and you seem to be, *why*? Did he have enemies? And more to the point: did he have the *same enemies* as the other fellas?"

"I know what you want to know. I know you want a smoking gun. I wish I had one to give you. I can only tell you what I know." Frost removed the Dutch oven by the handle with his big gray-mittened hand. He fished a spoon from the pocket of his gray plaid overcoat. He stirred around the contents for a moment and took a bite. He then scooped up some more and offered it to Mori. It did actually smell rather good, he thought. "Pea Soup and salt pork." He said.

"Thanks." Mori said, patting his belly. "I filled up on bug."

Frost snorted, took a few more bites. Mori waited. A large gray and white bird flew in behind Mori and perched on a pine branch. Some snow displaced and fluttered to the ground. The bird didn't squawk, only looked at them, flicking its tail.

"Moosebird." Frost said. "Or, Canada Jay, I guess they call it. Legend says they contain the souls of all the old dead Lumbermen."

"Really?" Mori said, looking at the bird. "You believe that?"

"Mumbo jumbo." Frost said through a mouthful.

"Huh. He's pretty quiet."

"They don't say much most of the time."

"Shoot. Maybe I believe the legend then."

Frost snorted again and began to walk back down the trail to the bunkhouse. "Be right back." He said.

Mori was left alone with the bird, who eyed him, waiting for one false move.

"Which one are you?" he asked the bird.

The moosebird flicked its tail and flew away, leaving another small dust of powdery snow to fall from the swaying branch.

Frost returned with an ancient looking blue metal coffee pot and two paper cups. He set the cups on the bench beside him and the pot where the Dutch oven had been, which had burned out of flame to nice bright orange coals.

"I started in these woods when I was seven as a picker..."

"Picker?"

"Picking spruce gum." Frost explained. "You go out and find where the tree has taken a slash or been chewed on or whatnot and it oozes out the sap. I was good at it too. Found 'em the size of hen's eggs. But it's a job for kids and women. I never had a feeling I would do anything else but make a living here. I knew I'd be in these woods for my whole life. It's been some forty years now. More. I've been all over Vermont, New Hampshire, Quebec, New Brunswick. But mostly here in Maine where the tall pines are. I've seen all kinds of men out here. If a man reaches his breaking point... out here, you would know. Back when I was starting out, men stayed the winter in the woods and rode the logs down the river with the thaw. Now there are good gravel roads and men can go back into town for the weekend. See their families if they have them. Or more likely, get a drink, get a game of cards or go to the knocking shop..."

"Did you say 'knocking shop?' You mean a whorehouse?"

Frost nodded.

"In that tiny burg?" Mori was incredulous.

"Of course. I know this doesn't prove anything. But I know. I seen a man take a pistol and go off into the woods and nobody seen hide nor hair of him again. And Delisle wasn't like that."

"So, you don't buy the whole 'Mohawk suicide ritual' thing?"

Frost practically spit.

"Mumbo jumbo?" Mori asked.

"Horseshit." Frost said.

"I spent a lot of time reading over what the library had about Mohawk tribal customs," Mori said, "I mean, such as it was. There wasn't much information but I couldn't find any mention of such a thing."

"You could have just asked me. I'm Mohawk. Delisle was Half Mohawk. Shit..." Frost took the coffee pot up and poured it out into two cups. "That don't even make sense."

Mori accepted one of the paper cups of coffee. "What doesn't make sense?"

"The guy whose ticket got punched last year. Moody. He wasn't even Mohawk. Abenaki, I think. And Quebecois. Shit, he was half Frenchy."

"Did you know him? Can you tell me about him?"

Frost shook his head, "Nah, not really. He stayed down with the Frenchies. Pretty sure he was Catholic though. I know Delisle was. Suicide is a mortal sin to them."

"True. But that doesn't mean..." Mori took a sip of the coffee. It was ghastly. But it was hot and strong. "...you know. What about the John Doe?"

"Who?"

"The last guy. No name. Not one anybody knows anyway. Was he Catholic?"

"Dunno." Frost said. "He wasn't even here a month, I don't think. Wandered into camp looking for a job. Didn't have the proper gear. Had to get old, bummed boots, mittens, hat and all that. Would have froze dressed like he was."

"How did *nobody* know his name? How is that possible?"

Frost managed to make the question seem silly without a gesture or look. Just a snort. "There's a guy down with the Frenchies names *Jacques Canuck*. You think that's his real name?"

"I… no?"

"Good guess. You gotta know this already. Don't you? A lot of guys… up here to disappear. Camp Boss knows… he doesn't care about us or our shit. Jacques Canuck is called that because he had a French name hard to spell and the camp boss thought it was funny. And I'm 'Horace Frost' cuz it was the first thing I could think of when they asked me."

"That's not your real name?"

Frost sipped his coffee but didn't reply. "Anyway, your 'John Doe' we called him 'Cheetah.' You know: like Tarzan?"

"Why?"

"Only word I ever heard him say."

"So, you heard him speak? There was speculation he was a mute."

"Nah. May as well have been though. Never heard him say anything else. And he didn't seem like he understood what anyone was saying half the time, so we thought maybe he was, you know, touched. Upstairs. And he damn sure wasn't Mohawk. I don't know what he was but he wasn't Mohawk, I can tell you that. If he was Indian at all. Anyway, like I said, we only ever heard him say that so that's what we called him. 'Salcheeta!' he said. We was in the chuck wagon, see...oh, that's what we call the dining car, and I guess he was hungry and got excited and..."

"Wait, what was it that he said again?"

"It, uh, sounded like Cheetah. But *Sal*-cheeta. Something like that."

"*Salchicha*?" Mori asked.

"Yeah, coulda been. I think that was it."

"Were you all making sausages at the time, by any chance?"

"As I recall...yeah. How'd you know that?"

"*Salchicha* is Spanish for 'sausage'." Mori said.

"Huh." Frost said. "Spanish, you say? That'd be strange, out this way."

"It would indeed."

Frost (or whatever his name was, Mori thought, now pretty sure a signed statement wouldn't be forthcoming) dusted the snow off of a short log from the end of the pile. He chopped it into short bits like it was slices of bread and revealed the reddish-purple wood inside. He put these on the fire and they released a pleasing aroma like rosemary or tea, Mori thought. "Cedar." The Indian said.

"Is that a symbolic thing, or...?"

Frost snorted again. "Nah. It just smells good."

Mori nodded. "Look," he said. "Everyone so tight-lipped... just because they don't want to be noticed? It seems... I mean, doesn't anyone care that it might happen again?"

"Sure. They care that it might happen again. To them."

"So, shouldn't they..."

"You think telling those cops would solve that? Look, I don't know what anyone knows, if they know anything at all. But I know fellas talk and what they say is that they don't want to end up taking a midnight ride..."

"What does that mean? Who said that?"

"Nobody said. It's just out there, it's on the wind..."

"*Dios Mio...*" Mori said, rubbing his temples again, repeating the refrain of his favorite frustrated childhood babysitter.

"If you want to know what I think," Frost said, "It's the whites."

When he didn't elaborate, Mori asked him to please do.

"The Whites see an Indian. Get him drunk or catch him coming out of the bar. Knock him on the head, throw him in the bed of their pickup, strip him naked and dump him in the woods. Probably the young ones. Teenagers maybe. Strong enough and still mean enough. White boys."

"Maybe. But that's not even a spree killer your describing or a lust killer or anything we could give a motive to. That is a person or, more likely, persons killing four men in cold blood, if you'll forgive the turn of phrase, over the course of more than a year... it's planned, premeditated, it's anticipated... what kind of person just kills another for... what?"

"Cuz they hate Indians. Motive enough for some."

"A mob of rowdy Caucasian boys methodically hunting down middle-aged Indian fellows on *four different occasions*? Mobs are spur of the moment. They're... frenzied."

Frost sipped from his coffee cup and then threw the last swallow onto the fire where it made a quick hiss. Mori found the smell of the cedar warm and pleasant, but the turn of the conversation ominous and unsettling.

Frost heaved a sigh filled with weariness, then looked Mori in the eye sharply. "Sometimes they do it for the thrill of it... but also to remind you that your body belongs to them. They can make you hurt or die and there is nothing anyone can do. I guess I should say, nothing anyone *will* do." He threw some bits of wood on the glowing coals, just to have something to do with his hands, not because the fire needed stoking. "Not always. Sometimes things are good, people are civil to each other, at least... but sometimes things break down. People lose hope, they fear one another, they don't trust each other or the things they've built, and life becomes cheap. Now, this war... millions dead. Has life ever been this cheap?"

Mori didn't know how to answer.

"Or worse, men get bored. Things running too well... too quiet... men think they need to make noise to prove they're important. Prove they're somebody."

Before long, men started drifting into camp. Most were veteran lumbermen like Frost and they regarded Mori cagily until Frost made introductions. Mori asked some of them the same questions but there was little anyone seemed able to add. He drifted with them to the cooking car and though there was an official cook, they all sort of pitched in, opening canned beans, frying bacon, heating cornbread. The woodstove got stifling as men pulled tabs on beer cans, played cards, ate and drowsed under a heavy odor of sweat, pine and moist clothes. He shook Frost's hand and left to get back to the Nash and to civilization, such as it was. It had gotten dark fast, Mori doubted it was much after 6 pm but the blackness was inky and the only lights to see him out came from the car and when he passed the camp cars. Eventually he made his way out of the woods and back to the highway, all of it looking so different in darkness.

When Mori got back to town he pulled into his hotel and ordered down for some bacon and egg sandwiches and hot tea. The night had chilled him through to the bone, though the cloud cover had insured that it wasn't as cold as it had been. He took a very quick, very hot shower and looked up Honeywell Hardware in the slender phonebook. Three town listings, Mori thought, and the phone book barely a half inch thick. Not for the first time, he felt a little ache inside for the bustle of people, crowd noise, car horns, street lights to cut the darkness... and carnitas. He would've driven back up into those woods in the dark if he knew that at the end there was a *taqueria* up there that was serving carnitas with a little avocado sauce and lime on tortillas made that morning, all wrapped in grease paper like...

"Hello?"

Lost in thought, Mori hadn't realized he'd found the number and dialed. "Uh, oh. Yes. Hello. Good evening madam. Is Trudy at home?"

"I should hope so. At this hour." the woman said. Trudy's mom, he presumed. She sounded as if she were loud most of the time.

"Well, if it isn't too much..."

"Trudy!" Mori heard the phone clatter onto some surface and he realized he wasn't being listened to. A moment later Trudy picked up. "Hello?"

"Hi, Trudy. Sorry I took so long. Were you inconvenienced?"

"Nah. Got a lot done with the Judge and his wife at their house actually. He needed some filing done. I helped the missus with this paper drive she's doing. Anyway, I knew you'd take forever, even if you didn't get lost." Trudy had a rapid-fire way of talking that Mori usually found a bit exhilarating to try to keep up with. Tonight, he had to concentrate to not lose her and he realized he was overtired.

"Your mom sounded a little irritated. Too late for some stranger to call I guess."

"Stranger? Oh no, he knows who you are. That's why she was being snotty."

"Oh."

"Nothing specific, don't worry. Just general disapproval. That's just how she deals with having a 19-year-old daughter, or knowing that there is a Japanese person in town. Japanese-American person. Sorry. Tsk tsk, clutch the locket, fan the forehead so as not to faint, furrow the eyebrow, and think how these things aren't done and harrumph!"

Mori chuckled. "So how do I get you the car tomorrow?"

"Pick me up here?"

"Okay. Sure thing."

"They want to have you over for dinner, by the way."

"What? Your parents?"

"Parents?! No! God no. Ha! That'll be the day. No, no. The Judge and Mrs. Norris."

"Oh. Sounds good."

"Get some sleep, Tiger." Trudy said. "You sound tired."

CHAPTER 17

February 3, 1943

Without saying a word, Mori waved Trudy into his room where she could hear the radio playing within. She shut the door and followed. Mori waved her over again to the General Electric table top radio and adjusted the small brown volume nob. They listened closely.

"*... statement from the government of the Soviet Union later in the evening said as follows: 'Our forces have now completed the liquidation of the German Fascist troops encircled in the area of Stalingrad. The last center of enemy resistance in the Stalingrad area has thus been crushed...*"

"Krauts." Mori said, explaining. "They surrendered at Stalingrad. Russians licked 'em. I'll be damned. I haven't had time to pay attention to the news lately but… the Desert last year and now this… maybe the war is turning."

"Maybe." Trudy agreed.

"And I haven't even gotten into it yet."

They were hovering close to the radio on chairs sitting across from each other. Trudy pointed at the robins-egg blue face of the radio. "Did you hear what the announcer just said? 45,000 Germans just surrenders and like a quarter million dead. Be careful what you're eager to get yourself into."

"I heard. I know. I might feel different if I weren't being *kept* out… either way… I don't know. I ought to be in the thick of it, anyway. I'm not some bloodthirsty he-man. And I know it won't be a picnic either. But I need to get in and do my bit."

The day was not a fruitful one. They drove to the cannery where one of the dead men had worked. It was bustling and smelled strongly of fish and motor oil. Most of the workers were very young or very old, men and a few women. Nobody remembered much; a whole year had passed after all… On the plus side, Mori thought, after speaking to a foreman and a few others, nobody seemed to have been leaned on by Captain Ballard. Maybe he forgot. They drove away and back to town under a gray, leaden sky.

"Why is it so dark?" Mori asked, looking up.

"Don't you read the papers?" Trudy said, "Solar eclipse today."

"No kidding? Huh. I guess it should be darker still, then."

"Well, we're not, um, whatya call it? Directly under it."

"Totality."

"Yeah. Not even close. Still kinda dreary though, huh?" Trudy whistled a little and deftly maneuvered the Nash over the slapdash plow job on the road. "Winter is a marathon around here. Half the year, it seems like, bundling up and trying to survive it... I swear L.A. must be... well, I bet you miss is more and more, eh?"

Mori thought about going through to the airport just blocks away from old haunts only to be whisked across the country. Still, he wondered what it was like out there now for people with skin like his. Who was left? He's read about shopkeepers putting out "No Japs Allowed" signs. So many – most of them probably – sent to a camp like he had been.

"Haven't you been reading the papers?" Mori asked, with a grin to put her at ease. "I may have to stay away for a while."

"Oh." Trudy said, red-facedly, "Right."

Trudy pulled the car into a gas station, the "Esso" sign barely visible under a sickly yellow light. She asked the attendant for 4 bucks of gas and promised another buck if he wiped the car down and cleaned the windows.

"Don't forget the whitewalls either, okay?" she said. Then, turning to Mori, "I don't want the judge to think I don't take care of his car, ya know?"

Mori was beginning to find Trudy a very welcome distraction. At first, she'd just been a friendly face and a way to navigate without a map, but as time went on, he'd begun to find her both insightful and deceptively smart. Bouncing ideas off of her proved clarifying for him, and despite his outwardly confident display, she was his ally in what was for him still a strange land.

The Judge's house was a large, stately, old colonial. The driveway was neatly plowed and in the dim light of the headlamps the fresh exterior paint shined a bright white with hunter green shutters. The house was on a high hill overlooking the town, with a long slope of hard packed snow descending to the barren road below.

"I used to sled down that hill on my toboggan." Trudy said, pointing. "We all did. The kids in town I mean. Judge never told us to clear off his land or anything like that. Mrs. Norris would bring us out hot cider sometimes. You'll like her. She's a peach!"

Trudy had been correct in that assessment. Mori found Judge Norris' wife just as good-hearted as the Judge himself. Her appearance was simple and unadorned, but she was the soul of efficiency and her words and movements were knowing and authoritative. She seemed, Mori thought, to anticipate what others were saying before they said it and to have already formulated an answer. When they arrived, she handed them each a tiny brandy glass after she had relieved them of their coats, hats, scarves, and gloves. "Just the one, Trudy dear." She said, nodding toward the miniature glass. "And don't tell your mom. Just a warm-you-up."

Mori emptied the glass in a shot and it burned nicely down his throat, sending warmth to the extremities. Lillian appeared from stashing the winterwear and took it from him, cradling it in her palm.

"This is Agent Mori." Trudy said.

"Of course." She said, nodding and sizing him up, with a penetrating gaze. "Talk of the town. No introduction necessary."

"Talk of the town?" Mori repeated. "You don't say?"

"Well, now, of course. The Japanese-American FBI agent lands in this tiny town… it may as well have been little men from Mars."

"I haven't noticed too much awkward… fanfare." Mori said.

"Oh no. We're all too good at our quiet, New England puritan ethic: head down, mind your own business – what a laugh! You'll never find a bigger bunch of busybodies!" the whole time she'd been looking him over, trying to form a judgement. Mori was at least relieved when she gave a short, almost imperceptible nod and put a hand on his shoulder to lead him into the dining room. "Judge!" she called out, "Trudy and Asa have arrived. Come to dinner!"

To Mori, "You don't mind if I call you Asa, do you?"

"Not at all." He said, and meant it. "My friends do."

"I hope you like Yankee pot roast."

"I bet I will."

"You will." Trudy said.

"Some people put tomatoes in it. I don't know who would do such a thing, but they're not from around here…"

The judge came into the dining room, fiddling with a pipe. They shook hands. "Glad to see you back in good health, Agent Mori."

"Thank you. And for looking out for me."

The judge waved it off. "Not at all." He said, showing Mori to a seat at the table.

Lillian took Trudy by the hand. "Give me a hand, won't you dear?"

"She'll be wanting to serve dinner now." The Judge said.

"Oh dear," Mori said. "Are we late?"

"No, no. She just runs a tight ship."

The Yankee pot roast was, as promised, excellent. The four of them spoke awhile over the hearty aroma of the meal and then coffee. Trudy sipped daintily from her cup and made Lillian chuckle several times. They didn't end up speaking about Mori's reason for being there until the meal was nearly done.

"She" the Judge said, pointing to his wife with the stem of his pipe, "is why you've been dragged all the way up here, Agent Mori. We were of a similar mind about how the investigation was going, or not going… But Lillian has a restless conscience and a… what to call it? Tenacity…"

Lillian only shrugged and gave a look over the rim of her cup.

The Judge took a long pull from his pipe and exhaled a slow white cloud that smelled of cherry and vanilla.

"Their hearts don't seem to be in it." Lillian said. "Because those poor fellows were Indians, I think. Or, at least…" she waved her hand and sipped her coffee, gripping the cup with the tips of her fingers of both hands.

Mori looked from the Judge to his wife and back again. He decided to voice what he believed were their suspicions, ones he himself had but didn't want to think, let alone say aloud. "Ballard and his men. Claypool and Falkenham. Do you think they are… strait arrows?"

"I've known Lou Falkenham and his folks for... well all of his life anyway. He's alright... he tries to do the right thing..." the Judge said.

Lillian said. "Yes. Elenore - that's his mother – she's a bit of a gossip but they're a good family. Good as any of us, anyway. I can't see Lou caught up in anything... nefarious."

"Charlie Claypool is a creep." Trudy said, stuffing a bit of strawberry-rhubarb pie in her mouth. They all looked at her.

"Well, he is!" she said, chewing. "he was a few years ahead of me in school, but you hear stories. He held other boys down and shaved their heads. Grabbing girls under the bleachers. He beat up a boy in my class. You know little Humphrey Lufkin? No?" the Judge and Lillian shook their heads. "Well, he broke his arm. That's what I heard anyway."

Lillian said, "Trudy is a good judge of character."

"What about Ballard?" Mori asked.

"We don't know him all that well either. He's new. Our police chief is away training recruits... he's an army man, you see, from way back. Ballard is filling in. He doesn't seem like a fool to me. But I can't speak for his character. I just don't know. He seems like a hard man. But then, the job is a hard one after all, even in a town like this..."

"Could he have done it?" Mori asked. Perhaps too abruptly. "I'm sorry," Mori replaced his coffee cup in the saucer and pulled at the lapels of his jacket to straighten them. "But..."

"Trudy, dear, let's go and clean up a bit. Okay?"

Reluctantly, Trudy got up and went to the kitchen. It was a strange gesture for Lillian to make, since she was sharp and not a shrinking violet of a female, but perhaps she thought her husband would speak more freely without them there.

As if reading Mori's thoughts, the Judge leaned in and said, "Isn't she a hoot? Like she won't drag what we said out of me later…" he struck a match and relit his pipe.

"But to answer your question, Agent Mori… I don't think he could have. And in fact, I know he couldn't have, in one case."

"How's that?"

"One of the unfortunate men last year. Curette, I believe his name was. The second, um, the second fellow to… When he… met his end, Ballard and I were in Augusta."

"I don't understand."

"Meeting of the Legislature and then I lectured at the University. I was there four days and Ballard was my driver. I'm too blind to drive anymore, to be honest. I hadn't given up and admitted I couldn't see the road well enough and, well, obviously I hadn't hired Trudy yet. So then, I managed to convince him it was part of his official duties. That way, I didn't have to admit… Well, Lillian was down with a cold and so… I Shanghaied the local cop into duty."

"I consider you a fairly good alibi." Mori said.

"I know the possibility, of course. I mean, I hate to even say it aloud though…"

Mori adjusted his tie and straightened his pocket square. "Well, a good thing that the Captain couldn't have – well, anyway. Still… murder on the other hand, well, it still seems more likely than the line they're taking now. Don't you think?"

"Did you really think Ballard did it?"

"Just that it was possible. I suppose his hostility could be simply what he says."

Mori looked around at their home, appointed with sturdy ancient heirloom furniture and soft, cream-colored drapes. The smells were comforting, burning wood from the stove, the lingering aroma of the roast, tobacco, coffee, moisture of melted snow, the wicks of candles... Mori began to feel heavy limbed and a little sad about his suspicions. He said, "You know, Judge, it took guts for you to call."

"Oh, I don't know. I don't think so. Just a call to an old student."

"Yes, but in a town this size... murder, suspicion. I know these fellows were drifters and all but to me it seems they were preyed upon because of that. Because someone thought they wouldn't be missed. That the events of the wider world would make their deaths seem unimportant. They see the cracks in society and they try and kick them wide open. Or they're just opportunists, some sickness making them feel they need to kill... and if we don't remedy the situation, the law goes..." Mori made a motion like an umpire calling a runner out at the plate and whistled low like air leaving a balloon.

"I agree. But why do you doubt Ballard's theory so? Don't you think it holds water?"

"Not really, no." Mori said. "Not that the Captain has shared his methods of reasoning with me. He's been firm on the point of not sharing with me, in fact. And he's told people around town not to talk to me."

"Oh, for pity's sake..."

"So, if he has some evidence that makes him think what he says he thinks, I haven't found it yet. They would have to be all a part of some sort of cult-like deal. He seems to think, or at least he's saying, that it was a sort of tribal custom. I'm not an expert but none of the reading up I've done on Mohawk tribal customs suggest that this sort of suicide is one of them."

"No." the Judge said, scratching his white hair on the crown of his head. "I've never heard of such a thing either. But like you, I won't claim expertise."

"I've spoken to someone who I would consider an expert though…"

"And this expert…?"

"Horseshit." Mori straitened. "Pardon my French. That's what he called it."

The Judge chuckled. "I see."

"And another thing," Mori leaned in, pointing one of the polished silver forks like a lecturer in class, "They weren't even all of the Mohawk tribe! We've got one John Doe, don't know a thing about him, one fellow a half Mohawk and one not a Mohawk at all. Abenaki tribe, at least according to my expert."

"Yes, well, that is odd. But remember too that the Indian population in these parts has been dealing with the white man since the Mayflower. They don't generally have names like "Sitting Bull" or "Geronimo" or have grandfathers or even fathers who can tell them about fighting white men just a half century or so ago. Their names are indistinguishable from the whites, really, and if they retain Indian customs, generally they can get muddled. If it is some cult type of thing, well, perhaps the tribal differences aren't as big a difference as you might think."

Mori nodded, and conceded it was possible, but remained unconvinced.

"I'm with you, though, if I'm honest." The Judge said, over the rim of his cup as he raised it to his lips. "I suspect foul play. What do you think? The sort that kills for sport? Indian hater?"

Lillian and Trudy returned before Mori could answer.

"Lovely to have guests for dinner." The Judge said. "Lillian would usually chastise me for drinking coffee this late."

Lillian smoothed her skirt as she sat. "That's *Postum* in your cup dear."

The Judge licked his lips with a little disappointment. "So it is."

"Asa dear," Lillian said warmly, "The Judge found this in the Boston paper, the Press-Herald didn't carry it, but that's why we get the Boston paper, to get more of the outside world than they think we need or… want sometimes. Anyway…" she'd brought in a newspaper crisply folded to quarter size and pointed to an article near the bottom, just two small paragraphs. She handed it to Mori then sat primly. He read:

US ARMY TO FORM ALL JAPANESE UNIT

Americans whose ancestors are Japanese are to be organized into a major combat unit to help the United Nations besiege Hitler's "fortress of Europe" under a new military policy announced here yesterday. Individual Japanese have been admitted to the American armed forces, mainly as translators and technical advisors, but there are no Japanese-American units of the size contemplated by the new program. The combat team is to include infantry, artillery, engineers and medical personnel, and the unit would presumably number several thousand men.

A hint of how the program might be expected to work came from Hawaii where Lieut. Gen. Delos C. Emmons, announcing the plan to induct 1500 Japanese-Americans as volunteers for the new unit praised the war service already performed by members of that racial group. A spokesman for the Lieut. General's office said that the plan was based on recognition of "the inherent right of every faithful citizen, regardless of ancestry, to bear arms in the Nation's battle." Japanese-Americans can now, by order of the war department, enlist...

Mori's eyes glazed over a bit after the word "enlist." Could it be true? It had to be. Right there in black and white.

"So…" Mori stuttered, "so, that is, I could…"

"Walk out of here, go to the nearest enlistment office and sign up like any other American citizen." The Judge said, folding his hands around his waistcoat pockets. "Since that is what you are, after all."

Mori almost stood but remembered himself and shifted back on his chair.

"Well, it is a little late for it now, dear." Lillian said, smiling. "And I imagine you'll have to square things with the FBI. Can they spare you?"

Mori smiled, nervously twisting the silver fox-head cufflinks that had been his fathers. "I think they'll make do alright."

"Wait, what's this now?" Trudy said. She had been invested in her pie a al Mode and was just now understanding the turn the conversation had taken.

"The Army has lifted the ban on people with Japanese heritage like Asa here." Lillian said. "He can join the service, Trudy."

"What about the case?" Trudy said.

"Well, of course, I have to finish what I've started here."

"And that could take some time, right?" Trudy said.

"Well, according to my petty cash reserve and a certain Agent Bullock in Washington, I don't think it had better take too much longer honestly... but I'll see it through."

"Of course." The Judge said.

Trudy sat her fork down next to her half-finished dessert silently. Lillian patted her hand.

CHAPTER 18

February 4, 1943

Mori had the misfortune to need to go to the front desk early enough that he caught the Night Manager still on duty. The latter's eyes grew narrow and disapproving as he approached.

"Hello." Mori said, giving near his best toothy smile. "The telephone in my room isn't working. Are they working in the rest of the hotel?"

The Night Manager said nothing for a few moments. Then cracked his knuckles and laid his hands flat on the desk in from of him, then the tips of his fingers curled up as if he was about to scratch away at the surface. "Heavy snow." The Night Manager said through gritted teeth.

"How's that?" Mori asked.

More silence. Another man came from the back room, dressed in the same uniform as the Night Manager: a green jacket with darker green piping. He was younger, redheaded and freckled. When Mori saw "Andrew" on his nametag, he could only think "Andy Hardy."

"Oh, so you're… him then. Sorry, I meant…" Andy Hardy straightened his tie and recovered. "Sorry. Been on vacation. Just heard about you. That you were staying. A Ja… an FBI… uh, guy, so… anyway."

The Night Manager has cast his eyes down at the desktop. To make sure his fingernails hadn't dug through the heavily shellacked surface, Mori supposed.

"Asa Mori." He said, extending a hand to Andy Hardy, who looked at the Night Manager, hesitated, then grinned and shook the hand. "Agent Asa Mori. FBI."

Andy Hardy grinned a little more. "Swell."

"Heavy snow?" Mori asked the Night Manager, who had managed to dig his claws from the sign-in book on the desk.

"Take care of this… person, Andrew, won't you." He didn't even grace Mori with more daggers from his eyes before disappearing into the back.

Andrew watched him go. "Geez, he's giving you the high hat, ain't he? Sorry about that. I'd say he isn't usually like that but… well, he's worse anyway."

"I'm acquainted enough with him to know, actually." Mori said. "I assume he meant that the heavy snow had knocked out the phones?"

"Yeah, that's right. But they're working on it." Andy Hardy said. "The ones to the rooms will still be out for a while. The one in the lounge is on though. Different line, I guess. If you want, you can give me the info and I'll put the call through. I'll let you know when the operator gets the call through. Long distance, I assume?"

Mori smirked. "How'd you guess?"

He wrote "Agent Philip Bullock, FBI headquarters, Washington, DC" on a slip of paper and handed it to Andy Hardy.

"Wow." The kid said.

"I'll be in the dining room having a coffee."

"You've got it, Agent Mori."

It didn't take nearly as long as Mori imagined, especially considering the weather. Mori was almost sad to be pulled away from his coffee and the view out of the window onto the blinding white of the snow-covered hill outside.

Andy Hardy brought the phone into the deserted lounge and sat it on a dark wood table next to a high-backed easy chair. He handed the receiver to Mori and motioned for him to have a seat. Mori nodded thanks and sat. The noise of a few last-minute relays filled his ear and then the operator reminded him that he could get the time and charges for the call after his party hung up if he wished. He thanked her, gave a sigh, then tried to project calm and professionalism through the phone, if such a thing were possible. He had feared what Bullock might say, and what his reaction to the progress, or lack thereof, might be.

"Mori..." Bullock sounded... amused. "I have a story. Wanna hear it?"

"Sure." Mori said. "I mean, Yessir."

The connection was only so-so but Mori listened intently over the buzzes and pops on the line. Bullock said, "So, a few days ago, I get a call from the local cop up there in Lobsterville or whatever the heck town you're in is called…"

"Captain Ballard?" Mori offered.

"That's the one. Yeah, he's a character."

"A character." Mori said. "Yessir."

"Well, this Ballard is none too pleased. Has a weird calm but irate at the same time kinda voice, you know what I mean?" he doesn't wait for Mori to answer. "He asks me if you are who you say you are and I say yeah. He asks me where I get off sending a goddam Jap to his town to butt his yellow nose into his official business, yadda, yadda… I say you aren't there to interfere in any way, just to follow up for the Bureau as part of a report… something. I don't even know what I said. Anyway, I *G-man speak* him into shutting up long enough to get off the phone and start thinking ways of tearing you a new asshole."

"Sir, really, I can exp…"

"Hold your horses, Mori. Just hold on and listen."

"Yessir."

"Okay, so, yeah, tearing you a new one. So, I leave my office because I'm busy, Mori. I had, and HAVE, more to do than worry about this. Which is why I sent you in the first place. To handle it. I thought you were a smart guy who could wrap the thing up but you made an enemy of the local police chief…" Bullock's tone softens and Mori decided not to interrupt.

209

"So, you're lucky." Bullock continues, "not twenty minutes later, as I said, I'm leaving my office and I run into my boss, see? And he says, oh hey, Phillip, he calls me Phillip, for some reason, Phillip, he says, I just got a call from my old mentor, Judge Wassisname."

"Norris." Mori said.

"Fine. Norris. Whatever. And he says he couldn't be more pleased and you were a fine young agent and all that jazz… said he so was glad I sent someone so competent, etcetera."

"Oh." Mori said. "So…"

"So what? So nothing. That's it. You were only up there to impress the old man. So good job. Just avoid the town cop and get out of there. You're almost done, aren't you? Suicide, right?"

"Suicid*es*." Mori said, emphasizing the plural. "And no. I don't think so."

Bullock was silent on the other end for a moment. "What do you think, then?"

Mori fretfully flipped the heavy black phone cord on the carpet, hearing it flap on the art deco woolen weave. "I think they might have a thrill killer. A compulsive type. Or just an Indian hater. A flat-out race hate murderer."

"You're serious?"

"I am."

Bullock was silent another moment. Mori was glad that Bullock was a professional, and didn't dismiss his assessment out of hand.

"Just a hunch?"

"I wouldn't say just."

"What evidence have you got?"

It was Mori's turn for silence. What *did* he have? "You see, Ballard, that is, Captain Ballard, he's not only refused to share what he has he's also going around telling people not to speak with me..."

"I guess I'm not too surprised. Telling people not to talk to you, eh? What a prick."

"So, I've kind of had to start at the beginning and..."

"So, what have you *got?*" Bullock said again.

Mori opened his mouth but he can't form the words. At last he said, "Not enough."

Bullock sighs and the long-distance crackles and hums. "Look, Mori. You did me a favor, and I appreciate it. You did your job; you got the Judge to feel like his concerns weren't being ignored. But I think it's time to wrap it up. You can't have much petty cash left, can you?"

"Well..."

"You're keeping receipts, right?"

"Yes. Keeping receipts."

"Look, take a couple days and see what you can find. But keep your head low, keep making nice with the judge and then split, okay? Obviously, you don't have to go back to Manzanar."

"No. I can even enlist."

"Yeah, we got a notice about that. You can enlist. See that? I know that's not enough time to… look, the local is probably right anyway. No disrespect to your hunches but… bottom line, if you can't get anything ironclad in the way of evidence in the next, what? Two, three days? You'll have to wrap it up. Okay?"

Mori said okay.

He sat there a few minutes after ringing off, thinking. He'd have to speed things up. He left the phone on the arm of the chair and left out through the front door before he'd even gotten all of his winter clothes on in their right places. He was pulling on his gloves and adjusting his fedora low above his eyebrows as he reached the main road. It wasn't far to the police station.

Snow was falling on the common. It smelled vaguely of the sea which he hadn't seen from anywhere in town but knew was near enough. The plow had been through but a new, fresh dusting had covered it over and the skating rink and bandstand were barely distinguishable. He saw the police station across the railroad tracks and up the little hill. He gave a little grunt of displeasure at the thought of having to go back.

He went inside quickly, like taking off a bandage. Claypool stood up from his ancient desk to look at him with smirk. Captain Ballard had been feeding a log into the wood stove. He stood up as well. "Well, look who it is." Ballard had a strange nervous energy that was hard to interpret for Mori. Veering from seeming smarmy and bullying one moment to worried and put upon the next.

"I need to share some information." Mori said.

"Funny, I wanna share something with you! A little record I picked up when I was in Bangor!" Ballard shut the front door of the wood stove and set the hatch in place then walked to a side table with a portable phonograph. He lifted the lid and then the arm and blew on it. "You know how the needles can get dusty."

Mori said nothing, began to remove his gloves.

Ballard set the needle down and the sound began to pop and crackle until there was the sound of a warbling male singer. Up tempo, dance hall type of ditty.

Ballard sang along: *"Oh, we didn't want to do it, but they're asking for it now! So, we'll slap the Jap right into the lap of the Nazis!"*

A small grin curved the corner of Mori's lip. Was this really, he thought, all this guy had to come at him with?

"Thumbs up England! We're proud of you! We'll show 'em there's no yellow in the red, white, and blue!" Ballard shook his hands out like Al Jolson singing along with the line. Claypool clapped his giant meaty paws together one time in satisfaction like a toy wind up monkey. Mori waited as Ballard and Claypool began to wave their fingers in the air as if conducting an orchestra. He stole a look at the clock.

"Patriotic!" Ballard said. He lifted the arm again. "Wanna hear it again? It's a catchy little tune. Fills me with patriotic spirit, I tell you!"

Mori walked with purpose to the record player and removed the record while it was still spinning. Ballard looked alarmed and on edge is if Mori was about to smash his record. Instead, he carefully slid it into the brown paper envelope that had been sitting on the table. He placed the record gently on the table.

"Just a minute now..." Ballard began.

"In your report, the one you had Officer Falkenham give to me, you briefly mentioned a source for this theory of yours that they were all suicides. Mohawk tradition, it said."

The glee drained from Ballard. He stretched and pushed back his hair. "What of it?"

"Who was it?"

"Why should I…"

"They weren't all Mohawk, Captain."

"So, what?" Claypool called out.

"Hard to have a Mohawk tradition if you aren't Mohawk, isn't it?" Mori asked.

Ballard goes from angry to exhausted looking in seconds. "How do you know what they were?"

"Police work, Captain. Did you not know, or did you not bother to find out?"

Ballard straightened up, puffed out his chest, but there was resignation in him. He exhaled loudly, looked about to shout, then suppressed it. "We… relied on a witness. An expert. Indian expert."

"Indian expert? Who?"

"Tribal elder. Well, he was…"

"Let me meet him."

"Listen, now…"

"Now. Today." Mori pointed his finger at the center of Ballard's chest, like scolding a child.

Ballard's eyes seemed to catch fire, but then, just as quickly, it went out. He nodded, closed his eyes, ran a hand over the stubble on his chin. "We'll go get him. Fetch you at hotel when we do?"

"Let's go get him now." Mori said.

Ballard started to grin. "Well, that's the thing. Might take a little while to rustle him up. Not even sure where he's staying. But if you want to ride around between Claypool and me and shoot the bull for... oh, however long it takes..." Ballard delicately doffed his Captain's hat and pulled on the lapels of his puffy winter coat, "Well, be my guest."

"Hotel it is." Mori said. He looked around. "Where's the other one? Falkenham? Off today?"

Ballard scoffed. "Lou decided to look for greener pastures."

"He quit?"

"He quit. Yes. Do you want to discuss my staff or can we go? I gotta lock up, come on."

Mori watched them silently move away and gruffly shamble into their patrol car. He watched the exhaust belch and the tires skid on the slushy road. When the car was out of sight he turned and looked at the front door of the police station. He had no way in to ransack any files or evidence they might be hiding, but then he thought, there wasn't likely to be any. But why, he wondered? Did they already know who the killer was – or did they not care? Something was gnawing at Mori. He couldn't put his finger on it. Maybe he didn't want to.

He decided to go and see Falkenham. It was a hunch and likely wouldn't come to anything, he thought. But then again...

He asked around and at the post office they had Falkenham's address. It wasn't a far walk. A small blue clapboard house with a man out front, shoveling snow off the walk. It was the man he'd come to see.

"Whatya say, Lou?" Mori said. "Can I call you Lou?"

Lou Falkenham straightened up from his backbreaking chore and looked back at his house. A bit of snow fell from the eaves. He looked back at Mori, and stuck the long, curved scoop of the snow shovel into the thick snow bank covering the lawn. He held onto it like Neptune with a trident. "Sure. Lou is fine."

"So, you quit, eh?"

"Not here." He said. "My folks are inside. Let's take a walk." He pointed a gray woolen mitten down the road and started off. Mori joined him.

They walked away, down the road, houses spaced well apart, the deep color of the evergreens barely noticeable under new powdery snow. The road had been plowed but was slowly getting a fresh covering.

"You quit." Mori said.

"Yeah." Falkenham said, looking at his boots.

"Something better come along?"

Falkenham shook his head. "Nah. It just wasn't for me."

"When was this?"

"Yesterday."

"Yesterday? Sheesh. Do you mind if I ask why?"

"What difference does it make? Why do you want to know?"

Mori just walked. He had found people don't like the silence and want to unburden themselves to fill it. The snow crunched under their boot soles.

"I wasn't cut out for it."

"No? Why not?"

Falkenham shrugged. "Just... wasn't what I expected. Wasn't cut out for it." He said again.

"This doesn't seem like the sort of place to cause a man such trouble."

Falkenham shook his head. The earflaps on his rust-colored cap fluttered. "It may seem like that. Especially to someone from *Los Angeles, California...*" he said it intending scorn, but it just sounded sad. "But here... you can feel closed in. Cut off. Disconnected. You have to rely on people. You have to rely on a policeman... or whoever. Your community. Your country. I mean, the war... I can't even go because of my goddam epilepsy so I thought I could make a difference here, but it just... it comes apart and nothing makes sense..." He waved his hand dismissively. "You couldn't understand."

Mori rubbed his gloved hands together and chuckled a little. "No? I don't know what's eating you but I can give you a little lesson in things coming apart, as you say. And not making sense too, for that matter.... *Los Angeles, California...*" Mori mimicked Falkenham's tone. "It may surprise you to learn that between coming here from DC and being back home in LA I had a little layover. A tin roof shack in the Sierra Nevada's. Mind you, this wasn't a vacation I chose for myself. Rather, the Army

217

thought I might be more comfortable for the duration of the war cooling my heels behind barbed wire and guard towers."

"Yeah," Falkenham said. "The relocation camps, I know…"

"Relocation, yeah… Do you know? You ever see a bunch of people that look like you climbing onto a bus with soldiers behind them? You can't believe Uncle Sam would do anything… *terrible* to you. You want to believe the story that it is for your own good, even though you know damn well it isn't. But then, you never thought you'd see the day people that looked like you would get loaded onto buses and shipped off to god knows where either."

Falkenham looked at his shoe tops and kicked at the snow.

"And they only came for people that looked like me. Not people that looked like you. Not even with your name. Not even a distant *maybe* relative of the renowned General von Falkenhayn."

Falkenham shifted in the snow, his overcoat rustled and snow gathered on them both. A house in the distance puffed out some smoke lazily from a silver metal stovepipe.

"So, I know what can *break down*. I know. So, what do you do? What do guys like us do? If the pieces here are broken, put them back together."

"Yeah? How? A bunch of G-men gonna come running?"

Mori wasn't sure if he hesitated or not but he replied. "Sure. Why not."

Falkenham shook his head. "It doesn't matter. I can't help you. Can't help myself. I don't know what you want to hear. There's nothing to say anyway."

"How long were you on the job, Lou?"

"About six months."

"Not very long."

"Like I said, it just wasn't for me."

"Did those men commit suicide, Lou? Because I don't think they did…"

"Of *course,* they did. What the hell are you talkin' about?" Falkenham shook his head. He sounded convincing.

"Four men. All the same way."

"It's an Indian thing. I don't get it. We can't understand it."

"I'm not buying that line anymore. So, why'd you drag me out here, Lou?" Mori gestured to the empty road, snowflakes falling so lazily they seemed suspended, disrupted by Mori's gesture. "You could have said nothing in front of your house."

"I dunno. I dunno… Jesus…" Falkenham has jammed his hands into his coat pockets, a nervous gesture as he was wearing heavy woolen mittens. He dislodged them again. "Maybe I just didn't want to put on a show for the neighbors and have them all wondering why I'm spilling my guts to the Jap G-man!"

"You haven't spilled a thing. What do you have to spill? Let's hear it already."

Falkenham smiles, resignation, frustration – Mori can't pin him down. "There's nothing to tell. I just… it wasn't what I expected."

"Don't you think you were a good cop?"

"I was alright."

"And Captain Ballard? Is he a good cop?"

Falkenham shrugged.

"Claypool?"

Falkenham scoffed. "I'm not… how should I know?"

"Who would know better than you?"

Falkenham paced. "I don't like beating up drunks. I don't like pulling over girls and patting them down for…. I don't like keeping money from evid…" he stopped, shaking his head. "No." He said. "They're not good cops."

"Did Ballard or any of you carry out any investigation at all into the death of these men?"

For the first time, Falkenham looks Mori in the eye. He's shaking his head a little, perhaps involuntarily. "I don't know anything else." He said. "I was only there 6 months. I didn't…" he looks away. "Ballard just treated me like an errand boy. Take the shit shift. Do the typing. Get lunch."

"Lou…"

"I don't know anything else, goddamit."

He'd closed down, looking back at his shoe tops, voice hard and distant. He started to walk back the way he'd come.

Mori caught up and they walk back to Falkenham's house in silence.

CHAPTER 19

February 4, 1943

Mori and Trudy waited for Ballard and Claypool to return. She'd arrived around lunchtime and they'd been waiting a few hours. They sat in the wingback chairs in the lobby of the hotel. In front of them was an ottoman with ornate, spindly, coffee-colored legs, on top of which sat Mori's upturned fedora. He had taken his card pack from his inside pocket and was flicking them into it, almost never missing. Trudy took her turns and though at first some went flying off in unexpected directions, she was getting better and barely missing the hat herself.

"Use those first two fingers." Mori instructed. "Just spin it strait in." They were at the game for over an hour.

"You're pretty good at this." Trudy said. She was dressed up today. A cobalt blue skirt with a matching belt and jacket with red and white starbursts that looked like peppermints on the front on either side with a matching peppermint striped blouse. Shoes the same color with bows on the top. Her butter-colored hair was swept back to the right with a fake flower clip and Mori even detected make-up. He was used to her ready-for-business attire of leather cap, trousers, and pea coat.

"You get good at things like this when you've got too much time on your hands." Mori said, then flicked two more cards into his hat quickly. He then covered his eyes, flicked another, and it deposited in the hat dead center.

"Show off."

"You're decked out today. What's the occasion?"

"It's Thursday night, USO dance."

"Thursday, eh? All kind of a blur."

"Yeah. Should be a swell time. Maybe. Anyway, I promised some girlfriends I'd go but... You know. I didn't want to go home and have to change an all that."

Trudy got up to retrieve some of the cards that have not flown straight. She bent primly at the knee and lifted them from the carpet. She cleaned up nice; Mori had to admit. And the idea of cutting a rug made him wish he could, somewhere simpler, in a simpler time.

"A dance, you say? Man, I haven't had a dance in... well, it's been a while."

"Why not come along? It's all according to Hoyle." Trudy said, handing him the cards. "Promise. Although not the sort of exciting nightlife you're probably used to. It'll be dull mostly, at least until the punch gets spiked. Which it will. Take that to the bank."

Mori actually thought back to one of the camp dances at Manzanar. They were always doing things to keep their spirits up. He remembered dancing with that one girl who could really jitterbug… what was her name? Keiko something… He wanted to show Trudy around the dancefloor so badly he could almost feel her moving beneath his hands as the thought of it crept into his head. He tried to push it out.

"Probably not a good idea."

"I'll save you a dance." Trudy said, drawing out the word 'dance' enticingly.

Ballard and Claypool walked in, tracking snow onto the rug. Neither removed hat or gloves.

"Duty calls." Mori said.

"Lookit you." Claypool said, giving Trudy the eye. "You look good dolled up. You usually dress like a boy." If he'd been licking his lips it wouldn't have been less subtle. He had a lewd smile that made the high, round cheekbones, already pink from the cold, shimmer like pebbles under his eyes.

"Yes, thanks, officer." Trudy said, crossing her legs and pulling the hem of her skirt over the knee.

"If you wanna see Joseph then let's go!" Ballard said with a low grumble. He barely stopped to see if Mori was following before turning back the way he'd came. Claypool's enormous frame turned just as quickly.

"I'll drive." Trudy said.

Walking to the door and pulling on his overcoat, Mori said, "I don't want you to miss the soiree or anything. I can just…"

She slid into her pea coat and buttoned it deftly. "It's not for hours yet. Anyway, like you said, duty calls."

Turns out they were only going to the police station, just a short drive into town. They all piled out in the small triangular parking lot like rival gangs shaking down the same joint. Ballard grunted and motioned to the door.

It was, as always, oppressively hot inside. How they got such heat to come from that small wood stove was a mystery to Mori. He unwound his scarf and shed his overcoat quickly. He noticed in the single cell, the one he well knew the nooks and cracks and broken cement and warped wood of, a man. Tall, probably taller even than Claypool. He was clearly Indian, skin a leather tan with long salt and pepper hair pulled back, probably into a pony tail tucked into the back of his enormous red plaid coat. He had a brown woolen cap in his hand, resting on his knee. There was no expression on his face, just a blank stare, straight ahead.

"Joseph." Ballard said, pointing, as if that was all the explanation needed.

"Joseph." Mori repeated, looking from Ballard to the man. He looked at Trudy. She shrugged; didn't know him.

Mori approached the cage. "Why's he in there?"

Ballard made a clicking noise with his tongue. "Well, I wasn't gonna leave him just sitting around in here while I went to track you down."

"Sir," Mori said to the man, "would you like to…"

"I'm fine." The man said. His voice was low, level, deep, but barely below a whisper. He didn't look at any of them when he spoke.

"He's fine." Ballard said, puffing out his gut as he sat in his creaking chair.

"Captain, get him out of there, for crissakes…"

Ballard scoffed but did as asked. Joseph really was very tall. He sat in a chair opposite Mori with a strong scent of beer and wood smoke. Claypool seemed to stalk the back of the room. Trudy seemed to find the exact opposite side of the room to settle when he did.

"So, Joseph… can I call you Joseph?" Mori asked.

The man nodded. Looking sometimes at the floor and sometimes into the distance, but at nothing in particular.

"What's your last name?"

Joseph shrugged, just a little. "Smith."

Mori smiled. "Really?"

Joseph didn't reply.

"Like the uh, the Mormon? The founder of the Mormon Church?"

A slight shrug. "Dunno."

"Mr. Mo… *Agent* Mori, you see, Joseph doesn't have any family and hasn't ever had any as far as we know, and not so many records to speak of, so… I mean, how important is a last name when that's the case?"

"That true, Joseph?"

"Yeah. It's like Ed says."

It took Mori a minute to realize that by "Ed" he meant the Captain. "'Ed' you say? You know the Captain pretty well?"

Ballard sat up straight and interjected, "Well, I've arrested him enough times for being drunk in public and let him sleep it off in the cage, he ought to know me by now."

Mori suppressed his irritation and looked at Joseph. "That right?"

Joseph let his eyes flick over to Ballard, then only for a second to Mori, then a kind of half nod before looking at the far wall.

"Joseph," Mori said, sitting forward to the edge of the chair, "The Captain says you told him these men, the Indians that have died here over the past two winters… you said they killed themselves. You stand by that?"

"I didn't know the men."

"What?"

"I met one of them. Years ago. Didn't know the others."

Mori looked at Ballard, then back art Joseph, "Then how did…"

"I knew the road they took…" Joseph began to nod.

"What? The logging road? County Road… what was it? What does that have…"

Joseph shook his head. "No. The road. *Onekwansha Oskahwe'ta Ohaha.*"

"What?" Mori and Trudy both said.

"That's Mohawk language." Ballard replied.

"What... does that mean?" Mori asked.

Joseph looked at him, but only for a moment, and rocked in the chair a little. "The road." He said again. "The road of the bleeding foot... The bleeding foot road..." he nodded.

Mori said, "What is that? What does it mean?"

"*Onekwansha Oskahwe'ta Ohaha*... When a man has nothing left. No family. No tribe. No place in this world. He walks to the next as he came into this one... "

"Stark naked?" Mori offered.

Joseph continued unfazed, "... across the snow, across the ice. No longer a burden to world, and no longer burdened by it. The man decides when his time is done by walking the road."

"And you say this is a custom of your tribe? You're Mohawk?"

The man nodded, just slightly.

Mori found nothing like this in his trip to the library. He knew the available literature hadn't been exhaustive (or, for that matter, very good at all) but still, not even some mention of so strange a custom? Then too there was Frost's view of it... Joseph Smith was hard to get a read on. Mori couldn't detect any obvious signs of deception, stoic as the man was.

"Why do they call it that?" Mori asked, though he knew the answer. "The bloody... foot... you know... Why?"

Joseph blinked his small dark eyes and began to remove his ancient boots. They slid off surprisingly easily and then he took off his gray woolen socks, holes in the toes and heel. He lifted his left leg onto his right knee and showed Mori the sole. It was leathery and a long time healed but scars remained. Perhaps decades old scars. Small, white snakes across his foot, little ridges, little snares, the indication of his feet once torn to shreds. Some of the toes were still black. He did the same motion, changing to the other foot, then began to replace his socks and boots.

"The ice and snow, they make the flesh soft... then the ice slashes it to bits..." Mori whispered, repeating what the doctor in Bar Harbor had said. He looked up, "But here you are. As alive as any of us..."

Joseph, having bent at the waist with an old man's gut, sat back catching his wind. He nodded.

"How can that be, if..."

"I took the walk," Joseph said. "Ten years ago, or so. I was done with the world. I took the walk until I... broke. I fell to the ground, passed out... but I was found. I woke up in a barn. Covered in blankets... Good people saved me. I don't know that I'm glad about it but they were good people all the same." he paused, and Mori noticed for the first time that a couple of the fingers on Joseph's hands were black too. Hypothermic dead tissue. The left pinkie was gone above the second knuckle. "It wasn't my time after all."

"My goodness." Trudy said.

Mori wasn't sure where to begin again. He pulled on his cuffs and tried to will himself not to sweat in the heat of the place. "Are there many Mohawks in these parts?"

Joseph shook his head. "Not many Indians of any kind anywhere."

"I mean…"

"No. Some. We drifted. Mostly from out west. Adirondacks. Lake Ontario. Out that way."

"This… ritual. The bloody foot road… is it… typical? Would any Mohawk tribesman know it?"

"I can't say what they might know." He said, barely above a whisper.

"In reading up on, well, your tribe, I… didn't come across any mentions of…"

"White men writing books about what Indians do. What they think. You're not white, are you? You look more like me than them. What would they write about you? Would they get it right?"

"Christ." Ballard said, and lit a cigarette. "Don't worry none, Joseph. Mori here is from the *federal government FBI civil rights desk* so you've found the right man to bitch about the white man to!"

Mori ignored the Captain. It was getting easier to tune him out. "You said you knew one of the men? Which?"

"Didn't know him. Met him. Worked a few weeks at the lumber camp. Years ago."

"So, his mental state wouldn't be known to you. So how do you…"

"I don't know. I just know they walked the road. That's all."

This, Mori thought, was all Ballard had hung the deaths of four men on. It wasn't that Joseph was unconvincing, he was quite convincing, but considering he admitted to having attempted suicide and Ballard's claim of frequent drunkenness (and the gin blossoms on Joseph's nose and cheeks) it all seemed, Mori thought, a bit *flimsy*.

"What if they weren't Mohawk, Joseph? Would them taking the walk... would that surprise you? If they weren't Mohawk?"

Joseph seemed to stiffen a bit, or perhaps Mori imagined it? He didn't speak for a few moments. Finally, "Once we were Mohawk, Ammonoosuc, Abenaki, Narragansett... then we were just Indians. We've clung to what we could." Joseph exhaled what might have been what passed for a laugh. "Hell, my real father was Cree. I think."

"You're saying this... custom. The blood foot road... could have crossed tribal lines, so to speak?"

Joseph looked first as Ballard, then Mori, only briefly, then gave a stiff nod.

Mori went through the questions again, to see if Joseph was remaining consistent. He didn't say much but it didn't change much either. At last, Ballard grew tired of the interview and said "Awright, well you got what you wanted, Mori, okay? Claypool, why don't you take Joseph back to his place?"

Joseph rose quickly to his high height. "No need. I'll walk." And he was out the door.

Mori watched, making mental notes.

"Well," Ballard said. "Satisfied? You heard wh..."

But Mori just held up his hand toward Ballard and it made the Captain stop talking. He walked to the door and watched Joseph walk away through the pebbled glass.

"You gonna let me look as Joseph's arrest record?" Mori asked.

"What arrest record?"

"You said you've arrested him a bunch of times."

"I said I picked him up and let him sleep it off. Nothing about arresting anybody… And no. You ain't going through my files."

"What a surprise. You ready Trudy?"

She was. And darted for the door gladly.

"See you around, Trudy." Claypool said lasciviously.

"I'd say 'not if I see you first'," she whispered to Mori, "But I'm not sure he'd understand and might take it as a come-on."

"Not even a thank you!" Ballard yelled after them.

Mori kept walking as he buttoned his overcoat. "I need real evidence." He grumbled. "I need to look at the bodies. At least the ones still above ground."

"Yeah," Trudy said. "About that…"

CHAPTER 20

"What?" Mori said.

"If you want… I think I know a way." Trudy said, tying the belt of her peacoat, then slipping on her kidskin gloves.

He looked at her quizzically.

"Not so quick on the uptake for a detective, are ya? The bodies, Sherlock."

Mori threw a glance back at the police station. "Let's get back in the car." he said.

Once in the Nash again with the heat on and the police station receding from view, he turned to her. "How?"

She smirked, while keeping hands at ten and two. "Well, it's like this: When I was a kid there was a rumor about what they did with bodies around here during the winter. After all, they can't dig into the ground to bury anyone, it's frozen solid. I mean, I would think at the hospital, you know, the morgue or what have you, right? But Jeanie Shields – she's this girl I went to school with – she says no. She says they put them in this room they have dug under the railroad tracks on Forest Lake Road. Well, not under, but there's this area where it curves leading up to a, whattya call it? A trestle? Then there's the road that runs underneath, and off the side, set back, is this… room. Now, I think that's silly, but she says her dad works for the county and they don't want to truck bodies to Portland, where the nearest hospital is, and they wouldn't have room anyway, so any bodies from anyone that dies after the deep freeze sets in are put in there until they can break ground in the spring."

"Trudy," Mori proceeds cautiously, "That seems a little… how old were you when you heard this?"

"Oh, we'd all heard the rumors forever, but when Jeanie said that about her dad? Dunno. 12? 13? Something like that."

"Don't you think it is a little… unlikely."

"No. Not at all. I know it's true, actually."

"How… could you know that?"

"I broke in and looked for myself."

Mori was taken aback. "You… how?"

"It was a door. With a lock. Easy peasy."

"How…"

"My folks run a hardware store. Remember? I've been making keys since I was eight years old. But in that case, I didn't need to file one down or anything. We had a bit key that opened it."

"Bit key?"

"Like a skeleton key. That's…"

"I know that one. Okay. Wow. So, then what?"

Trudy shrugged. "We went it. Me, Bill Oates, some other girl, can't remember her name… not Jeanie though. She chickened out…"

"And you, what? Saw a body? Bodies?"

She smiled, excited now, taking a turn a little faster than she should have. A little skid but she righted the Nash. "Sorry. Yeah. Well, kind of."

"Kind of?"

"I let us in after I found the right bit key, we went in with our flashlights… the girl stood by the door. I think it was Doris… Wassername… anyway, doesn't matter… And, okay, I chickened out a little, I guess, but there were these wooden tables but only one had a wooden box on it and we figured, I mean, it looked like a coffin, So Bill had brought a tire iron, figuring, well, you know, and he opened it and he got pale and I said, you know, what is it? Is it a body? I asked him who it was and he didn't say, he just started to leave. So, I ask again, was it a body? And he starts shaking his head and saying we gotta go, we gotta go… he was so affected, I'll be honest, I'm not sure we put the coffin lid all the way back down."

Amusing as it was and as eager as Mori was to get a look at the bodies, if he could, he felt he needed to point out the holes in her story. "So, you didn't actually *see* any bodies?"

Her eyebrows made a V and she made a quizzical curl of her bottom lip. "Nooooo, not really. No. Bill did though. Want to ask him?"

"Don't think we have time for that."

"Good. I think he's in the Army now anyway."

Mori wondered if this errand would be worth the time spent to do it. It couldn't be true, could it? Seemed an awful lot like Trudy remembered this event from her childhood and perhaps it wasn't quite what she'd thought it was at the time. At any rate, he couldn't think of anything else to do.

"I've got to go to the hardware store. Get the bit keys – I can't remember which one it was. Been a long time. Real long time. And I'll pick up some blanks and a file set in case it's been misplaced or they've changed the lock and I have to make one – that could take a while…"

And she was already on the way…

"Do you have a camera and some flash bulbs?"

She nodded. "Sure."

"Bring them along too."

Forest Lake Road was another narrow meandering lane through deep woods that seemed as if it got no traffic. All of life seemed to come to a screeching halt by nightfall in these parts, Mori thought, and as it was late afternoon, people were nestling in for the night.

"There it is." Trudy said, and pulled off onto the shoulder. She'd pointed at a black door that covered a green-painted brick wall that made a sort of squared arch right in the living earth. It was at a curve at the bottom of a steep slope running down from railroad tracks, barely visible through the foliage, and growing dark. Trudy shut off the car and the light reflecting off the slight fluttering snow disappeared.

They walked across the road, barely more than a path the width of a narrow car, through the unpaved snow up to the door. Though set a good way back from the road, they would still be visible if anyone drove by. Seeing him look around, Trudy said, "Nobody will come by. And even if they do… nobody cares."

"Awright, Trudy. It's your town."

She smiled at that. They got to the door and Trudy examined the lock. "I don't remember if it is the same or not." She said.

"Well, it doesn't seem like it's been changed in… ever."

"Yeah, good point. Bag?"

Trudy pointed at the brown rucksack on his shoulder that she'd hurriedly filled with tools, a pry bar, and the camera Mori had asked for. Her mother had asked her what on earth she needed a camera for and Trudy reminded her that it was Thursday night and she was going to a dance and thought a few snapshots might be fun for anyone shipping out (it was a harmless little lie, she thought.) While her mother fetched her some extra film, she sneaked the folded oilcloth filled with locksmith tools and bit keys into the rucksack.

Mori handed her the bag and then used his boots to clear away the snow in front of the door to give her some work space.

"Thanks. You read my mind." she said.

She sat the bag on the freshly cleared ground and unrolled the oilcloth on top of it. "Okay, old one, but pretty standard mortise lock," she said, poking the keyhole in the door with her finger. She then examined the tools and keys. "I'm going to hope for the best and think dad still has the right bit key..." she fished thru a ring of clanking keys, wasn't pleased, then tossed it down in favor of another. She examined them, talking to herself, "stem is right, wrong collar though...no... oh wait, let's try..." she inserted a key. It slid all the way in but didn't turn.

"Close." she said. "But no cigar."

She deliberated over a few more, tried them, swore. "Sorry. Ugh. I really don't want to have to file a key for this. Freezing out here. It might take twenty min... wait. Hold on..." she slid in a key, slowly, showing off. "Hear that?"

"What?"

There was a muffled clinking noise as the key turned and she beamed. "That... was the bolt being thrown." Trudy turned the knob and it gave a little. "Tug hard, it's stuck." She said to him.

Mori grabbed the rusted doorknob and pulled. It was reluctant to move in the cold and rust and infrequent use. It was dark inside.

"Flashlight in the bag." Trudy said.

Mori pulled it from the rucksack by the cold, ribbed, tarnished silver handle. He flicked it on and shined it inward.

"Another door." He said. There was indeed another door. Also painted black, cracked peeling paint scabs. The small space in front of them looked like a small antechamber, perhaps added after the inner one, and seemed to contain nothing and was barely eight feet from the other door.

"Hold your horses." Trudy said. "Yeah, I forgot about this. A lot of times these old ones will take the same key or…" she walked up to it, rather fearlessly, Mori thought, and gave the knob a turn. It was unlocked, but didn't budge much. "Human nature, right? Why lock both doors?"

"My girl Friday." Mori said.

"Got nothing on me."

"Clearly."

Again, Mori stepped to the door and muscled it open, and this one was just as reluctant. The smell that floated out was of must, mold, and… formaldehyde? Both of them were slightly queasy immediately.

Mori let the amber light flick over the surfaces inside. Not an enormous space, perhaps twelve by twenty feet, with a high, vaulted ceiling of cement. The walls too were of the same color cement, but seemed to smell strongly of the earth they held out. There were five rather crudely (but sturdy looking) constructed tables, about three feet high. On the three of these nearest the door were wooden boxes, each about six feet long by two and a half feet wide. They were rectangular and not constructed, Mori thought, with the distinctive shape – wide shoulder area, tapered leg area – of a coffin…

And yet…

"Wow," Trudy said. "Now that I'm back, it feels like yesterday. Hoo boy."

Mori turned to her. "Maybe you should go. You're gonna get your swanky clothes all messed up."

"I'm fine."

"At this rate, you're gonna miss that dance."

"What am I gonna do? Leave you to hoof it back? Three miles back into town you know."

He affected a somber sort of tone to try and impress upon her the gravity of the situation. "Trudy," he said, "Right now it's just breaking and entering. If it comes to it, I can cop to that and take the heat. But you have to live here. I can't say I know offhand what the law is in the state of Maine for tampering with the deceased but I'll bet it ain't a slap on the wrist."

She nodded. "I know." She said. "But in for a penny, in for a pound, right? Let *me* worry about me, Ace. You just do what you came here to do."

He smiled and turned the light back into the chamber. There were more of the man-sized rectangular boxes leaning against and facing the back wall. The covers, some with nails already in the lid, were in a similar stack next to them. Mori shined the flashlight on the boxes on the table. To his alarm, the room was suddenly flooded with pale white light. He looked up to the ceiling, startled.

"Sorry." Trudy said, "Found a switch." She was standing next to the door and had flicked the lone switch in the chamber up. It was a silver switchbox bolted onto the wall with the wiring in a silver tube running up the wall, the ceiling, then to a bare bulb in the center of the vault. "wish I'd know that was there when I was a kid."

It wasn't actually very bright, but was still better than the flashlight. Mori clicked it off and put it in his overcoat pocket before approaching the ends of the tables and the… boxes. He noticed labels on the end. "Milton Bean." Mori read.

"Oh yeah," Trudy said. "Mr. Bean. Sure. Passed away around Christmas. That's a kick in the head, isn't it?"

"Holy Toledo, that means… you were right."

"I told you."

Mori read the next one. "Just says 'unknown.' That'll have to be… Sal…"

"Sal?"

Mori waived it off. "Never mind. Okay, next one… there it is. Rupert Delisle."

"Holy smokes." Trudy said.

Mori dove into the rucksack again and retrieved the pry bar. It was small, perhaps not a foot long, with a forked end bent under. A "cat's paw" Trudy had called it.

"What do you think they do if more than five people die over the course of a winter? Just put them on the floor? I mean, around here it probably doesn't come up. We don't have a bunch of deaths or anything, it's quiet. God knows it's quiet… Not a bunch except, you know… I mean, except what brought you here, of course. But we have our share of old timers too so… And the ground doesn't thaw until May. At the earliest. Well, maybe April. No. Heck, probably June…"

"Trudy," Mori said, applying pressure to the graying, cracking wood of the lid and hearing the nails squeak and give way, "Are you chattering because you're nervous."

"Yeah. Yeah, I am."

"Do you want to, maybe, step outside?"

She did, but she said, "Not a chance."

241

Mori lifted the lid and the nails, tight in the wood, they gave more and released with more squeaks and cracks. Trudy exhaled a great cloud of breath as the already frigid chamber seemed suddenly even colder. Trudy helped him lift off the lid and put it aside as he warned her to be careful of the exposed nails. Trudy looked inside, started to say "holy cow" but stopped on the "h." Mori looked the body over.

"Which one is this?" Trudy asked.

In his rush, Mori hadn't thought to choose and hoped it wasn't the Mr. Bean Trudy had known. He looked at the end of the coffin (which he now called it in his mind, despite the shape.) "Delisle." He said.

"Why is it lined with metal?" Trudy asked.

The coffin was indeed lined with tin sheets tacked over the inner surface. "Probably to keep out the rodents." Mori said.

The appearance was about what Mori expected. Dead embalmed flesh a sickly purple, rust, and jaundice yellow color. Features Mori would describe as "Indian." His jaw hadn't been wired and so was hanging down, making him look even less alive, and appalled about it. Delisle, in life, had had a large, beak-like nose with pockmarks that indicated, perhaps, severe acne as a younger man. Doctor hadn't mentioned that. What had he said? Broken hand… Mori leaned over, nearly overwhelmed by the harsh chemical smell. He picked up the hand, which alarmed him by being as cold as the air around him. He could see what the doctor had said quite easily. Fingers bent at odd angles, bones not set before the death, flesh not healed and now ragged… broken during the death, Mori thought…

During the murder, he corrected himself.

Could have been a slamming trunk. Nothing really to prove it, but the thought occurred to him.

But what can you prove? He scowled at his conflicting thoughts. Focus. Get as much information as you can and get out.

Mori unbuttoned the man's shirt, an ill-fitting plaid number. Chest the same sickly color, life drained away, embalming suspending the decay. Old scars but nothing out of the ordinary for a laborer. He buttoned the shirt again and tucked it prissily back into the blue work trousers. It looked like, and probably was, Mori thought, spare clothing that had been scrounged for burial. No suit and tie... what difference did it make, Mori thought. It still made him angry.

He moved on to the feet, removing the boots, which were several sizes too big and slipped right off with no stockings beneath. The skin was frozen in tatters, unhealed, shredded. He put the boot back on and didn't remove the other. He decided a picture wouldn't be necessary either. His patience for this was wearing thin. He knew he should be disgusted, but the whole thing was just making him angrier. He thought about how his father would tell him anger was a good thing – but control it, harness it.

He dug the camera out of the rucksack and primed it to shoot a photo of the head and shoulders and the mangled hand. It was an Argus box model 50mm. The overhead light wasn't enough, so he inserted a flashbulb. He took the first shot of Rupert Delisle's face, making sure the hand was also in the picture. He pressed the shutter and there was a metallic ping, a blinding flash, and he heard Trudy exhale in alarm.

"You okay back there?" he asked.

She nodded. She had inched back close to the wall. He started to replace the flashbulb but thought better of it, letting it cool while he started in on the lid of John Doe. The magnesium from the bulb just added more odors to the vault, already awash with them. Mori hoped Trudy could hold out. He hoped the same for himself. He worked quickly. More prying at coffin lids, nails screeching their reluctance as if they were bad spirits issuing warnings.

Trudy picked up the camera, removed a handkerchief from her overcoat and used it to remove the flash bulb. "Funny," she said. "I think I have a couple of shots on this roll of me and some friends ice skating. Should be a hoot dropping it off at the druggist to develop, huh?"

"I'm going to develop them tonight." He said, laying aside the second lid and shining in the flashlight beam. He smiled, "Don't worry, I'll save your snapshots."

Mori shined the flashlight on the face of the unknown man. Same sickly dead color. Maybe a bit darker. He had been a short, portly man, dark widow's peak. Hands small, curved (neither broken like with Delisle) and coarse, ragged nails, black-tipped: the ravage of hypothermia.

Mori started to think aloud, "He looks... different."

"Than the other guy? I should hope so."

"No, I mean... does he look Indian to you?"

Trudy scoots up to the edge of the coffin. "I guess so. Jeez, Ace, what's he supposed to look like? Headdress full of feathers? Loincloth? Peace pipe in his jaw?" Although this jaw hadn't been wired either and though not agape as with the last body, it did have a leftish lean.

244

Mori waved her off. "Never mind." But the man did look – what? Familiar but different? He couldn't put his finger on it.

He unbuttoned the shirt, clinically, almost daintily, then flipped the shirttails open. Wiry chest hair, short, barrel-like torso. "Wow." Mori said. "Bullet wound."

"What?"

"Yeah. Here…" Mori poked the stiff flesh, "Right side. Looks like…" he leaned over, lifting the corpse a bit, "Yup. Went right through."

"Don't fall in. So… what? He was shot too?"

"Well, a long time ago. Old, faded scar. But it is a good identifying mark. Bullet wounds are often reported, often end up in police reports…"

"Gotcha."

This was the man with the tattoo, the doctor had said. John Doe. Or Sal Cheetah. He checked the biceps but nothing much there, then began to hope the tattoo was above the waist. He buttoned the shirt again and started rolling up the sleeves to check the forearms. Bingo. The discoloration of freezing and embalming had distorted what had clearly been coloring to the tattoo but it was still obviously… Mori froze.

He said, "Oh my god."

"What?" said Trudy, "What is it? You're pale. What's wrong?"

"It… how? It…"

She asked him, "what?" Again.

"*Nuestra Señora de Guadalupe…*" he said.

"How's that?"

"Our lady of Guadalupe."

"I… I'm going to need a little more information still."

He used his pinky to point at the rigid flesh on John Doe's right forearm. When he pressed on it, it felt like frozen beef roast. He would buy new gloves, he thought, in the back of his mind. "It is a religious icon. A Catholic symbol, like… It's the Virgin Mary, okay, but a very specific one. This one is the Virgin of Guadalupe. See? The tunic, here. Then, she's standing on the crescent moon, which is being carried by an angel, here…" he points to the base of the tattoo, a dark-haired cherub, wings outstretched, "And then, the *Virgen de Guadalupe…*" he points to the central figure, a somber young girl – Mary the virgin – eyes closed, head cocked downward piously, hands together in front of her in prayer. The discoloration of the skin as well as age had caused the tattoo to look blackened a bit but Mori was sure the tunic had once been blue with probably golden stars adorning it. "And all this around here is the sunburst."

"So, it's a tattoo of the Virgin Mary?"

"Sure, but the one that appeared four times to Juan Diego in 15… something. 1530, or thereabouts. In the hills outside of Guadalupe. If you believe in that sort of thing."

"How…" Trudy rubbed her gloved hands together and stamped her feet to warm up. The vault was like a freezer. "I mean, are you sure?"

"No question. Half the friends I had growing up had a *Virgen de Guadalupe* framed and hanging on the wall. Or their parents did, anyway. It's a huge deal to a lot of Mexicans where I come from. And Mexicans in general."

"So, he's..." she pointed at the body.

"Mexican." Mori said. "Bet my life on it."

"But..."

"Also, Frost said he spoke Spanish. Or at least he said something that seemed to me like Spanish. And I mean," Mori gestured now to the body. "*He looks* Mexican. To me, anyway... but I'll bet the killers couldn't tell the difference. They thought they were just killing another Indian. Although, I guess they were sort of right. By the looks of him he's indigenous. Or Mestizo."

"You said killers? More than one?"

"Maybe. Yes, I think so."

"Oh my." Trudy said. He thought he saw her shivering. "Mexican? How did he get all the way here? What does it mean? Wait, if he's Mexican then..."

"Exactly. The bleeding foot road wouldn't be a cultural tradition of his, now would it?" Mori looked at the man's feet. No shoes at all this time. Apparently, there wasn't even a spare pair lying around to bury him in. Torn, frozen flesh. Mori grimaced and felt a need to leave. He tried to arrange the arm so it was in the frame with the man's face but the frozen meat and bone and rigor mortis wouldn't permit it. He snapped a picture of the face. Another blinding flash and explosion of magnesium. He had to stand on the table for the next picture, in order to get both the tattoo and face in frame, his boots teetering on the narrow edge. Another flash.

"Give it here." Trudy said. "I'll change the flashbulb."

"Never mind. We've got what we need. Let's get out of here."

Mori set about quickly replacing the lids on the rectangular coffins, lining up the nail holes as best he could. Somehow, they'd forgotten to bring a hammer and Mori was forced to drive the nails back in with the pry bar. After the loud clanging of the first nail, he removed his glove and used it as a cushion to suppress the sound. Definitely need new gloves now, he thought.

They collected the gear into the rucksack and made again for the door. Mori pointed at the light switch and Trudy clicked it off. Mori replaced it with the sickly yellow of the flashlight and the head back out through the doors, which he pulled tightly shut. Trudy reminded him not to lock the inner door. It was pitch dark outside, with barely a hint of moonlight through the overcast night sky, hanging like a sodden blanket of the darkest inky gray. It had somehow been colder inside the vault than it was now, outside. They walked in silence for a moment, trying to shake off the claustrophobic feel and to banish the smells of mold and chemicals from their nostrils.

"Not sure I feel much like dancing now." Trudy said, breaking the silence. The snow was building up again and she was starting to regret her choice of shoes as well.

"No, you should go. Seriously. You're off duty now. Go."

"I don't know. Kinda late anyway." She said, somberly.

"You said the punch was getting spiked. You could probably use a good swig of something right now."

"Decent point, Ace." She said. "You might have talked me into it. What are you going to do?"

"Break out the chemicals I bought for just this occasion, shut myself in my hotel bathroom with the lights off and develop some film."

Trudy slid into the driver's seat and Mori deposited the rucksack on the floor at his feet and sat beside her.

"Well then we'll both have a real gas of a time by the sound of it." She put the Nash in gear and they drove off over the fresh snow.

CHAPTER 21

February 5, 1943

Developing the film hadn't taken long and Mori was actually able to sleep well enough, though dreams of jitterbugging with Keiko led to a Rumba with Sofia and then it was Trudy swinging with him and he woke up before the dawn somehow both content and lonesome. He walked to the druggist to make prints first thing at seven when it opened. He was able to take over the tiny darkroom by flashing his FBI badge ("provisional" going unnoticed or uncommented on) and swearing the old druggist to secrecy. A ten-dollar bill for his trouble helped ease things along. Three morbid prints barely dry in a buff-colored envelope stuffed in his inside overcoat pocket and it wasn't even eight a.m.

He got back to his hotel and Trudy was waiting in his room. Feet on the floor but laying back on the bed. She moaned and raised her hand to wave but didn't sit up.

"How'd you get in here?" Mori asked.

"You saw me operate yesterday and you ask me that?"

He nodded. "Fair enough."

"I kid. The morning guy let me in. He likes you."

"He likes *you*." Mori said. "He's fascinated by me. Like an animal at the zoo. Or a car crash."

"Speaking of... where to today?"

"Well... say, you look a little green. Doing okay?"

"I think somebody spiked the punch. I know. I'm as shocked as you." Trudy said. "So yeah, I may have had a little gin. Or quite a bit of it. After our... adventure yesterday I thought a little would do me good. Then, somehow, I got convinced that a lot would do me good. And I was right, for a while. I feel now like I may have been wrong."

He smiled and patted her knee. "Poor Trudy."

"Poor Trudy." She repeated.

"We have to go to Portland. But don't worry. I'll drive."

Trudy sat up and fixed her leather cap over her hair, more unruly than usual. "Portland? Why Portland? That'll take hours."

"You want to stay and... sleep it off?"

"No, no, I want to go but… what's in Portland?"

"The closest Western Union with Wirephoto."

It did indeed take hours, but by noon, after a long meander down the Maine coast, picturesque like Mori had never seen, Trudy snoring mildly next to him, he was in the lobby of the Eastland Park hotel on High Street in downtown Portland, looking back and forth between a pair or posters hanging near the phone banks. One said, "Enjoy a climb on Munjoy Hill!" and the other: "Keep him flying! Buy War Bonds!" The latter had a lantern-jawed Caucasian pilot looking heroically to the sky as he climbed into his plane, cap and goggles on, and little rising sun flags down the rivets of the plane fuselage to indicate how many Zeros he'd shot down, Mori supposed. Six visible. Not a bad score, he thought, but pulled his hat down lower over his forehead in case anyone passed by and looked too long.

The operator came back on the line. "Holding for Phillip Bullock?"

"Yes."

"One moment please." He heard some clatter. Wires and plugs, beeps and scrapes. A series of beeps, nine, maybe ten, then, "Go ahead, sir." Good thing about Portland being a decent sized city: much faster long-distance lines.

"Mori." Bullock said. He could hear his sort of boss exhaling loudly. One of his ever-present Pall Malls, probably. "Is this your call to let me know you're wrapping it all up and leaving?"

"Yes. Nearly. Well, not… exactly. But close. I need a favor."

"Oh Christ."

"I'm going to Wirephoto you a couple of pics. Can you get me an identification?"

"Mori, you may not remember this but the only reason you're doing what you're doing is because I don't have time or people to do it. What makes you think I can spend god knows how long pouring over files to ID some stiff for a case that doesn't exist?"

"It shouldn't be too difficult, actually. Probably has a record. There was a gunshot wound, a distinct tattoo, and he's almost certainly Mexican, or of Mexican descent..."

"What? Did you forget what part of the world you're in? Mori..."

Mori interrupted again and laid out the case for Bullock, with updates.

"You sure about the tattoo?"

"Hundred percent."

"Did you think about something... unexplainable?"

"That maybe he just liked the look of it and had it tattooed on his arm? And that he didn't speak Spanish at all? Yeah, I thought about it... anything is possible. I think my theory is the far more likely one."

"Okay, okay. Don't bother sending it to me. Send it to the West Coast. Send it to the San Francisco office. You remember that, don't you?"

"Vividly."

"Okay, well, send it to Harvey Feynman out there. I'll give you the details." He did.

"I think if he narrows his search to the southwest. Probably California, maybe Arizona. Far as Texas maybe, I…"

"Yeah, Mori, I know. You were supposed to be leaving today, weren't you? Wrapped up and all that? Don't push it."

"Of course, I'll be waiting here at the hotel for his call."

"No. He'll call me. I'll call you at the front desk. If we don't get anything today, I'm not going to push it. If he doesn't have a record or he ain't on file…"

"Understood boss."

"Boss!" Bullock swore then hung up without saying goodbye.

The Western Union office was only two blocks down, where they promptly informed him that their Wirephoto technician was at the Associated Press office that day, and gave him the address. Mori went there and flashed his badge around, spoke very fast and managed to convince them to send the photos to the FBI office on the AP's machine. When he implied it was business that might concern the war effort, they didn't even charge him. Satisfied, he returned to the hotel, tipped the clerk to keep him up to date and began to wait.

Mori wondered how long it might take. Pouring over mug shots and files. All he could do was wait. Trudy was in the lobby cafe blowing on the surface of a hot chocolate. He felt eyes on him from hotel patrons. He'd already spoken to three different people telling them, working into the conversation with little subtlety, the familiar little white lie that he was Korean. He didn't like doing it but it was better than risking anyone paying too close attention. He was hoping the rumor would get around as quickly as his real story had gotten around Trudy's hometown.

"Ordered you a coffee." Trudy said. Indeed she had and it was still hot.

"Thanks." Mori said.

"So now?"

"We wait."

"How long?"

Mori shrugged. "Not sure. Bullock said he'd have his man look at it today – and *only today* – but the day is young out on the West Coast... it could take ages to go through all the mug shots or files necessary to find..." Mori stiffened and sat up straighter. "I don't know. I know I'm right about this though. I need the confirmation to confront Captain Ballard though. He won't budge on my word alone. He may not budge anyway."

"Budge... how?"

"We have an inescapable conclusion. Joseph Smith it lying. It is likely, for my money, that he made up the whole "bloody foot road" business. Or is embellishing wildly, or... what have you. Anyway, he has lied. So WHY has he lied? Covering for someone most likely. Or himself. So, either he did it or he knows who did."

"You thing that old guy murdered those men?"

"... or he knows who did."

"He was pretty big. And those eyes. Man. Dead eyes."

"Okay, Trudy, let's stay focused on what we know."

"He lied."

He raised his coffee cup and drank. Bitter, sweet, hot, perfect.

Trudy sipped, tapped her fingers, sighed. "Could take all day, huh?"

It didn't. They got bored and took a walk. Quick turn inside a bookshop until the owner started eyeballing Mori. Then to a record store. Trudy bought a copy of "Don't sit under the apple tree" by the Andrews Sisters and they were barely gone two hours when Mori checked in at the hotel desk.

"Yes, Mr., uh, that is, *Agent* Mori. You missed the call about ten minutes ago." The desk manager said. "Shall I put in a call now?"

"Yes. Please. I'll take it in the lobby."

"Very good."

Trudy hustled along beside him to the lobby. "How much did you have to tip for them to be this nice?"

"Five bucks."

Bullock sounds bored on the line. "Well, you're lucky, Mori. Harv went right into a federal file and found your guy. Immigration charge from 20 years ago, so it was in the federal file. He's Mexican alright. Arrested in El Paso… actually a couple of times. Second time was when he took that bullet. State trooper plugged him trying to run. Tattoo listed as 'distinctive marking,' doesn't say he was ever taken to a hospital for it but it does say he was deported a few weeks later. Then later a charge for selling reefer, vagrancy…"

Mori covered the mouthpiece, looked at Trudy. "Bingo."

"Ruiz." Bullock said. "That's your guy. Roberto Manuel Ruiz. File has him arrested a few years later in Mississippi, working as, it says, 'tomato picker,' another reefer charge. They use the reefer charge to throw Mexicans in the clink all the time down there. Anyway, then he got a drunk and disorderly in Pennsylvania a few years ago… sounds like your guy was moving north and east – god only knows why – following the work, maybe, or trying to run away from the local bulls. Who knows? Anyway, that seems to be the story of your Maine Mexican. So, what's the deal then? This for the old man?"

"The old man?"

"The judge, Mori. The judge. A going away present to show you 'cracked the case' and all that?"

"Sort of…"

"Look, I told you that you didn't need to do all that. Old man is happy. I know you're an eager beaver but reign it in a bit. And get out of there. I need that ID back. I'm not sure I can count on you to destroy it."

Mori paused, "Yes sir."

Perhaps trying to soften things a bit, Bullock said, "But keep whatever you've got left of the petty cash to see you to wherever you're headed… you were gonna enlist, right?"

"Just as soon as I'm done."

"Well, there ya go." Bullock said. "I still need receipts though."

"Of course."

"I'll wire the rap sheet to you. Ain't cheap you know, the wire service."

"They did it for me for free."

"Free? How'd you manage that?"

"Appealed to their patriotism, I guess."

Bullock gave a short guffaw and the line crackled with the noise. "Maybe you should come see me after the war, Mori. You seem the resourceful type."

"Maybe I will." Mori said. "If I'm not a million miles away."

They raced back to town, though "racing" included necessary care over roads with icy patches and new fallen snow and so it was still dark by the time they arrived. Mori instructed Trudy to take him directly to the police station. "Wait here." He said.

He walked directly in, always overcoming the urge to knock, as it seemed more like a house or a shop than a public building. Ballard was alone inside, finishing out his shift for the night, Mori figured. Not now.

"Jesus Christ!" Ballard said when he saw Mori. He was sipping from a coffee cup and rolling his eyes.

"Roberto Ruiz." Mori said, extracting two sheets of paper from his inside pocket. He unfolded them and handed them to Ballard.

The Captain, looking quizzical, snatched the papers. "How'd you get this?"

Thankfully the only picture on the page was an old mug shot taken by the Texas State Troopers many years back. But it was him alright, and Ballard's face showed the recognition. Mori could smell liquor as the Captain spoke and wondered what was in the coffee mug. He read a bit, not quite taking it in.

"So?"

"So? Your John Doe is Mexican. Record in Texas. Whoever killed him couldn't tell the difference and took him for a local Indian… doesn't seem anyone around here could tell the difference. And if Doe is Ruiz, then he sure as hell isn't walking any 'bloody foot road' out of Indian cultural tradition or whatever."

The color drained from Ballard's face and he pushed his greasy hair back. "That don't mean… I mean… It could be…"

He finished none of those statements. He took a sip and tried again. "Maybe it's them Indians too. Maybe…"

"Captain!" Mori shouted, incredulous.

"Alright, goddamit!"

"Joseph lied. We need to know why. We need to arrest him. Now."

Ballard stared at him a moment; his face inscrutable "He's gone."

"Gone? What do you mean gone?"

"He said he was leaving town. I saw him today, earlier, and he said he was leaving."

Mori suppressed the urge to lambast the Captain, realizing he didn't have much authority anyway. "Just like that? Picking up and going?"

"Well, he's the sort that don't like trouble, you know. Having to talk to us before and the FBI now, well, it probably spooked him. And I ain't got anything to hold him for, so why would I?"

"Well, you've got something now. He doesn't drive, does he? He can't walk out of here it'll be ten below zero tonight…"

"Taking the train." Ballard said.

Mori looked at his watch. "There's only one train out of here. The B and M, headed south in about 35 minutes."

"What? You sure?"

"I just came in on that train a little while ago. Unless they changed it, which I doubt… anyway, you can check the newspaper if you want but we should make an effort anyway." Mori headed for the door.

"You going to the train station?"

"Of course I am!"

Ballard held up a finger, "Hold on. I'll call Claypool and have him meet us there to help out."

Mori nodded, a little surprised to have any cooperation at all. "Alright. Good."

Ballard had the receiver in hand and was twirling the rotary dial quickly, making it release a mechanical purring. "Wait for me in your car. I'll be right there."

Mori said okay and wondered what he would be waiting for. He went back outside and slid in beside Trudy. "We have to go to the train station."

"Train station? Okay, you got it." She started to put the car in gear.

"Hold on." Mori said. "Ballard's coming."

"With us?"

"No. He'll take the squad car I should think." Mori said, pointing at it. "He just said to wait for him…" Mori looked at his watch.

Ballard exited the station and approached the Nash. Mori turned down the window. "Alright," he said. "Claypool is on his way there. He lives closer anyway. So, there's that."

"Okay." Mori said. "That it? You ready?"

"Hold on." Ballard said. "You need to know your role. You don't arrest or…"

"Captain, for Christ's… I know. We don't have much time. I get it."

"Alright, good. Just so you know…" he paused. "You think Joseph murdered those guys and made up that story?"

"I don't know. We'll find out together I guess." Or at least, he thought to himself, you'll be there when *I find out*.

"Yeah." Ballard said. "Ain't that something?"

"Let's go." Mori said, turning the window up again.

They got the station with time to spare, but not much. Mori could see it much better this time than when he'd arrived in town that first night (no blackout drill tonight, it seemed.) What he couldn't see was either Ballard and the squad car, (though he expected to arrive before him,) or any sign of Claypool. And he had no idea what the big man drove. There didn't seem to be many people on the train, at least by what he could see of the section illuminated up by the interior lights. A few cars. The relative grandeur of the station building and that they seemed to have daily rail service made Mori think someone must have once believed this area of Maine was going to become more of a busy hotbed than it was.

Trudy parked and Mori hopped out. "Stay here, Trudy." He said.

"What? What if you have to get on the train? It looks like they're about to leave."

"I know. Stay here. Please. Keep an eye out."

Trudy slapped the hood of the car and a bit of clumpy snow flew up and landed again. "What? Keep an eye out for what?"

"Trust me. Stay here. Once the train is gone, go home."

Trudy said "dammit." And then watched Mori buy a ticket at the station window and board, giving the Boston and Maine Minuteman a lucky pat with his gloved hand as entered, the porter waited to raise the step until he was inside.

He heard, "Oh, you again!" from one of the stewards in a square billed cap, though he didn't remember him from his trip up. Mori found himself once more in an empty train car. Rows of woven blue seats with blue leather headrests. "Hey," he asked, "Is anyone on the train yet?"

The steward nodded. "A few. Not so many yet. I think there are a couple in the dining car. A few others… We don't take on many until Rockland and of course, when we get to Portland, but…"

"Have you seen a couple of big guys? I'm talking real tall gents. One might've been in uniform? Town cop. The other an Indian, gray hair pulled back, probably."

"No. Haven't seen anyone like that."

"Would they have had to pass you to get on board?"

"Um, well, no. I just came up when I saw someone at the window. We don't punch tickets 'til..."

"Okay," Mori said, patting the steward's shoulder. "If you see either of those fellas would you let me know?"

"Sure thing."

Mori started down the aisle, checking even for a coat or a bag left to claim a seat but he saw none. He headed for the door to the next car. It was mirrored so he couldn't see in. Another coach car. A few people this time; three in fact. Mori looked them over but could tell right away none were Joseph. Two older men that look like salesmen and a priest. He proceeded to the next car. Through the door and into the lounge car. Cushier blue leather benches this time. A bar in the back, round with a padded exterior and a shellacked top of gleaming ebony. One man reading a newspaper – looked a bit like Adolphe Menjou, Mori thought, or was it just the moustache? The bartender gave him a nod and a stare. Mori returned the nod and pressed on. Next two cars were sleepers. He lingered. The train jerked, exhaled, came to life, began to roll. Still, nobody came out of any of the berth doors. He wandered to the back and opened the door to the last car. It was a glass domed observation car. This connection area sent a rush of wind and snow at him, unlike the other car's connections. Unlike the rest, which had the rubber accordion connection collar, the observation car has a metal gate hugged by it on either side. He went into the observation car. Empty. Dim light, swivel chairs, gleaming brass triple columned smoking stands. The railroad must be losing a fortune, Mori thought. The night sky would be quite a sight through the roof with the lights out. He wondered if he should head for the front and check the baggage car and the RPO. He went back through to the sleepers and paced down the aisles again. Still nothing; he doubled back.

In the second coach, where Adolphe Menjou's moustache doppelgänger sat, Captain Ballard came through the mirrored door. "We got him." He said.

"Joseph? You've got him? Who's 'we?'"

"Claypool and me. Well, Claypool got 'im, really. I just got on board as the train was pulling out. They're in the next car."

Ballard being helpful and reasonably non-combative was as jarring to Mori as the news that Joseph was so readily found. He followed the Captain back into the first coach car where Joseph was sitting in an aisle seat with Claypool hovering over him. It was the first time Mori had seen Claypool not in uniform. He wore no overcoat, just a thermal undershirt stretched by his swollen physique and denim work trousers with unlaced boots.

"You were in a hurry." Mori said.

"Wassat?" Claypool said.

"Nothing. Anyway, you found him. Where was he?"

"Hiding in the luggage car." Ballard said, answering for his officer. "Isn't that right?"

Claypool said it was but Joseph looked up like it was he who was being addressed. He nodded.

"Why didn't you just buy a ticket." Mori asked.

"Joseph here has been hopping train cars since they were all steam engines and…"

"Captain," Mori interrupted. "Perhaps let Joseph speak for himself."

Joseph looked from Mori to the Captain, then off into the distance. "No money."

"Where you headed with no money?"

"Find work."

Claypool started to pace, slowly. Ballard was sweating. "Joseph, now," Ballard began, "that story of yours, about the bloody foot… thing there, the naked Indian walk, well, now, one of them weren't even Indian."

Joseph was the only one sitting, a massive man dwarfing his seat. The rest of them hovered over him. "I didn't know the men." He said.

"And yet they all died with the same scars as you." Mori said, pointing at Joseph's boots. "A custom among Mohawks and non-Mohawks and now Mexicans, apparently. At least according to you…"

Joseph said nothing, looked off at the windows, where the occasional snow-laden branch could reflect enough moonlight to catch the eye.

"The *bleeding foot road,* you know, I was just thinking, what if you didn't walk it because you wanted to end it all but because someone was *making* you walk it? That's a hell of a thing, ain't it, Joseph? You think it would crack a man's mind if that happened to them and they lived to tell about it?"

265

Joseph didn't reply.

"You're a big fella, Joseph. A very big fella." Mori removed his overcoat and folded in neatly, laying it over one of the coach seats. He did the same with his jacket as he continued, "You worked at a few lumber camps in your time too, eh?"

Half a nod.

"That work makes a man strong, no question. Strong enough to overpower another guy. Shove him in a trunk or the bed of a truck or…"

"I didn't know the men." Joseph repeated in the same tone, low, removed. "And I don't work in lumber yards no more. You'll get your back broke, fingers under an axe… your toes smashed… and it's too dark out there, too many men in the bunkhouses. I don't like being cooped up. Closed in."

"Claustrophobic?" Mori asked. Astounded that Joseph had said so many words in a row.

Joseph shrugged. Stared.

"Think you'd try a little harder to stay out of my cells then, Joseph." Ballard said. Claypool tittered. Joseph looked weakly at Ballard, but only for a moment.

Mori asked a few more questions but if Joseph answered at all, it was just to restate that he didn't know the men. The steward came in and Mori handed him his ticket to get punched. He waved at the others with a nod. They'd flashed their badges to get aboard, apparently.

"When is the next stop?" Mori asked.

"Rockville." The Steward said. "About 45 minutes."

Mori nodded. "Local cop will give us all a ride back if we get off there?" he asked Ballard.

"I'm sure he can. Don't know the man, but I doubt we can all pile in a cab. If there is even one to be had. You must hate it here, Agent Mori. No cabs in the middle of the night. No city lights and no Japanese food. Whatever that might be... "

Mori looked from Claypool to Ballard. "Oh, it has its charms, this little Burg..."

Claypool smirked, which caused the muscles in his neck to jut out and his tiny mouth and eyes to recede even more. "You been driving around with a nice piece of charm for a week now, ain't you?"

"Get your head out of the gutter, Claypool."

"Well, Claypool, you watch Joseph. I'm going to get a beer or two from the lounge. Mori, you want to get something?"

"With you?"

"Sure. Come along. We can chat."

Mori would have killed for a coffee but drinking it with Ballard for company made him think it would turn his stomach.

"I'm fine."

"Oh, come on. You can tell me your theory. If you have one. I'm interested. You can tell me how I fucked this whole thing up. I'm sure you'll enjoy that. And you can get a little bit of something to warm you up. Hot toddy or something..."

"Coffee will be fine." He'd make it quick. He wanted to get off the train in a hurry.

267

"Fine, fine."

Mori looked at Claypool looming over Joseph. He was going to say to let him know if Joseph said anything but any speaking to Claypool seemed like activating a personality that always made Mori uncomfortable and a bit disgusted.

They made their way back to the lounge. Adolphe Menjou was gone. The bartender, a thickset man with his hair in a shaved crescent around his head like a monk, served Ballard a beer in a frosted mug and dribbled coffee from a silver percolator into a china cup, leaving it in front of Mori with a delicate clank. Mori left four quarters on the bar.

"Much obliged." Ballard said.

"Did Joseph come to you with his story? The…"

"Yeah. Well, sort of. I had to pick him up at Shorty's, that's this place out on Route 3, okay? Bartender called me. Said Joseph couldn't stand up even, so I fetched him. Threw him in the cell. I told him I had real things to do without babysitting him. I had dead men to deal with. He said he knew what they done. He knew why. I said bullshit. He passed out. But then when he came to and sobered up and I reminded him he said it was true. Then he showed me his bare feet like he did you. Told me it was a Mohawk custom. I believed him. Why not? He isn't one to tell tales. He keeps to himself and except for the drink he doesn't get out of line that I know of."

"You think he could kill someone? Like this, I mean. This sort of… cruelty."

"I would have said 'no' not long ago. But who knows? These Indians… you can't know them anyway. They see a white face and they zip up tighter than a drum. And they do have some damn odd rituals and whatnot. You guys have that too, don't you? The suicide thing? If you're dishonored or what have you? Don't you have to slice your guts open?"

Mori drinks his coffee a little faster, hoping it will help the headache he is fast developing. "I think you are referring to *hara-kiri*, ritual disembowelment, yes?"

"I guess. If you say so."

Mori had had about enough of chatting. "I'm going back. Try to talk to Joseph again." He swallowed the rest of the coffee.

"You haven't even told me your solution to the whole thing yet, Charlie Chan."

"You mean Mr. Moto." Mori said, without looking over his shoulder. "Idiot."

He grumbled all the way back, past the dining car, the sleepers, the second coach car and then the to the first.

Now empty.

Mori stayed still for a moment. Cartoonishly, he looked behind himself, as if they might be in the six feet between him and the door he'd just come back through. Then he went to the seat Joseph had been occupying. Except for a wet spot of melted snow on the carpet, there was no sign anyone had been there.

Mori began to head toward the baggage car when Claypool came crashing through. "Have you seen him?"

"Joseph?"

"Yeah, of course Joseph!"

"How have you lost him?"

"I turned my back for two seconds! I didn't even see what direction he went in!"

"Two seconds? How?"

"Look, the porter came back in. Said how ya doin? Then I remembered I wanted a smoke, so I called after him into the baggage car. I didn't even go in; I just stood in the doorway and bummed the smoke and turned around and... poof!"

"Jesus Christ." Mori said. "Well, he obviously didn't go past you that way, so he headed toward us, toward the back. Stay here in case he doubles back. I'll sweep the back of the train."

Mori headed back once more through the mirrored door, and felt the now familiar suction of wind and cold through the accordion rubber barriers outside the stretched fabric artificial hallway and even through the metal grate walkway over the car couplings. He was back in the second coach car. He knew there would be no sign of Joseph but hurried through anyway. Into the first sleeper. At the other end he saw Ballard coming about a third of the way up the aisle.

"Joseph has gone missing." Mori said.

"What?" Ballard looked pained.

"Surprised?"

Ballard shrugged. "Not... entirely. Claypool is kind of a dumbass."

"Let's go get the steward."

Claypool remained where he had been standing. In the exact spot Mori had left him. No movement or even sitting down. "We're going to have to check the sleepers." Mori said. "We'll need the steward."

"We can't just barge into…" Ballard began.

"Captain, that is why we are going to get the steward. Also, there is hardly anyone even on this train yet so we'll probably be disturbing around four people."

"Okay, okay. So, he didn't come my way, and, what… Claypool, what did you see, I mean… what happened?" Ballard asked.

"I was in the doorway bumming a smoke from the steward."

"Okay," Ballard said. "So, he must have gone that way." He pointed to the back of the train. Or…"

"Or?"

Ballard cocked his thumb like a hitchhiker and pointed sideways.

"You think," Mori said, "That Joseph Smith, a man who professed to us not just a fear of confined spaces but also the dark, a man pushing, what? 60 years old? More? You think he climbed out a window and is clinging to the frigid exterior of the Boston and Maine hoping to hop off at the next stop unnoticed?"

"No, I don't think…" Ballard said. "Especially when you put it like that. I'm just saying it is an idea. And Joseph is strong as an ox. Don't let age fool you."

The steward came through from the front again. He seemed to be checking on them, Mori thought, and was actually glad of it. "Sir," Mori said. "You know who these men are?"

"Um, yes, they've shown their badges."

"We're going to need access to the berths in the sleeper cars. The stowaway has slipped away, I'm afraid."

"Stowaway?"

"The man who was with this officer." Mori said, pointing at Claypool.

"The Indian?" The steward frowned thoughtfully. "Shouldn't be a problem. There's only a few occupied right now. Won't fill up 'til Portland. We can knock on those occupied. Ask the passengers if they've seen the fella."

"Thank you." Mori said. "Take Officer Claypool with you. Captain, would you accompany me please?"

"Uh, Mori," Ballard said, sidling up to Mori as he walked to the door to the back cars, "Why not take Claypool with you. I can look with the steward. Like I said, he's a real screw up…"

"Let him do the grunt work then. Come on."

"But, I…"

The walked back through once more. Mori stopped at the bar again in the lounge and asked if the bartender had a flashlight. He went below the bar and pulled out a green metal can with a light attached with a handle.

"Wow. Looks like this was from the last war." Mori said.

"It was." The bartender said.

Mori then asked for two shots of rye. He downed one and pushed the other to Ballard. He drank it quickly. Mori set two dollars on the bar and picked up the flashlight.

"I'll bring this right back." He said.

With Ballard trailing, Mori went to the section between the lounge and the observation car at the very rear of the train. Here he could see up into the night sky via the non-compatible coupling. He unfastened the canvas barrier with surprising ease and it retracted into the metal sheath that housed it. There was a chain on a clip hook and on the other side of that, a ladder climbing up the backside of the lounge car. He unclipped the barrier chain and let it fall. It clanked on the metal walkway and snaked off into the dark, swinging from the other eyehook that held it.

"Here goes nothing, eh?" He said to Ballard, who only watched from the doorway.

Nimbly, Mori swung over onto the ladder and, clicking the flashlight on, he slowly climbed up. It was only a few rungs but the wind and snow seemed not so much to blow at his face as attack it as he neared the top. He got to where he could see over and onto the roof and swung the light over, turning it one way and then the other. And though he knew there was a whole train ahead, he couldn't see halfway beyond the car he was currently scaling. The snow only reflected the light back in his face. He wished he hadn't forgotten to put back on his jacket and overcoat to shield him against the onslaught of the wind and blowing snow. The train clacked and swayed and he gripped the freezing metal of the ladder rung with his left hand as he pointed the flashlight this way and that, visibility still nearly nil.

"See anything?!" Ballard called up.

"Can't see a thing!" Mori said.

"You gonna go out on top? You'll have to, won't you?"

Mori looked again, pointing the light as best he could, searching for anything, anything at all.

Not a chance, Mori thought.

He climbed down, careful not to slip. He climbed back onto the metal walkway and pulled the chain back up, then clicked it back into place. He pulled the canvas barrier back into place as well.

"What if he's up there?" Ballard said.

"He's not."

"How can you be sure?"

"He'd be dead." Mori quickly passed the captain and went into the lounge, soaking up the heat from the radiator. There was a couple seated there now. They watched the odd pair briefly then went back to smoking and chatting.

"Well," Ballard said, hitching up his belt. "I guess it is pretty bad out there. Last place he'd wanna be. Not safe."

Mori nodded. "Indeed. Safety first. Speaking of which…" he pointed at the Captain's gun holster, which was unsnapped.

Ballard flipped the strap over his Colt .38 and snapped it in place.

"Let's keep looking." Mori said.

Which they did. For the next 20 minutes or so, until they pulled into Rockville, which was barely a station at all – just an old clapboard building. A few passengers got aboard as Mori caused a delay, asking the steward to pause while he checked the exterior, though it was all for naught. Mori knew to almost a certainty that no trace would be found.

Ballard and Claypool had ceased even the pretense of looking for Joseph. They stood on the bare Rockville platform smoking. The steward informed Mori the train had to depart. The engineer sounded the horn twice, long and loud.

"I'll go fetch the local cop." Ballard said, flicking the cigarette end toward the trees, like a weak firework in the night. "Get us a ride back to town."

"I'll come with." Claypool said, eyeballing Mori.

Mori stood still on the platform, not moving. He breathed hard and deliberately, timing the breaths, feeling the cold enter him, to be expelled again, warmed by him. He was calming down slowly, as he collected snow on his overcoat and hat brim.

"Hey." Came a voice from behind him.

It was Trudy. She emerged next to him on the platform as if an apparition from the very darkness.

"Where did you come from."

"I've *been* here waiting for you, what are you talking about?" She slapped his arm playfully, but with something like affection. She seemed... relieved. "I'm kidding. The Nash is a good car but it can't outrun a train. Though I tried."

"Why?"

"Need a ride back dontcha?"

"Trudy…"

"I… I don't know what to make of it. But I came because I saw… I saw Claypool and the Indian fellow… Joseph. I saw them sneak onto the train after you'd gotten on. I… what does that mean?"

Mori's head hurt still. Fatigue was getting the better of him. It had been a long day. He shook his head and snow flipped from the brim of his fedora in little clouds. He should arrest them all, sweat them for hours, drag out confessions… but where? On what authority? With what concrete evidence? As he stood there in the dark in the sickly ocher light of the station with the heavy snow-laden evergreens surrounding them and feeling like they might as well be concrete walls closing in, he began to feel for the first time that there was nothing he could do and there would be no resolution, no justice.

"I don't know." Mori said. Except he was pretty sure he *did* know. It was the truth that had been staring him in the face since he'd arrived that he simply didn't want to see.

"Oh." Trudy said.

Mori looked at his watch. Almost 10:30. "Let's go back." He said. "Sort it out in the morning."

They didn't bother to tell Ballard they'd left. Mori knew he wouldn't have waited anyway. Thankfully.

CHAPTER 22

February 5, 1943

Less than ten minutes after bidding goodbye to Trudy, receiving a sneer from the night manager, shimmying into pajamas, and collapsing face first onto the pillow, he was in bed and asleep. The room was far too cold but rather than get up to turn up the radiator he pulled the comforter up to his neck.

He wasn't sure how long he slept, but it wasn't long. Hours? Perhaps.

Even despite his exhaustion, Mori was able to detect the presence in his room, but not in time to do much of anything about it. He saw thru the darkness the black clad figure moved toward him, growing enormous as it approached in a flash, taking up his entire field of vision. A man, eyes ablaze, face hidden by a balaclava, the scent of tobacco and sweat swirling in the ferocity of movement. Mori blocked the swing of a small club (or maybe a blackjack) at his head, but the other enormous fist crashed into the side of his face. He was disoriented for a moment and a hand was on his throat. He pried at it, gnashed and scratched. With his fist he attempted to punch out, hoping to connect with something tender or vulnerable but no such luck. His legs were trapped beneath the heavy blanket and the weight of his attacker. He tried to hold off the hand with the club and to mount some kind of offense with the other hand but every time he let go of the hand on his throat, he started to have no oxygen to work with and reflexively it went back to keeping his lungs with anything at all to breathe and keeping his windpipe uncrushed. His attacker bore down, thrashing wildly with superior strength and size and landed the club at last on his head. Thankfully, Mori managed to roll away a little and it caught him on the meaty part of the back of his neck. It was still enough to daze him. His hands were rubbery and he couldn't defend himself any longer. The clubless hand smashed into his temple, then nose, temple again and he saw no more...

Until regaining something like consciousness in near darkness. He was cold. Beyond cold – he was freezing, quite literally. He knew he was naked, the thick pajamas he'd been wearing had been taken from him. It might have been his own shivering that awakened him. He began to get an idea of his surroundings by assessing the various discomforts. He knew the rigid circle beneath him was a spare tire and the general odor or gasoline and exhaust – he was in the trunk of a car. He touched his face – sticky and crusted with drying (perhaps freezing) blood. Everything ached. His head felt heavy, as if overstuffed with cotton and searing shots of pain every few seconds. He tried to focus but there was only pain. The car drove on over bad roads, skidded through snow as his attacker seemed in a hurry and not inclined to take care over the slick surface. Maybe there was a tire iron somewhere. He couldn't see and his arms didn't seem to obey the commands his brain was trying to send. He wished he'd said to hell with all this business and gone dancing with Trudy. Let the Caucasians stare at them. The car hit a bump and waves of pain shot through him from all directions. He thought he cried out with the pain. Frigid metal beneath him began to grate and burn his bare skin, or at least, he became unable to ignore it any longer.

He began to think of plans to fight off his attacker. The car was going somewhere – it would have to stop. He just needed time to pull himself together. If he could only get warm... Was there a tire iron? Flashlight? Anything at all? He thought his arm moved, fingers spidering over the surface behind him. When they touched his own skin, it felt like meat in the fridge. Which it was, he thought, almost laughing maniacally. His legs were pulled up to his midsection as much as he could manage. He started to think that maybe he could get into a more upright position and once the trunk opened, he could spring out, fight, get away. Maybe steal the car. My head must be clearing, he thought. This is a plan. The only plan I've got.

The drive seemed to take forever. Every bounce on the road sent a fresh wave of pain. Every nerve became like a live wire. His shivering became worse, unable to contain or control. He tried not to cry out when it seemed like the car ran over some hard ice or a rock – something large enough to jolt a tire anyway – but he did.

The car slowed and came to a stop. Mori readied himself. He tried to clear his head. He couldn't stop shaking. Get to a crouch, he told himself again. Focus your energy; what you've got left. He wondered if there would be a gun pointed in his face. It didn't matter. Getting shot was better than going out like this.

He heard boots crunching on snow. Car door slam. More crunching footfalls. The metal scrape of key in the trunk lock. He tried to tense himself. The trunk swung up.

His attacker was on him in a flash. Mori was grabbed by the back of the neck with one hand and his manhood with the other. He hadn't been able to get to a crouch, or to even stop shivering enough to swing a punch or jab an elbow. He was lifted with the ease an experienced butcher might have with a frozen sheep carcass, off the truck and into the freezer and the meat hook. He couldn't even see who was carrying him, though he hardly needed to. At that moment, it didn't matter. The blood – his blood – is still obscuring his vision. He was aware that the iron grip on his testicles was crushingly painful but couldn't bring his mind to make that pain a priority. His voice failed him when he tried to cry out. He knew he was outside, maybe someone was in earshot, though probably not, but he tried to shout and no sound came out. Mercifully, his attacker moved his hand around Mori's thigh to get a better grip. Mori could smell, he thought, salty air? Was his attacker going to throw him in the ocean?

And he was thrown; he felt the welcome release of the iron grip only to be followed shortly thereafter with the most unwelcome crack of his flesh against ground. A snapped rib? The pain was shocking. He landed not in the ocean, even on the frozen surface, but something hard, jagged... a rock. He couldn't manage to cushion his head from it either and once more he lost consciousness.

It was once more, he thought, his own violent shivering that brought Mori back to conscious. He was amazed, in as much as he could be, that he had awakened at all. He could see only blurs. He raised his hands to his eyes to get the blood out. Hands and face were both cold as the rocks beneath him. Any movement at all caused pain to shoot from what he figured was a cracked rib. Or ribs. Every movement seemed to slice at him, tearing flesh. He could feel shredding with every turn or slide, attempting to stand, which he hadn't yet managed. His feet were frozen and he could barely feel them except for a dull throb, but he tried to concentrate on them, to focus hard and direct energy there. To make them solid and heavy to support his frame as he attempted to stand. With some effort, he got up, legs shivering so that he could barely hold upright. The ribs discharged fresh agony.

He ran his forearms over his eyes again to clear them. Frozen blood chipped away and the remaining liquid blood streaked down his arms and immediately stuck, frozen in place. He was able to see finally, at least, not that there was much that he could. It took time but his eyes adjusted and most of the blood had been smeared away. He could see in front of him, a flat, frozen expanse of frozen ocean. It must be very cold indeed, he thought. Seawater froze at a lower temperature than freshwater. He almost laughed that his brain was using its capacity for facts like that. Still, he was glad it was working at all. Also, he knew it was many times over cold enough outside to freeze seawater.

He tried to take a step but his shivering was so bad that it renewed his fear that he might fall over. His jaw clattered, the literal chatter of teeth, he thought, trying and failing to make a joke to himself; create thoughts, for them, stay lucid, stay awake, alive. He turned to look over his shoulder. A desolate road with one set of tracks in the snow and a wall of dark forest behind it. He needed to get back to the highway.

Like it or not, he was going to be walking Joseph's bleeding foot road.

He wondered if his feet were bleeding at that moment; leaking out his heat and life. The wind picked up and whistled across his bare skin, cutting at every bit of flesh. He couldn't keep simply standing. He braved the step, almost fell but didn't, felt more slices of flesh. He looked down. He was right. Each movement *was* causing slashes. The rocks had clinging to them the remains of mollusk shells and the ground beneath had shards of shells that had broken loose from the frozen ground and must be walked over to get away. His feet would be properly bloodied even before he ever reached a road.

He knew that it was good that he was still shivering. To stop would mean systems were shutting down. He knew the shivering wouldn't last and time was not on his side. He didn't know how long he'd been in the trunk but it had seemed like forever. How far was he from help? He had no idea. There wasn't much moonlight. He made his way daintily over the rocks, away from the craggy shore and saw his feet land in the tracks of the car that had brought him. He didn't pause, just kept on, up a small incline and through a snowbank, where he sank up to his bare thighs. He held his hands over his nether regions as he shimmied free and emerged out onto the road. He looked one way, then the other. Saw nothing. Heard nothing. He decided to follow the tracks back the way they had come. He had no way of knowing what was the other way. He didn't have much time left. The thoughts were getting fuzzier. His tongue felt like a sponge, sucking up all the moisture left in his body, weighing a hundred pounds or so. He started to speed up, legs almost unbent at the knee. Make as much time as he could before he collapsed. He needed to be careful to stay upright though. One fall, and he might not get back up.

All he could do now was walk.

PART 3

CHAPTER 23

July 8, 1937, Los Angeles, California

Asahito Mori was skinny at 17, and taller than most of the *Nisei* he knew. Or their parents, for that matter. He felt he looked rather like a praying mantis, sometimes, as he had a habit (soon broken, with a conscious effort) of tenting his fingers in front of him as he listened to people talk. He found himself doing this on that hot breezy afternoon when his father passed away and he didn't know how to react. It had been a surprise... and yet not. He'd been laid up in the bed for a few days – and off and on for weeks; young Asahito kept wondering if he should fetch a doctor, even though his father kept telling him not to.

The last couple of years had been hard. Lung cancer. Hideki had continued working (no choice, really) until April of 1937 but the coughing fits and the weakness overcame him. He became winded after even a few steps. Asahito insisted the Pall Malls weren't helping and Hideki agreed to give them up – though mainly because he worried if he could even afford them anymore. It was foolish to burn up 15 cents a pack every day, he thought. Who had that kind of money?

I should have known, Asahito thought, as a mercifully cooling breeze fluttered the gauzy curtain on the window and then his simple cotton shirt. Tears started to trickle down his cheek, but held back from a real release. He checked his father's pulse again. Cold skin. He held his little finger under the nose… nothing. The bristles of Hideki's usually immaculately trimmed and waxed mustache brush him… feels like a brush or a garment… nothing human. Should have known, he thinks again… the way he had been talking the night before…

"Your mother was so beautiful." Hideki had said. "You remember?"

Asahito sat in the wicker chair next to his father's bed. He nodded. He felt bad about lying, especially about this. But his mother had died when he was barely four, and he had no picture of her in his mind; only from the few snapshots of her that his father had kept. One picture when she was a younger woman and she and Hideki were both still living in Hawaii. Another was of Hideki and Fujiko, his mother, standing outside a carnival in Los Angeles. Fujiko struggled to keep young Asahito, probably not even 2 years old, still in her arms as the photo was being snapped. But they were all smiling. And she *was* beautiful, he thought, even if he couldn't remember. This was how Hideki spoke of her now and then: fondly, of her beauty, her quiet calm. But the younger Mori couldn't remember.

But then Hideki spoke of the war. The war Asahito only knew about Hideki's part in from a few grudging comments here and there, and never at length. "The... chaos at Port Arthur." The older man said, searching for the right English word. "It was... very great. Much loss of life. Much..." he shook his head. Asahito sat up straight and listened, this sort of talk was rare.

Hideki smoothed his pencil thin mustache and replaced his hands in a fold over his midsection. He was covered by a thin sheet, it was too warm for anything else, over his linen pajamas. "We had to take the hills around it first – from the Russians. They didn't even have names. Just numbers. The captain would tell us to take the hill. Hill 204! We would shout *Banzai!* and take the hill... I'm not sure if that is the right number, honestly. They all had numbers. Hill 174. Hill 202... I... I can't even remember. It doesn't matter. Months of this..."

Asa knew his father had been a soldier in the Russo-Japanese War of 1905. He mentioned it now and then, but always changed the subject almost at once.

"I was your age." Hideki said, looking at him with watery eyes and a kind smile.

Asa nodded.

"I remember hearing the captain speaking with the general. I was back in the medical tent. We all wore the *tabi*..."

"The what?"

"Socks. These rough cotton socks with sandals made of straw. I had western boots but everyone wore... anyway, I stepped on a, a... *neirubōdo*..."

It was rare for Hideki to not pause and pronounce words in English. He was fastidious about it, even if it meant a halting, deliberate pattern of speech.

"Boards," Hideki said, "that the Russians laid down in the brush and mud. Nails pounded into them and sticking up to catch our feet. *Nail boards*. I stepped on one. Many of us did…"

Asa nodded again, listening intently.

"What was I saying?"

"Uh, the general said…"

"Yes, yes… casualties. They knew… how rough it would be. Ten thousand casualties would be acceptable, I heard him say, as they passed outside. Ten Thousand…" he shook his head. "We took the forts on the *Wantai* Mountains. Then we started to feel we were close. That Port Arthur would be ours. And it would be… after months of sliding down the mud on the side of the mountain. After many of us threw ourselves at the positions to cut wires for the men behind us, only to be mowed down by the heavy Russian guns… we couldn't bury the dead. Too many and we couldn't risk the exposure. They rotted there on the hillside. The smell was unbearable. Some fiend among us joked that it was yet another weapon against the Czar. The smell of our dead. It drifted up to the Russians in their forts. They would soak rags or blankets in camphor and hang them out on the walls of the embankments to cover the small of our dead."

"Jeez." Asa said.

"We were mad. All of us. Crazy. We were drunk on what they told us. The Emperor. The Nation. We were possessed. I couldn't stay there…"

The circumstances under which Hideki had left Japan were a mystery to Asa. When he asked his father, it was usually met with either an affirmation of America "to breathe free air in the new world!" or the romantic "how else would I have met your mother?" The war and having fought in it didn't usually – ever – come up.

"From what I have read, and what I hear on the radio," Hideki said. "It has gotten worse there. And it will soon follow me here."

Asa swallowed hard and realized he was holding his father's hand. He hadn't realized. Hideki coughed. He did that a lot lately, but through most of the story he was telling, he hadn't.

"There was an officer... I knew him a little. He was older, but our families knew each other. He was... crazed. He led a charge that failed. Back in camp he was... inconsolable. He screamed and pulled out his hair, pulled at his clothes... he drew out his dagger. He lost many men but he didn't cry for them. He cried for himself. Because he thought he had failed his Emperor. Our Emperor. He was going commit *seppuku* right there to atone. At least he said he was. I believe he would have... but we stopped him. We all grabbed at him, held him down, wrenched away his dagger. Held him until he promised to think it over. To come to his senses. To at least volunteer for another charge to prove his worth. This he did. We were all mad..."

Asa could only utter "Wow."

Hideki looked at him fiercely, "Asahito, you will have to fight in your life. You can't avoid it. But don't be fooled. Don't be tricked. I would tell you to only fight for what you believe is right – but they were. *We* were, all of us, I think. We didn't know any better. That's what you need to know. You need to be able to tell what is right on your own. To have good judgement. That is the key..."

Hideki closed his eyes and suppressed a cough. He folded his hands again over his stomach atop the sheet. The world beyond the fluttering curtain turned to purple and orange dusk. Sounds of the city in the distance blended into a calming harmony. His father became so still that Asa almost shook him gently, but he was interrupted when Hideki asked, "Do you think Mrs. Delgado has finished making the tamales she was making earlier? She said to come and get some but I feel a bit tired. Bring her some of the oranges we promised her when you go, okay?"

Asa smiled, nodded. "Okay, Pop." He said.

Not even twenty-four hours later, Asa was standing over his father, checking his pulse, checking his breath. That morning before work he had been thinking of ways to convince his father to see the doctor again. He sat back down in the wicker chair, clutching the cold hand and he wept, silently.

CHAPTER 24

February 5-8, 1943, Maine

Mori's shivering became more like the slower version of a palsied person's twinges; spasms he couldn't control, but they slowed, all that his tired muscles could manage. As he became less lucid, all he could think was if only he could cover himself, but he had nothing. Not so much as a cloth, and his skin was attacked by the freezing air, every last pore raked by the arctic winds. He mainly kept his hands over his crotch but the fingers were so cold and stone-like that they seemed to do more harm than good. His feet hit the ground, slabs of meat that felt to him like overfilled sacks, dragging on the icy road beneath him. Dead quiet around him. He could hear only the wind and buzzing in his head. Brain panic, he thought. Trying to figure out what to do. Take heat from extremities, move to the core. Die bit by bit, heart and brain last... He tried to speed up and keep upright. He had no idea how far he needed to go or how long it had been. He walked, trying to be quick, trying to stay upright.

His eyes had adjusted to the darkness but he had started to see spots, white starbursts like the traces after watching fireworks. He had only been able to hear his own feet shuffling and teeth chattering. Now he heard only buzzing like extreme tinnitus. He was finding bending his knees harder and harder. He propelled himself forward. Stiff legs scraping forward making him resemble some obscene puppet.

Icy white hell, is all he could think. He started to imagine someone, inexplicably, having thrown a big, heavy overcoat out of their car earlier and it would be waiting for him just up ahead. Or a basket of laundry tipped out the back of a truck... just ahead he can see clothes. Relief. Salvation... but there weren't any. He began to find breaths difficult. His lungs ached and felt like they were sodden, as if he were somehow drowning.

Then he fell.

He had been on a near run, stiff-legged, unable to corral his senses, unable to control his speed. He pitched forward, onto the snowy road, face and shoulder taking the brunt of the impact. He thought he started bleeding again probably as he thought he felt a tiny bit of warmth on his skin that disappeared as quickly as it was felt. He released a wheeze but again could not cry out, and his limbs didn't seem to be able to respond to the commands of his brain to rise once more. His shoulder began to ache and he imagined all his bones shattering, skull to little toe, and his skin simply peeling away and his muscles and organs spilling, frozen solid, as if onto a butcher's table. He couldn't see. He couldn't raise his arm to wipe at his eyes.

Time passed. Hours? Minutes? He couldn't tell.

He didn't *see* the light so much as feel a vague but distinct glow. He heard a voice, he thought. He began to imagine those movies where the angels were all loitering in togas and bent wire wings and glittery judgement books – hadn't he helped run the smoke machine on one of those? He couldn't remember. Maybe that was the one where Sofia had been an extra in the low-cut, billowy dress?

He felt hands on his body. Not warm but warmer than he was. What wasn't at this point? They tugged at him.

"Help me!" He heard through the tinnitus. "You've got to stand up! I can't lift you! Help me get you into the car! Oh, dear god!"

Trudy.

It was her voice, her hands, he knew now. And he obeyed, as best he could. He commanded his brain to command his legs and arms and – was partially successful. He managed to get to a kind of crouch. Then to lean in that position against the warm hood of the car, slide over across the passenger side headlight. He thought he may have grabbed the silver hood ornament at one point, probably leaving blood on the thing. At last she managed to usher him into the passenger side seat. It was warm – downright balmy. His skin began to prickle. The prickling got worse and started to feel like searing and stabbing. He reached out, trying to close the vents but couldn't seem to get his hands to work. Trudy did it for him then reached over into the back seat, saying "Omigod!" over and over.

She handed Mori a blanket – small, plaid, ideal for a picnic or grandma's legs if she was chilly in her chair but hardly enough to cover any more of him than his solar plexus and groin. He shivered and it fell off, Trudy had to keep pulling it back into place. His shivering intensified.

Trudy drove as fast as she dared. "We've got to get you to the hospital."

"No hospital." He croaked.

"What? Why?"

"Don't know… who to trust."

She didn't know what to say. What could she do?

"Get out of town." Mori said.

She thought briefly of taking him to the doctor in Bar Harbor that they had visited. Mori had seemed to get on well with him. But he wouldn't be there in the middle of the night and it was too far and she was beginning to wonder if Mori would make it. His skin was so discolored and blood-smeared. She started to panic a little… think Trudy! she chastised herself. She began to drive and to think. She needed to get him somewhere warm, that was all.

"I'm sorry." Mori said.

"What? Why?"

"Getting… blood all over… seats."

Trudy pulled the blanket over him again and he tried to clutch it with his hands, shivering and seemingly frozen into talon-like curls. She couldn't tell what was blood, black and purple skin, bruises… she didn't want to turn on the interior light to find out.

"Don't worry about it." She said, voice shaking.

He didn't remember, later on, much of the hours to follow. Trudy drove and he watched her, a tear on her face reflected the moonlight. He felt he should try, but couldn't summon the energy to reassure her. She stopped and he was alone with the car engine running, then, shortly thereafter, she ushered him into a dark room. It was warm but his skin was still ablaze with the extreme transition of temperatures. His body tried to go from frigid – to what seemed to be flames flashing across his torso and then to severe chills. At one point Trudy lowered him into a bathtub. Mori noticed a bare light bulb giving sickly, low-wattage light and mossy green tile. The bath was warm but he continued to shiver. Trudy washed him, taking care to not irritate the myriad cuts and bruises. She dabbed at his cheeks, eyes, and lacerated ear from the beating he'd taken. He had dozens of little cuts from the mollusk shells on his back, flanks, thighs... his feet were a mess. Inflamed but, Trudy noted, they hadn't blackened or sustained permanent damage. Or so it seemed. He needed a doctor but she listened to him. She was the only one he trusted. He was very conscious, *when* he was conscious, of his shivering, and chattering teeth. He thought they might shatter like a cartoon character biting down on a rock, only to fall out with a tinkling like broken glass.

Hours passed and Trudy fed him something hot. Pea soup with fat back, she'd said. "Warm you up." She was right. But only for a while.

He managed to sit up and saw Trudy nodding off in a chair that was a similar mossy green to the bathroom tile, if darker. "Where are we?"

"Motel." Trudy said, sitting up and rubbing sleep from her eyes. She was fully dressed, rumpled peacoat and all. Red circles under her eyes betrayed her exhaustion.

"How did we... get here."

"I drove out of town. We're in a town called Machias. We got here about dawn yesterday. Sorry I had to leave you in the car for a little bit yesterday. I could tell the check in lady was curious as to why a single girl was traveling before dawn and needed a room. I gave her some cock-and-bull story about my dear sainted granny being in the hospital and I was just too tired to go on. Then I had to give her another one when I didn't check out right away about how my papa told me to stay put, that granny was okay but they were going to come to me… I'm not sure she bought it."

"I can see how a naked and bloodied oriental-looking fella might further heighten her curiosity."

"Boy howdy."

"No longer naked, though, thanks." Mori said, looking down at the grey sweater he was wearing.

"That was my dad's. When he could fit into it. It was in a trunk in the attic so it's probably got a nice moth ball odor to it."

It did. And was itchy. But Mori thought that might have been his skin. He thanked her again anyway.

"You saved my life." Mori said. "Probably a couple of times. More. Hell… I…"

"You're welcome." Trudy said, smirking and yawning. "For the sweater. And the save."

"How did you…?"
"Know where you were? You got lucky…" she pulled her feet up under her and sighed. "I dropped you off and went home. My folks were having a fit! They read me the riot act. How late I was, how I was shirking my responsibility to the family… see, they were driving over to New Hampshire to visit

my grandparents for a week, right? And they wanted to give me the keys to the store and a list of stuff to do and all that and I was late so they bawled me out. I was not in the mood after the long day we had, you know? So, I drove around... okay, not around. I drove back to see you. I... I knew you were probably going to bed, and I wasn't even going to knock. Heck, what would that have looked like, me knocking on your door late at night after a fight with the parents... anyway, I pull in, turn off the lights and I'm just sitting there, you know, thinking. The parking lot is pretty well deserted and I see these two guys carrying out another guy. Drunk, I figure. Probably what they wanted people to think, if anyone saw. But they obviously didn't think they were being observed cuz they put the guy in the trunk. That guy was you, by the way. I guess you figured that out. I think you still had your clothes on at that point but it was dark and you were kinda far away..."

"Did you see the men?"

"Not at first. Didn't recognize the car either. But it was a Plymouth. Maine plates. License plate number 82-627. The driver got in and I didn't see him. But the other guy went back inside and he had to step under the light over the door and I saw him then. Guess who?"

"The hotel night manager." Mori said, slumping a bit. Beginning to tire.

Trudy tsked. "Yeah. That's the one. Jeez. And I wanted to do a big detective reveal."

"Sorry." Mori said.

She smiled and shrugged, yawning. "Yeah, so, I was starting to get a bad feeling about what I had just seen, obviously and the only thing I could think to do was follow."

"That was brave." Mori said. "Very brave."

"Or stupid. But... I knew it was you. Somehow. I mean, I was surprised they got the drop on you but, still... I knew."

Mori tried to think of something to say but only shivered a bit.

"So, I followed, like I said. Kept the lights off though. Didn't want to get spotted. Surprised I didn't run off the road a dozen times or so. He drove to the seashore..."

"Different road." Mori said. "Just for me."

"And I saw the car stop, from a distance, couldn't see what was happening though, then the car turned and headed back. I had to backtrack and duck into a side road I'd seen about a half mile back. When I saw the lights go by, I drove to the shore. Well, to you. You'd made it quite a way but..."

"Yeah, I know. I'd fallen down when you got there. Probably for the last time."

"You'd have got back up again. You've got more fight in you than just about anyone I've ever met."

"So do you, Trudy."

She smiled, and her head lolled tiredly on her chest. "Thanks."

"You looked beat."

"That's cuz I'm beat."

"Have you been sleeping in the chair?"

She nodded.

Mori nodded beside him in the bed. "Get in."

"I am not that kind of girl."

"The kind that needs sleep and warmth? Yes you are. Get in."

"At least buy me dinner."

"Any of that pea soup left?"

"Ugh. No thanks." But she climbed in, fully clothed, only kicking off her boots.

Back to back, they were both asleep again in minutes.

Mori had some kind of relapse. His shivering became worse. Trudy asked him if he was okay and he mumbled that he was but she wanted to get him to a hospital or get a doctor to visit. She tried to imagine the reaction of the town doctor walking in, little black bag dropping from his hand at what he saw… She wished she hadn't drawn the curtains closed quite so well. She couldn't tell what time of day it was – it couldn't be night, could it? She realized she was holding him. His shivers radiated through her body. She knew she'd cried a few times since she'd found him on that road – not loud wailing, just tears she barely noticed and couldn't contain. She hugged him tighter, hoping somehow to will away the shivering. She brushed away the black hair, drenched in sweat, from his forehead.

After the shivering and incoherence continued, Trudy slid out of the bed and paced around it, looking at the shivering figure under the thick woolen blanket. She went to him and pulled back the covers. "Ace." She said. "Trust me."

He nodded, though she wasn't sure he was paying close attention. She reached to his waist and pulled up the sweater over his head. His skin was clammy with sweat, yet cold. She then chastely rolled down the ancient pair of her dad's pajama trousers and tossed them on the floor. Silly to avert her eyes, she thought, considering what she'd seen already, but she thought she owed it to him to try. She replaced the covers over him and began to remove her own clothing. Dungarees, sweater, underthings... an unceremonious pile on the floor. She was cold instantly, and cast a glance to the radiator by the window, trying its damnedest to heat the room but not quite managing it. She felt she ought to feel self-conscious, unsettled, or perhaps even... guilty. But she didn't. She slid in behind him and wrapped her arms around him, pressing her bare flesh against his, pale bluish-white, goose-pimpled, battered, and torn. She pressed against him, as if willing herself to generate more body heat and transfer it, breasts, stomach, hips, legs. She rubbed his arm and chest with her free hand and curved her legs against the back of his. She pulled the blanket tightly to them.

He said, "Trudy..." as if to protest but didn't move.

They slept again for a short while. His shivering reduced. Their bodies were still entangled, they'd turned to face each other and their foreheads touched delicately now. Mori woke up with Trudy's arms tucked under his, her legs crisscrossed with his. He saw a tiny spot of blood on her breast, probably from one of the mollusk shell cuts on his back, he thought. He took his thumb and wiped it away. She watched as he rubbed thumb and forefinger together. His eyes met hers and she didn't look away. Mori thought he should speak but couldn't find words.

Trudy smiled a little. "You're, uh, poking me."

He looked down.

"In the leg." Trudy said. "Guess we've got your blood pumping now."

Before he could reply she kissed him ardently on the mouth, leaning in, nibbling his lips. She held his face in her warm hands, pulling him to her with hunger and longing. He kissed her back, overcoming his trepidation. She moved her hands down past his waist and held him in her hands, feeling his eagerness. She guided him to her and whimpered a little when he was inside at last. They rocked slowly and with only slight movements, staying beneath the covers, slowly achieving a rhythm, holding it awhile, murmuring and sighing with pleasure and, after a bit and resting in almost the same position, falling off to sleep again.

When she awoke, he was finishing dressing, except for his winter outer clothes and hat. He had rummaged through the quickly packed bag of things she'd brought from her parents' attic: a denim shirt beneath the itchy sweater, heavy canvass trousers, too tight ancient boots and wool socks. He smiled at her. "This'll do for now. Can't wait to get back and get my own things on. Although you'll have to tell your dad how grateful I was for the loaners."

"Don't think I'll mention it, actually." Trudy said. She sat up in bed, pulling the blankets snugly to her collarbone. She looked radiant, he thought, even in the dim light. Pink-cheeked, clever, his savior… he could never repay her. "Or you can tell him at the wedding."

"Wedding?"

"Ours, silly. I mean, we gotta now."

He smirked.

"What?"

"*What* what?"

She smirked back. "Didn't I have your leg pulled for a second?"

"Maybe a second." Mori said.

"So, getting dressed, I see… Are you okay?"

"Much better." He said, truthfully enough.

"What are you planning to do?"

"Get all this out in the open. Finish what I started."

"But it's the middle of the night." Trudy said. "Isn't it?"

He nodded. "It is."

"Are you going to, I dunno, call in the cavalry?"

"I think the cavalry wouldn't come."

"Are you… up for that? Are you well enough?"

He thought. Nodded. "Yes." It could be true. It didn't feel as true as he wished it did. His head started to hurt.

"Guess I'd better get dressed too then." Trudy said.

CHAPTER 25

February 8, 1943

"Wait here." Mori said. "I won't be long."

"Are you sure it's safe?" Trudy asked. "I mean, this is... where they got you."

Trudy was idling the engine in the hotel parking lot of Mori's hotel. "Yeah, it'll be fine."

"I asked the Judge to say that you were not to be disturbed. That's all. I didn't want to alarm him or give away whatever you might be doing."

"Clever as always, Trudy. You did just the right thing." He wanted to lean in and kiss her but now that they were fully clothed, back in the car, and he wasn't shivering uncontrollably, it seemed no longer an option.

"Thanks." She said, smiled.

It was a great smile, he thought. He wished he'd met her in another time and place. He wished that he could talk it out with her and see where they might stand – but he couldn't. Even with everything else, his race and hers, the small town, and the fact that he was headed to the first recruiting station he saw when he was done with this town, the switch inside of him that went cold and dead when he was angry enough was now flipped on. She would see that part and not care for it one bit, he thought. He got out of the car and headed for the hotel before she could finish telling him to be careful.

Of course, it was cold, but he had a new appreciation for it now – and a loathing. But right then, he barely even felt it – his blood was more than hot enough. He made fresh tracks across the new powder and up onto the porch. He swung quickly through the heavy double doors and across the lobby, deserted as usual. He threw a glance over at the bar and saw nobody. The Night Manager emerged from behind his curtain with some papers in hand, smoothing the lapel of his green jacket. A sinister grin curled Mori's lip when he saw it wasn't the man's night off.

Lucky me, he thought.

The Night Manager saw him and couldn't contain his surprise. He dropped the papers he had been holding and only was able to mouth something like "What are… but…" before Mori leapt the counter and delivered a two footed kick into the man's gut, sending him flying back through the curtain. The man landed in a chair sideways, falling over the wooden arm of it. Mori was on him in a flash, bashing his fists against his head. He blackened both eyes and broke his nose with a satisfying crunch.

The Night Manager screamed and Mori backhanded him, causing the man to fall over a box and onto the floor. His voice was lost now and he could only croak, "Stop!"

Mori did stop. He let the man get to his hands and knees. "You let him into my room, yes?"

The Night Manager paused and wiped away a tendril of blood and mucus dangling from his nose. He nodded.

"With this key right here." Mori said, and reached up to the board on the wall where spare keys were kept, dangling from little brass hooks, each with a little brass plate for each room number. He snatched and pocketed the one to his own. "Afraid I'll have to borrow this one. Had to leave my room so abruptly last time I think I left mine behind…"

The Night Manager remained on all fours. His combover was flapping like a ship's flag. Danger, perhaps, or surrender.

"Claypool, that is, right? Officer Claypool."

The Night Manager nodded again, sitting back on his haunches.

"Say it." Mori said.

"Yeah, it was Claypool. I let him in with the spare key."

Mori went over and lifted him into the chair. The man's head lolled a bit and his bulbous nose continued to leak dark red. He removed the man's tie, carefully undoing the shoddy Windsor and held it draped over his right hand. "Why would you do a thing like that?"

"Fuck you." The Night Manager mumbled.

"Say again?"

"*Because fuck you, you goddam Jap fairy!*" the man screeched, spraying Trudy's father's sweater with nasal blood and spit.

Mori didn't bother to respond. He jammed the man's tie around his mouth and tied it tightly at the back. The Night Manager struggled but remained seated and Mori came to the front of the chair, wound up, and delivered a knockout blow to the man's temple. He was out. Mori checked the pulse just to make sure. Alive. He hunted around and found some lengths of velvety cord, probably used for tying curtains, and secured the man to the chair. He was about to leave, then turned and looked at the unconscious Night Manager. Then he put his foot on the arm of the chair and kicked it over, tipping the chair and the unconscious man sideways.

He hopped back over the counter into a still empty lobby and proceeded up to his room. He decided to be as quick as he could and not leave Trudy waiting but also – he was impatient. He didn't know how the rest of the night was going to go but he was eager to get on with it. He shed Trudy's Dad's tatty old things and took a look at himself in the dim light over the bathroom mirror. Cuts and bruises. Nothing permanent. He pinched the skin on his chest but it felt normal. Maybe a little tougher, a little less sensitive. Some aches and tingles on the outside, a deeper pain in his muscles... he snapped to attention. There was no time for this. He put on his dark wool suit and matching waistcoat, striped shirt, azure and brown checked tie and even a pocket square. Even if he had wanted to dress a little more appropriately for knocking heads, he didn't really have anything else. Before he put on his socks and boots, he sat and crossed his leg onto his other knee. He examined the underside. Not shredded to bits, no blackened nails.... Still seemed red though. Spongey. They hurt, but they wouldn't for long.

He buckled his boots, whirled swiftly into his overcoat, and secured his hat. Time to go.

Mori asked Trudy to drive him to her family's hardware store. He had such a look of determination that she decided against any of the usual small talk. "I'll pay for anything I need to, um, borrow." He said. He wasn't sure how he could at this point. He'd run through just about all of his petty cash. Might get something for selling his overcoat and boots when he left, he supposed.

She let him into the store and went to turn on the lights but Mori waved her off. In the sparse light he went to the sporting goods corner and retrieved two Winchester 12-gauge pump action shotguns and two boxes of shells. He told Trudy to stay put and lock up and walked off into the darkness with a flutter of snow left spinning in his coattails.

He walked with the shotguns hanging from the crook of each arm to Falkenham's house. There was a light on inside. Mori tapped the tip of the barrel on the door and waited. He saw movement at the curtain to his left and a fraction of Falkenham's plain face. "Whatya want?" he said, nervousness in his voice.

"Come on out, Lou. I'm not gonna shoot you."

There was a pause while, Mori supposed, the ex-cop debated his veracity. Personally, Mori thought to himself, he would have aired on the side of caution, but Falkenham opened the door a crack, peeking out from behind the door with eyes on the shotguns. "What do you want? Do you know what time it is? My folks are asleep and…"

Mori leaned one of the shotguns on the door jamb and took a box of shells from his pocket, setting them next to it. "I've come to arm you, Lou. I could use a hand."

"A hand? You're nuts. What are you planning to do?"

"Nothing at all. If everyone acts right. This is just for persuasion." He said, hoisting the other shotgun. "That is, as I say, if everyone acts right."

Falkenham looked at the gun, then at Mori, then did it again. But he didn't pick it up.

"I wish I had time to see you wrestle your way out of this moral quandary, Lou. I do. But I feel a little pressed for time." He started walking away, off the porch and back the way he'd come. Falkenham watched as Mori loaded a shell into the breech, pulled the action, then began loading five more shells into the magazine, pushing them home with his thumb. He watched Mori disappear again back into the night like an apparition, only he'd left the gun and shells to prove he'd been real.

There was no light on at the police station but Mori had a feeling he'd find someone there. This town is great, mused Mori, you can walk around for a good while with a loaded shotgun and even if there was someone around, they probably wouldn't say anything – try that in LA and see where you end up…

Mori tried the door handle and found it unlocked. He walked in, the long barrel of the Winchester preceding him. He felt he clearly wasn't alone but there was only a small light from the bathroom on the far wall and a strange sound…

Snoring.

Mori saw a figure asleep at a desk – it was Ballard. There were a few empty bottles in front of him – beer bottles by the look of them. He still hadn't raised the shotgun to attention or even clicked off the safety. Still, he poked Ballard with the business end and the Captain stirred.

"Who... who the hell?" he struggled to say.

Mori pulled the little cord on the desk lamp.

Ballard made a noise, an exhale, a resignation, almost a laugh. "Got you good, didn't he?" he said, pointing to Mori's face.

"Yeah, he got me alright."

Ballard starting shaking bottles, all empty. He went in the desk drawer, slowly, trying to appear innocent for Mori, and pulled out a flask, not a weapon. He swigged and suddenly, as if realizing his position, became agitated and nervous. His face was sweaty and pale gray. "I knew you'd be back..."

"Did you?"

Ballard started to talk then paused. "I have no need to unburden myself, Mori, if that's what you want. You can try to prove whatever you think you can with your FBI buddies but..." he trailed off.

Unburden, incriminate... whatever you want to call it, Mori thought. He knew Ballard was on to something – he'd need more than he had. And he was out of time. So, it was a confession he needed. Could he scare Ballard into it?

"Do I look like I came here to talk?" Mori asked, popping the safety off and sliding the action on the shotgun loudly.

"You ain't gonna shoot."

"No?"

309

"Knock it off."

Mori leveled the gun at Ballard's chest. Then took aim, moving it up so he was looking right down the barrel at him, right in the eyes.

"You cocked that thing, you know. Put it down. You ain't gonna shoot. It might go off by accident. You ain't gonna... I know a straight arrow when I see one. You ain't..."

"I guess the straight arrow froze and got broke. Any idea how that happened?" Mori choked up on the shotgun, settling it into his shoulder comfortably.

"You know that wasn't me!" worry crept into his voice.

"Do I?"

"Claypool! You know it was Claypool roughed you up!"

"Roughed up? That's a funny way of describing attempted murder."

Ballard took another swig of courage. "It was all Joe's fault."

"Joseph Smith? Where is he now?"

Ballard rubbed his hand through his hair, seemed about to pull it out, he grimaced. "I liked him, actually. Joseph, I mean. He was a drunk Indian like the rest of them but he was alright." Ballard swigged again. Mori could smell the cheap hooch. Whiskey aged in a gas can, by the smell of it. Mori noted the past tense.

Ballard continued. "We had a few drinks and Joe told me this story about how he got rousted by some boys years ago and chucked out in the snow buck naked. I was arresting him, see, and we had a few and chatted and it just stuck in my head, this thing that happened to Joe. But that was before Moody…"

"Winfred Moody. The first one."

"Yeah." Ballard confirmed, taking a pull on the flask. "The first. Moody, he had a mouth on him, boy, and he…" Ballard gave an angry smirk and he balled up his fist as if pretending a punch at the dead man. "He got my dander up one night when we was throwing him out of this bar out on the county road… he was a son of a bitch with a few fire waters inside him, let me tell you…"

He paused, as if waiting for Mori to ask just how much of a son of a bitch, of if he realized he was spilling his guts, but Mori didn't reply, and he seemed like he was on a roll. "I didn't want to drag him all the way back to the station, and he'd just, hoo-boy! He just pissed me off…"

"How did he do that?"

Ballard got a sort of faraway look in his eyes. "I think it was right after Pearl Harbor. I think I was just pissed at the world. Mad at the goddam Japs…" he pointed as Mori.

Ballard stiffened. "Funny thing though – I don't rightly recall. Don't matter. He had a mouth. It was something like: I had no right; I didn't roust the white drunks. I didn't need to pull the pistol… all that bullshit. He kept calling me officer instead of captain, you know, but then he'd say 'officer' like it was a dirty word… so…"

"So?"

"So, I told him to strip off and get out in the snow. I guess Joseph's dumb story got stuck in my head. Just pulled right over after driving way the hell out…" Ballard started to sound

311

agitated. "And *goddam Claypool* thinks this is the funniest damn thing he's ever seen. He's got a look on his face like... I don't even know."

By now, Mori had lowered the shotgun and replaced the safety. He saw the barrel twitch as he had a shiver sent through his body.

"So, we drive off and leave him, I'm cursing him. Claypool is laughing. We pull over and I say I'm gonna give him some time to think it over and let him freeze his pecker off. But I fell asleep, you know..."

"You'd been drinking." Mori said, matter-of-factly.

Ballard looked at him sharply, but confessed. "Yeah. Some. I wake up and it's almost light. Snowing like crazy. Claypool is gone..."

"Gone?!"

"Yeah, I wake up and he's gone."

"Where?"

"He said he didn't want to disturb me. So, he let me sleep. I yelled at him, that we had to go back and pick up Moody and how the hell... but he just got this blank look... smiled. He's simple. He's – a little out there. *Way* out there..."

"Do you think he went back to get a glimpse of Moody... dying?"

"I... I don't know."

Mori didn't either. Certainly, the fact that he himself was still alive seemed to indicate that perhaps he just abandoned his victims... but he wasn't sure. At any rate, he was glad he hadn't been watching when Trudy picked him up.

"Did you hide Moody's clothes? Did Claypool hide them? Destroy them? Keep them? Leave them?"

"I mentioned it a couple of times. He just said he handled it. I don't know."

"The next one, a few weeks later, you have an alibi. Airtight. You were acting as driver to Judge Norris. I don't see you coming back here to send another Indian down the bleeding foot road... quite a story that, by the way. You cook that up?"

Ballard nodded. "I thought about them stories of Eskimos sending their old ones out on the ice flow when they can't take care of them anymore. Had Joseph swear to it. He looked at me funny but I think he knew. Wasn't hard to get him to go along. Life can be tough for a guy like that in a town like this..."

With a man like you as the law, Mori thought.

"What about the Mohawk words? The ones Joseph used? Fake?"

"Search me." Ballard threw his hands up. "Actual Mohawk words, I daresay, but that was a little flourish Joseph threw in on his own. For you. He's clever... was clever."

"And I figure," Ballard continued, "he was looking to skip out when he made enough scratch. In the meantime, he could... say what I told him."

"The next one," Mori said. "Robert Curette. Claypool did him in solo, yes?"

Ballard nodded.

"And what did you say when you found out?"

"Well, I bawl him out, you know, what the hell happened? I ask. He says he had another uppity Indian needed a lesson. I say, a lesson ain't dead! You don't learn lessons dead. How are we gonna explain it? He doesn't know. Doesn't care. Doesn't say. Just leaves it up to me. He knows he's got me. Nothing I can do. Not without giving myself up too…"

After a pause, Ballard looks up at him. "How long did you suspect?"

"From the minute I heard what had happened. Then in a real way the first time we exchanged even a word. I'll be honest though, I tripped myself up for a long time because I didn't want to believe it. I wanted desperately for it not to be true… I wanted you to be good cops."

Mori thought Ballard was about to protest but instead he took a slug from the flask. "You're the problem."

"Me? I just got here."

"People like you. Japs. Negroes. Hell, you caught *a Mexican* up here. How the hell does a wetback son-of-a-bitch get all the way from down your way to up here. Hell, I left Tennessee to get away from the damn ni…"

"Yeah, and you thought he looked like just another Indian so you killed…"

"I didn't kill nobody, goddamit!" Ballard got up on his hind legs and the rolling chair beneath him slid back. "That was Claypool, I told you already!"

Mori leveled the Winchester at Ballard's gut again but kept the safety on. "Why don't you, uh, go back to taking it easy, Captain."

Ballard pulled the chair back and hunched over the desk once more. "All I'm saying is you all come here and…"

"Yeah, I know this story. Slant-eyes, Japs, Negroes, Mexicans, they came to your lily-white community and messed it all up somehow, blah blah blah, of course that the Indians you and Claypool killed had had family here about 1000 years before your white trash family darkened these shores doesn't seem important to you."

"I didn't kill nobody." Ballard said, pathetically sounding this time. "It was an accident. I fell asleep."

"Alright, just tell me the rest. This year. What happened?"

Ballard shook his head. "I can't kill anyone… I just… couldn't, so…"

"Couldn't? You were trying to get me out on the roof of that train and shoot me, weren't you, Captain? Left your holster strap off even after I came back down. How many more steps would I have to have taken?"

"Claypool was supposed to go with you and take care of you." Ballard said, almost whispering. You insisted he go with the porter. We were rushing and getting it all fucked up, trying to get to the train… I don't know why we didn't just say Joseph changed his mind or something and he wasn't on it… goddamit. I… I… couldn't kill anyone. I… that's why I didn't enlist. I didn't age out. I just… couldn't."

Mori wanted a confession but this was crossing into priest territory. "That isn't why. You're a real tough guy when you've got the upper hand… and a coward. Like most who're like that. But I believe you when you say you wouldn't kill Moody on purpose. That's why I'm still listening and not shooting. But you did create a monster, didn't you? Okay, that's not fair. You gave the monster an example, a direction to point his terror at. And gave him an opportunity to do what he wanted to without consequences. I mean, you couldn't report him even if you wanted to. Even if the deaths of those men meant a damn thing to you… a policeman. Now, this year: what happened?"

"What happened?" Ballard looked puzzled. "He started again. I thought he was done. I mean, I hollered at him, tore him a new one… last year, that is. And he didn't do it again. I figured he was just, I don't know, touched a little and, he got it out of his system. Hell, we didn't even mention it and things went back to normal. Then the city hired Falkenham and I didn't even think about telling Claypool to keep quiet cuz he didn't talk about it and I kinda… forgot."

"Forgot?"

Ballard shrugged, drank.

"Don't drain that thing. Stay sober enough to talk."

"Yessir Agent Mister Moto."

Mori almost turned the Winchester around and gave him a crack in the ribs but thought better of it. He walked to the door, which he'd left cracked. "How much of that you hear?"

Falkenham was standing there holding the other Winchester pointed at the ground in his right hand. "Most."

"You followed quick. Good. Does it square with what you know?"

"Yeah. It makes sense. Claypool as much as confessed a couple of times anyway. I think he wanted to tell someone."

"Wanna come in out of the cold?" Mori asked.

Falkenham looked at the building like it was a dark temple he'd been cast out of. He shook his head. "Nah. I'm fine out here."

Mori nodded and went back to Ballard, whom he'd been keeping an eye on lest he reach for a hidden weapon concealed on him or fished around in a drawer for one. He didn't move though. Just sat at the desk hunched over.

"That Lou?"

Mori nodded.

"Ha. The Kraut and the Jap. Figures. Oh, don't get me wrong. I got a little Kraut in me, I think. Grandmother on my mother's side was a Schmidt."

"Figures? Funny. You sound more like you'd fit in in Germany right now than you do here."

Ballard found this amusing. "It's a white man's country, Mori. You don't get it cuz as much as you want to sound like an American, dress like one, grease your hair back like a swell… you'll never be an American. You don't understand and you can't…"

"I don't understand?" Mori shook his head. "You think this country is blood and soil. You think because your ancestors came here a few generations before mine… maybe… and that you look like most of the other people here that god himself prepared this place just for Caucasians like you…"

"Well, he did…"

"You're the one who doesn't goddam get it." Mori said. "You're a fair-weather fan of this country. Four men were murdered here because they weren't white. Five! Christ, I forgot your friend Joseph. Murdered by people who were sworn to protect them. I have seen people that looked like me bussed into a camp behind barbed wire because they were considered a threat even though most of them were born here and don't know any other country, and don't want to." Mori drew closer and pushed the barrel of the Winchester into the center of Ballard's chest. "And when I get done here, cleaning up the home front from criminals like yourself, preserving law and goddam order, I'm going to volunteer to ship out to god knows where and probably get my head blown off while you rot in a jail cell thinking about how you couldn't go to war cuz you're a damn chickenshit! Now tell me another one about who gets what!"

Ballard smirked, sweat, drank, but said nothing.

"Unless they hang you." Mori said. "They still hang people in Maine, don't they? Or is it the chair?"

The phone rang.

With the barrel of the shotgun, Mori gestured toward the phone, to indicate to Ballard to pick it up. He identified himself and then listened, after a minute, he showed a look of both fear and... excitement? He said nothing and then hung up.

"Who was it?"

"Claypool." Ballard said, after a pause. "He wants to talk. Says we should meet him."

"Where?"

"He said to come right over. The hardware store."

Trudy. Shit.

Mori flipped the safety off again. "On your feet."

CHAPTER 26

"Howdy Lou!" Ballard said, putting on his cap with the ear flaps as they went outside. "How's tricks?"

"Cover him." Mori said, and took the lead on the short walk to the town common.

It was late and so the little bandstand was deserted, just like all the stores around the common. The ice rink would need shoveling in the early morning before the skaters arrived. There was almost no light except that reflected by the moon. There didn't seem to be any streetlights – another blackout drill? The three of them trudged through the snow, two of them pointing weapons.

When they got close enough, Mori could see the light from inside reflecting the splintered wood of the door, which had been kicked in. Mori approached carefully, mindful of an ambush, but he was impatient for Trudy's sake. Ballard started to say something but Falkenham jabbed him with the barrel end and told him, "Shut it!"

Mori pushed the door inward with the toe of his boot. He looked around but didn't see anything. There was a single light on in a conical hanging lamp overhead.

"Come on in!" It was Claypool's voice. He sounded eager but almost amused.

Mori edged inward, following the voice. Falkenham prodded the Captain in a few steps behind. They were in the open section of the store, paint and brushes on one side, tilted vats of nails and other fasteners and small hand tools on the other. Wooden barrels of sale items running down the middle. Claypool leaned on one of these, his considerable bicep wrapped like an overstuffed anaconda around Trudy's throat. She couldn't spare the oxygen to look worried, she could only struggle for breath, her cheeks a worrying red color. Her eyes were bloodshot and veins were visible from where Mori stood. Mori could see claw marks all over Claypool's arm, from Trudy's nails, no doubt, but now she only held on, as if willing his arm away.

"Alright, Claypool." Mori said, taking aim. "Let her go, for crissakes. This isn't going to do any good. You're done. This is all over. Ballard talked."

Claypool found this amusing. His little mouth puckered into an obscene little smile. "I could squeeze just a little bit more and that would be that." He said. "But if you put the gun down right now…" he stopped. Making no promises. Just the promise of a promise.

"You can't do it." Mori said, flatly. He wasn't sure what he meant. That Claypool physically couldn't commit the act? Mentally couldn't? He knew both of those things weren't true. Was he trying to persuade? Pleading with him not to?

"Can't?" Claypool was incredulous. "I think I might be able to snap her neck even. So, I'm dead sure I could choke her out. Hell, she's close now." He chuckled about this and lifted Trudy to her toes. She made a ghastly coughing noise and saliva hurtled from her nose and mouth.

"I mean that isn't how you do it." Mori said. "You strip them naked and let them freeze. I'm not sure you even watch."

Claypool opened his mouth and almost seemed like he was about to explain his entire method and psychosis but then closed it and just smirked again. "I can take care of trash that way or this. No matter to me."

"Then what, genius?" Mori said, still looking down the barrel of the Winchester. "You gonna kill everyone here?"

"I don't know." Claypool shrugged a little, as if mulling it over. "Don't seem that hard really. People just disappear all the time. People say they care but they don't, really. They're just glad it isn't them. You and this one end up in a hole in the woods and it gets around that you ran off together like lovebirds and nobody hears from you again. Who's gonna look? Her family? Disgraced cuz she ran off with the Jap phony fed. They may not want to believe it but they will. Captain Ballard knows they will. And Lou… well, Lou has reason enough to make everyone believe it. He's got family in town he don't want to end up… well, in a pickle. Or he himself. Lou tries to be a straight arrow too, Mori. Like you. But he's got a rubber spine."

"Hell with you!" Falkenham hissed. But Mori noticed his grip on the Winchester wasn't as firm as it had been. Ballard stood near him, a wild sort of looking creeping into his eyes as he tried to sober up enough to find his nerve.

"Lou, you're a friend. Really." Claypool said. This kindly-voiced reassurance seemed all the more profane as he choked Trudy nearly to unconsciousness. "Nothing will happen to you or your family. This ain't the business of outsiders anyway. Go ahead and put it down. Or just hand it to the Captain."

Falkenham's feet began to shuffle but he didn't lower the Winchester.

Mori had about a thousand thoughts ping-ponging through his head. He wondered if he could get a shot off and miss Trudy, Claypool was a big target and Trudy a small human shield after all, but he couldn't chance how much the shot pellets would scatter. He knew Ballard was sobering to be coordinated enough to make a move; that Falkenham was losing nerve enough to be duped or even turned, and Trudy was running short of time. He wondered what Ballard meant to Claypool. Anything more than a partner in crime? Certainly not a father figure. Didn't matter. He'd have to hope that what he was thinking would be, if nothing else, just distracting enough.

And, if nothing else, it would eliminate one threat.

"Trudy!" Mori said loudly. "Look at me!"

She couldn't move her head, in the vice that was the crook of Claypool's arm, but circled her bloodshot eye to his face.

He didn't say anything but gave her a pleading look and a little nod. Her eyebrow flicked quizzically.

Mori turned away from Claypool and Trudy and to the Captain, whose face was blank, not registering the turn of events, just about ten feet away. Without wasting a second, he pumped the action, lowered the Winchester, and pulled the trigger, kneecapping Ballard. The Captain's right leg swept out from under him and he fell forward on his face, screaming in agony. The loudness of the shot was as shocking as the Captain's screaming and seemed to echo. Mori didn't hesitate to turn the gun back to Claypool, pumping the action again. Trudy had used the distraction to kick backwards against Claypool's shin, driving her booted heel in hard. It had caused him to loosen his grip just enough that Trudy could lean away, creating a space for Mori to aim. He fired.

He'd been too aware of Trudy and afraid to shoot her and aimed high and left. Still, Claypool was struck, (on the cheek only, Mori thought, and barely a scratch) and his grip was undone and he only retained a hold on Trudy by clutching at her sweater, pulling her back to him. The struggling forbade a clean shot. Instead, Mori charged, butt of the Winchester as bayonet and caught Claypool in the jaw. Not squarely, but enough to cause him fall over backwards. Still, he retained his grip on Trudy's sweater. She at long last could take full breaths and gulped them in greedily but had to do so as Claypool was pulling her to the floor on top of him. The big man regained his footing in a heartbeat and shoved Trudy toward Mori like a human battering ram, and Mori had to raise the Winchester to avoid accidently discharging it in Trudy's gut. Claypool grabbed at the gun and started to wrestle it from Mori, the latter's finger still in the trigger guard, pressure applied, fired at the ceiling, a rain of dust, paint and plaster. Claypool nearly had the Winchester pried away when Trudy recovered and jumped on his back like she was a child getting a piggyback ride. Mori tried to hug the Winchester close and ended up getting bearhugged by Claypool and pummeled with kidney punches. Trudy grabbed his bicep but got swatted away, knocking over a stack of paint cans on a shelf behind her.

It was then that Falkenham recovered his senses enough to charge the melee and run shoulder first into Claypool, knocking him to the side, but not really phasing the much larger man. Trudy jumped once again on Claypool's back and the three of them wrestled the behemoth to the ground as he grunted and growled with pure rage. The Winchester had fallen away and

Mori thought it might be under Claypool's body. Claypool became momentarily preoccupied with trying to rid himself of Falkenham and did so, elbowing him viciously to the nose with a spray of blood and a nauseating crack. Unable to see through the blood and stinging pain, Falkenham rolled away. Mori used the time to grab Claypool by his closely cropped hair and slam his head into the wood plank floor. Trudy endeavored to use whatever strength she had to keep him down, but slight a girl as she was, it was an uphill battle.

Falkenham still couldn't see through his bloodied eyes and broken nose. Though Mori caused Claypool to be dazed by attempting to get through to the basement using the latter's head, he started to get up. Before he could block it, Claypool jabbed him to the gut and then, when he doubled over, uppercut him. Thankfully, he telegraphed it and rather than covering the gut, Mori absorbed the blow with his forearms. It still knocked him over. Claypool side-kicked Trudy and she went sprawling forward with a scream. Mori searched for the Winchester but it was too dark, he was too dazed... he found... a paint can. Before Claypool could turn and square on him, he swung it and landed. Right across the face. Claypool went down like a plank, exhaling a moan and cursing. Where was the damn shotgun? He started to call out to Falkenham to grab his, wherever he'd left it, but he saw the man had passed out. He saw Claypool about to get up again. Mori bashed him again with the can on the back of the head and this time the lid flew off and hunter green splatter went everywhere. Claypool absorbed the blow and fell again, lying flat on his belly but this time he was barely phased. His hands slipped in paint and he fell on his face. Mori looked around for the gun, for anything... he found a hammer. He dove atop Claypool, hammer in hand, using his body weight to keep him face down and hoped the slippery paint kept him from getting a footing. Trudy dove back into the fray, right on Claypool's head and shoulders, forcing him face first into the paint spill. He bellowed as he inhaled it, coating his nose and mouth like leaded pancake batter. Mori reached over the struggling hulk and retrieved with a quick clutching motion of his fist some long nails that had been spilled on the floor. He shimmied to Claypool's outstretched arm, lined up one of the nails dead center on the back of his hand and brought the hammer down hard.

There was a thick wet bellow from Claypool, who spit rage and paint but was now pinned to the floor by his left hand. Mori gave the nail another crash and it went deeper into the wooden floor, a spurt of blood erupted onto Claypool's otherwise green hand, making it a disturbing brown. Claypool's raging and thrashing had swept Trudy clear again and she watched as Mori slid across the back of Claypool, still trying to use his weight and the slippery paint slick to hold the hulk down and lined up another nail on the other hand.

"Omigod!" Trudy said, and covered her face with her hands.

Mori drove the nail home. More bellows. Two more clangs, getting the nail in deeply. The bellows stopped. Claypool passed out.

A minute passed. Ballard moaned, then was quiet. Mori helped Trudy into a wooden chair at the end of the aisle. She had her hand over her mouth, and though tear streaks lined her cheeks she was too in shock to cry now. She folded her hands in her lap, then said. "Those were like, 30 penny nails. Like four and a half inches... dang."

Mori couldn't help but laugh a little. *That's* what she was thinking?

"You don't say." He said.

"That was..." She shook her head. Didn't matter. "We're alive. I mean, anyway, we're alive."

He nodded. Falkenham was walking toward them, unsteadily. He leaned, then slid down the face of the shelves, hands on his face, which was a gory scene of still fresh blood and a nose inflamed and cocked to one side.

"I'm just gonna... sit here." He said.

Mori checked on everyone. Ballard and Claypool passed out from shock. Falkenham recently awoke from same. Tough little Trudy sitting, looking at Claypool's hands.

"Couldn't find any rope. Or... anything. I just grabbed what came to..."

"I know. You saved us. Me. You saved me."

"Just returning the favor."

"You want to get the story straight?" Falkenham asked, still sitting. "What I mean is: how much trouble are you in if you were here for this, Mori?"

"I dunno."

"If you want to *not* have been here... you can pin it on me."

"We got the bad guys." Mori said. "We ought to get medals." Of course, he knew it wasn't that easy and honestly, he didn't want to stick around to deal with it.

"Just let me knew what you want to do." Falkenham said.

It was a generous offer. Maybe Mori could find a way to make a sworn statement to the state police (I overheard everything officers!), make Falkenham the hero and slip out of town as fast as he could. He patted Falkenham's shoulder.

"Good man." Mori said.

He went and crouched by Trudy. She looked less pail, streaks of green paint, a torn sweater, some cuts and bruises – she'd be fine.

"Trudy, you… you've got moxie, kid."

She smiled a luminous smile, "Thanks."

"One in a million."

Trudy suddenly looked very serious. "My god. Look at this place. My folks are gonna kill me!"

Mori looked around. Claypool began to moan again. "We'll fix it." Mori said. "We'll fix everything."

CHAPTER 27

February 12, 1943, Maine

It actually took about four days: state police, sworn statements, files finally available – not that they were much help. Mori let Falkenham be the center of things; he would make a decent cop, probably, and Mori just wanted to leave without having to bring in any official FBI measures. The war was waiting and he was, he had to admit to himself, itching to get to it. He felt renewed purpose. It was clearer than ever what needed fighting.

Trudy drove up in the Nash, parked, and met him on the platform. She was running late. Honestly though, she'd delayed on purpose. She didn't know what to say. She didn't want to make a scene.

The train was boarding unhurriedly. They had spent the last few days giving statements and cleaning her parents' store. They called the ancient doctor who had seen to Mori after he'd collapsed on the floor of the cell and had him give Claypool a sedative. After which, Mori himself pried out the nails that held him down. After that, Ballard and Claypool were shipped off to the prison hospital. The doctor said there was no way Ballard was going to hang on to the bottom half of that leg, and amputation was pretty much certain. If he wanted to live.

His Winchester had been kicked under the metal frame shelves that held the paint cans. Mori had a laugh about that.

"Where is your coat... and your boots?! Aren't you freezing?" Trudy said, stomping her feet on the train platform.

He actually wasn't. He handed her an envelope. "I sold 'em. Managed to get the paint off the boots. Only got 15 bucks. And I put in another 20. But it should cover the shotgun shells, the paint, any small damage... Anyway, where I'm going, Uncle Sam will be buying my new coat. Matching boot and helmet, I hear."

"Ah, you didn't need to. We fixed it all up and..."

"I know, but I thought I should. And..."

"Ace," she said, "the train is about to leave and I don't want to spend the last bit of time talking nickels and dimes."

He nodded. He pulled out another bit of paper. A ticket. He handed it to her.

"What is this?"

"FBI bought me a round trip ticket. I've only used it one way. And it's transferable so... if you do decide you want to be an actress, just keep the destination and go. One way to LA.

Or if you find you want to go somewhere else… go ahead. Wherever you like."

She smiled and looked at the ticket. Just a slip of paper and a whole new life. If she wanted it. Did she?

The train whistle sounded and the porter called "All aboard!"

"It's just good to have options in life, is all." Mori said. "And you… you deserve to choose what you want."

They embraced, just for a moment. Then Mori hopped onto the stair at the end of the train car.

"And whatever it is," Mori said, "I hope you get it."

The train started to pull away. Mori tipped his hat at her and said, loud enough for her to hear, "You're one in a million, Trudy!"

Trudy gave a short wave and watched the train until it disappeared into the trees and he was gone.

Made in the USA
Columbia, SC
25 March 2021